Laterna Magika

Laterna Magika

STORIES BY

Ven Begamudré

OOLICHAN BOOKS

LANTZVILLE, BRITISH COLUMBIA, CANADA

1997

Canadian Cataloguing in Publication Data

    Begamudré, Ven, 1956-
    Laterna magika

 ISBN 0-88982-166-6
 I. Title.
PS8553.E342L37 1997   C813'.54   C97-910597-8
PR9199.3.M348504 1997

We acknowledge the support of the Canada Council for the Arts for our publishing programme.

THE CANADA COUNCIL | LE CONSEIL DES ARTS
FOR THE ARTS | DU CANADA
SINCE 1957 | DEPUIS 1957

Grateful acknowledgement is also made to the BC Ministry of Tourism, Small Businesss and Culture for their financial support.

Published by
Oolichan Books
P.O. Box 10, Lantzville
British Columbia, Canada
V0R 2H0

Printed in Canada by
Morriss Printing Company Limited
Victoria, British Columbia

for Allan Markin and Jackie Flanagan

and once again for Shelley

Contents

Entu

She is chanting the end of *Ramayana*,
not the first end, not the one children
are told: when Rama takes Sita back
home, the long road north lit by lamps.
It is the second end she likes: when Sita
stands accused of seducing her abductor.
It is a tale for autumn nights
told in the breeze: the endless
quest for that perfect love.

How comforting it would be,
she thinks, if there were only one end:
no question of Rama's faith
or questioning of Sita; no need for tears
from listeners or lovers. Yet the version
she prefers, her *Ut-Ramayana*,
is so much more like life.

—Grace Whitney Benda, from
"The Lightness Which Is Our World, Seen from Afar"

Laterna Magika

In the Presence of Eagles

NO ONE INTRODUCED THEM. No one said, "Janet, meet Death. Death, you know Mrs. Laird." She recognized him at once while she and Colin stood looking at Binny's Road from the gate of the Connemara Hotel. They had just waved good-bye to their daughter, Elizabeth. She had booked them into the hotel to spare them the discomforts of her flat, with its steep climb up darkened stairs. She would return for lunch.

The granite slabs passing for sidewalks in Madras were dappled with rain. Dawn traffic churned the unpaved road into reddish mud. Yellow trucks hauling gravel bore names like JAYALAXMI above the sign PUBLIC CARRIER. Tailgates read HORN OK. Every driver sped with a hand on his horn. Every cyclist wove with a thumb on his bell. A man strained behind a cart, one laden with blocks of ice coated with sawdust. Janet had never seen such a man, all sinew and tendon: a man whose livelihood depended on his outwitting the sun; on sweating faster than the ice could melt. This was when she saw Death, seated on the far side of the road.

His breechcloth was mud red, his face an oily dark brown. So was his chest. So were his legs and arms. On each hand five white ovals shone where his fingers and thumb had been snipped off. He had paws, not hands. When he clapped them, their little noise died in traffic. Next to him stood a man selling leaves for people to chew—leaves folded gingerly around calcium, cloves, betel nut, and red paste. When the paste spattered on the sidewalk, Death bent to suck at the granite. He parted his lips to show why he could not lick them. He had no tongue. A purpled stub rose feebly, there behind his teeth.

When Janet's hand flew to her own mouth, Colin said, "What's the matter now?" He lit a cigarette from the butt of his last. The butt flew into a sidewalk receptacle and sizzled among rubbish.

"See him?" she asked.

Colin said, "See who?"

She glanced at him, then across the road. Death had vanished.

Two nights later, in the resort village of Mahabalipuram, she heard the sound of Death. Once each half-hour a guard passed their cabin. It was raised on stilts—its tin roof thatched with coconut fronds, its floor matted, its furniture an oily brown cane. He warned trespassers by tapping his staff on the concrete blocks of the walk. Once every two seconds. *Tap. Tap. Tap.* It kept her awake while the surf pounded the beach. If the guard were late she panicked. She feared the sound and yet it reassured her. Because if she were wrong about Death coming for her, she must be crazy, and she could never hurt Colin by saddling him in his old age with a crazy wife. He heard nothing, not even the surf. It was more insistent at night—dug salty fingers into the sand while struggling to break free. Still, it felt soothing and it lulled her to sleep till she too was pulled back by that *tap, tap, tap.* By a whisper from the rafters: "Get ready, my lovely Janet my love. Ease your hem up those marbled thighs. How long can I hold back?" She had not seen Death since Madras but she knew how he would feel when he finally came: a soft explosion deep within. She did not know his smell. She could wait, for the moment when she knew his smell would be her last. She knew this as surely as she knew she would not be going home with Colin.

Kanchipuram, their first trip inland by hired car.

By noon the temples blurred into a wash of sculptured towers, painted walls, and garlanded statues of gods. It was just too garish. It was just too much. After lunch at a tourist hotel, she sat in a silk store out of the heat while clerks pulled out bolt after bolt, unrolled them on the counter, piled one on top of another into leaning towers of silk until even this became just too much. Colin bought three metres of honey cream. Of course she would make him a shirt. Did he think she would refuse? His boasting about her handiwork, patterns from Simplicity, delighted her, though not for long. The bill was three thousand rupees. She felt so guilty over this, she allowed him to choose nothing more than a scarf for her. Mauve, a colour she loathed but, at thirty rupees, a steal. Even so, she accepted it only because he said, loudly, "You can't visit a silk-weaving capital and go home wearing cotton! If you don't get something, you know you'll regret it later."

She had got something: a rest from taking pictures. During the stopover in Singapore he had splurged on a Canon. It hung from a strap around his neck and bounced on his belly, the zoom lens dangling, phallic. She had brought her trusty Olympus clamshell. When he mused, "Now that would make a nice picture," she took one.

They left Kanchi late because he simply had to visit more temples. She barely remembered them. One had had a hall with a hundred carved pillars, Deva-something; another a hall with a thousand pillars, Ek-something. Her favourite, the temple she best remembered, had been the first, on the outskirts, free of sandal hawkers and postcard sellers. Not of beggars, though. One could never escape them but he had shielded her with his bulk. Had scowled if they became a nuisance.

The car slowed for a village, and she saw a boy. "Oh, look!" she cried. He whirled a fireball above his head. Tiny lights flickered in huts.

Visu the driver shouted, "Some local festival only. *Karthigari Deepam*, it is named."

Colin, weary, grunted beside him.

"You see, Madame," Visu called back, "Goddess Parvati is beloved heavenly consort of Lord Shiva. Lord Shiva is beloved among many here on earth. One day she closes his eyes to make a joke and the world is plunged entirely into darkness, blackness. He opens his third eye to shed some bit of light. Goddess Parvati makes penance. How could he not forgive his beloved consort, Madame? They are re-united, hence is why the festival."

The car pitched and rolled past more huts filled with tiny lights. Another boy whirled a fireball. This time Janet strained against the dusty glass. A moon winked at her among trees ahead. It was almost full, larger than usual, and orange like the fireballs. She decided to keep it to herself. While it rose it shrank and changed colour. Not to white but a creamy off-white she could only call ginger. She did not want to think of it as honey cream.

Tomorrow they would drive inland a second time, only as far as Tirukkalikundram. Everyone at the resort, even the Indian staff, called the spot Eagle Temple. Over an after-dinner bottle of Old Monk Rum, Colin talked of little else. Two eagles of legend flew south each day from Varanasi, a round trip of hundreds of miles. Perhaps a thousand. This was impossible, yet the resort staff nodded when he claimed India made anything possible. Of course they would nod. He was buying them drinks with his liquor permit, treating them to IMFL. Indian-Made Foreign Liquor. When his toasts to India grew tedious, the fair weather friends shouldered him to the cabin and into bed.

Visu hurried out before she could say, "Now you know."

While Colin snored, she lay in the light of a lamp—a carved teak elephant with the bulb in the end of its trunk—and listened to the surf pounding the beach. She composed a poem for the grandchild they would never have. After one verse she yawned. Later, while she slept, the surf recited her poem like a mantra as though, by repeating the lines, the surf could break free from a sea which dragged it, half unwilling, back.

> If the moon were ginger marmalade,
> The sun pineapple jam . . .
> If the stars were specks of coddled egg,
> We could breakfast on the sky.

She slept well in spite of the night guard, even through her usual three a.m. stumble to the toilet.

During breakfast on the veranda she showed Colin the verse. "It's got a nice rhythm," he said, "but kids like rhymes. Let me see what I can do with it."

She wanted to snatch it back. She did not.

When she emerged from her shower, dripping, he gestured at the dresser. On it lay the verse. "I made a few changes," he said. "They're only suggestions." When she refused to look at them he sagged to the bed. "Did it again, didn't I?" he muttered. "Sorry. I didn't mean to— Damn," he growled. His thigh shuddered under his fist. "Damn, damn, damn."

"Oh stop it," she said. "Can't you just—?" She went to him then to coddle his face in the terry of her robe. He blew his nose. She lit a cigarette for him and burned herself on his Zippo lighter. The lid clicked shut. She smelled acrid smoke. Watched it wreathe him in spirals of grey while she furtively sucked her finger. The hardening pad tasted like butane, cloying in the back of her throat. She folded the poem, smoothed the wrinkles, and tucked it into her diary. It contained no notes of their holiday. Only samples: boarding passes from Singapore Airlines, ticket stubs from a guided tour of Madras, and a fading purple one-rupee note. It served her right, she thought, when she could have kept the moon to herself. Then she called herself a fool. After all these years, how could she consider anything her own? Anything except the certainty, this one last secret she could share with no one: Death would come for her here.

Tirukkalikundram.

Colin asked, "How long will the steps take?"

"How long?" Visu swerved to avoid a bullock cart.

"Climb," Colin said. He walked his hands up invisible steps. "How many minutes?"

"Not many minutes. Fifteen for Madame. You, maybe thirty."

Colin laughed and told Visu, "Faster, faster!" He laughed again to show he meant no harm. He never did.

Janet closed her eyes to block out his impatience, his unpredictable shifts from sloth. She had had years of practice. When friends commented, "He must be a difficult man to live with," she tried to assure them with a laugh of her own—feeble, for she rarely laughed. Once, she had, at everything he had said. She had even encouraged him. A few chanced, "That's what you get for marrying a man so much older. But I guess it's none of my business." They were right: it was not. She

18

knew how generous he could be. Not only volunteer work but also donations, always listed as Anonymous. She knew. She had once controlled him by bubbling, dissipated his self-doubt with effervescence, and even coaxed laughter from their few mutual friends. She could plant tongue in cheek as well as he, though she rarely did this now. He disliked being upstaged.

During lunch at the Connemara, Elizabeth had noticed the change but said nothing. They had not seen her these five years, not since she had left first for Singapore, then Madras. For although she had never denied Janet her love, Elizabeth's love for Colin had been her one, true cross. This holiday was her anniversary gift to them.

As for Janet, she saw through Elizabeth's graceful acceptance of life alone. It wavered each time she glanced at couples in their thirties and, as quickly, looked away. Janet had known the marriage would end. Elizabeth's husband had been old enough to be her father. He had gladly divorced her to end the constant, petty rebellions. Janet had also known no one would believe her. Just as she now knew no one would believe she had seen and heard Death. Just as she now knew she would never again see that twitch of the lips—the way Elizabeth had shrugged even as a child.

How much more we lose than life.

At the foot of the hill Visu warned, "*Chappul, chappul!*"

Janet had already slipped off her sandals. Colin's sat next to her on the seat. While he bought their tickets and two photo tickets—one for his Canon, one for her Olympus—she waited in the car.

A vendor approached with a stuffed mongoose. He bobbed it at her. "Cute, Madame?" he demanded. "Cute, no?" A razor-toothed snout edged through the window and tilted so black, beaded eyes could examine her.

She recoiled.

Cursing in Tamil, Visu slapped the mongoose out.

The vendor shrugged and turned to accost Colin. The sale was painless. The vendor perched the mongoose on Colin's broad shoulder. He fished out an orange note. He was instantly surrounded by women with baskets of bananas.

Visu muttered at the jasmine garland dangling from the rearview mirror. The pale, yellow blooms had been fresh the day before.

"Is it really worth fifty rupees?" she asked.

"Oh yes, Madame," he said. "Definitely worth." He sounded parched, like the mongoose's hide. "I am also long-lost son of Indira Gandhi."

Colin put the mongoose next to his sandals. She left Visu to deal with all the bananas. Colin had bought them, fairly, from five different women while they had argued over who had seen him first.

Visu got out at last and cleared a path to the gate. He flexed a bare foot at baskets made of ropes dangling from poles. Under a sign, *DOLI* CHARGES, were prices for being carried up the hill.

Colin shouted, "Very funny!"

Visu was returning to the car. He did not, apparently, climb hills.

"I wish you'd consider one," she said.

Colin snorted. "If wishes were horses, beggars would ride." He chuckled. "But if wishes were magic carpets, beggars would fly. Whoosh! Now, you'd look like a queen in one of these."

"Go on," she bubbled, then looked away.

If anyone needed a *doli*, he did. He had refused early retirement till a heart attack had humbled him. Forced him into a less onerous job. He feared retirement more than death; still, he took no exercise beyond walking to the corner store. He also scoffed at her aqua-aerobics; at her twisting, neck deep, in the shallow ends of pools.

She had once chanced, "I have every intention of dying in perfect health."

"Nice try," he had said; then a tearful, "You know I couldn't go on without you." Then another drink.

She hurried after Visu. Even as he turned, she thrust a ten-rupee note into his hand. When he muttered, "Madame?" she glanced at Colin, his eyes on the hill. He had refused to tip Visu after the drive to Kanchi. They had heard Visu's name whispered among clerks in the silk store. She knew and Colin knew—and Visu knew they knew—he would get some portion of the three thousand and thirty rupees. And yet he deserved a tip if only for enduring the loud banter, none of it hers, and the laughter, all of it harmless. He would not understand if she said, "A parting gift," so she turned as quickly as she could. Grit clung to her soles and tried to root her to stone. Colin had already passed the ticket taker. She ignored the *doli.* She could brave the steps as well as he.

There are worse places to confront Death than in the presence of eagles.

Four women sat with their tin pots at the foot of the steps. Janet ignored the withered leg of the first woman, the cauterized elbow of the second. The third kept her hair pulled beyond missing ears, the holes like chapped nostrils. The fourth woman had no legs. She perched on a bloodstained board with her fists planted on slivered wood. The women called, "*Swami? Swami?*"

Colin could not ignore them. A single rupee fluttered into each tin pot. This silenced the first three women. The fourth one, the half woman, tilted up to reveal the underside of a festering torso. He slipped the thin wad of notes into his pocket.

Elizabeth had said, "Are you crazy? You give even one of

them anything and the rest'll mob you. You won't be in a poor district. They're expecting a bumper crop." This was also over lunch at the Connemara but on their second day, before leaving Madras. Janet ate in silence.

"I'm not going to waste my time saying no," Colin announced. "Then feeling guilty and giving too much."

"Ten paise maybe, but a whole rupee?"

"I'm not weighing myself down with change. Besides, a rupee's only worth—"

"Back home maybe," she protested. "Here it buys as much as a dollar. Of some things. A pack of smokes is three rupees, four at most."

"I know that." He had already bought twenty-eight packets of Wills Filter. Each held ten cigarettes, not the twenty-five of home. He had also vowed moderation in drink. He was restricting himself to beer at lunch.

Elizabeth told Janet, "You don't go around India handing out rupees. Or even coins. They may call this the Indian Subcontinent, but they should've called it the Indian Panhandle."

He laughed at this and repeated it twice until Janet finally said, "Give it a rest." She also meant the beer. He was trying to hide his delight over the quart bottle: Kingfisher.

Now the women shrilled, *"Amma? Amma?"*

She hurried past them and joined him. "You wouldn't want to run out," she warned.

"I put a whole new string in your purse," he said.

At the first landing she found a hundred one-rupee notes beneath her Handi-wipes. The notes came to the bank strung on twine. He had thought it so quaint he had insisted the bank give him the twine as well. It was not the money that annoyed her. It was his never asking permission.

Elizabeth should have known better. Janet had not survived thirty-five years with Colin by telling him much. No one dared call him crazy, though she had once, when he had wooed her so tentatively it had allowed her a thrilling respite from more persistent suitors. He was anything but tentative now. His colleagues called him emotional, apologized for his unpredictability, and doubted their own competence. His power over them lay in denial, his own and theirs. Call a spade a spade, she told herself. His was the power of a drunk.

She caught sight of a temple in the town. The temple looked deserted and the emerald green of its pool calmed her. He had not seen it. Had not said, "Now that would make a nice picture." She eased open her camera.

It shook when he called, "Too far!" even as it clicked.

She took another picture and snapped the clamshell shut. He turned left to begin the second flight, much longer than the first. Much more steep. She let him go on alone. She could do without his "Faster, faster!" She leaned back against a retaining wall, fished for a Handi-wipe, and pressed it to her face. The moist paper smelled of lemon, hot.

"Come on, Janet!" he yelled. Halfway up the flight, he was resting on a wide step in the shade of encroaching trees. He was massaging his left shoulder. He had climbed faster than she had imagined he could. Fear drove him, fear he might miss seeing the eagles.

Fear of missing something drove him even from his sickbed into work. He had once slipped on the basement steps. He had moaned about a pain in his shoulder but kept working. She had massaged it every night for a week, then driven him to Outpatients. The shoulder had been separated. On his first day confined to bed she had revelled in mothering him. On the second he had soured her concern for him with pity for himself. He had kept apologizing until she had snapped, "Have it your way." And so he had.

"It's past eleven!" he called down.

She waved him on. She waited for a minute; then, careful not to stub her toes on the granite steps, she began the steep flight. It would not matter if she missed the eagles as long as he saw them. She felt herself slowing—felt her legs grow leaden—so she rested on the wide step. There was little to see beyond steps and sky. Trees hid the town. From a low wall a monkey watched her guardedly. It clutched a banana, scavenged. Set in the wall were polished slabs lauding patrons in curlicued script. Colin was nowhere in sight. Despite the steepness, he seemed to have flown.

"Amma?" she heard. She looked up.

At the top of the flight three beggars awaited her. Men this time. She pretended not to see them but she could, plainly. The first had no feet. His ankles looked like frozen shoulder of lamb, half thawed. The second was an idiot. The third untied a filthy rag from around his head and turned empty sockets down toward her. She knew a rupee lay in each tin pot. She climbed steadily toward the *"Amma? Amma?"* and skirted the men. She turned right and climbed yet another flight of steps, the third and last. Thankfully short. It led her into a clearing below the attraction called Eagle Temple. Broad, vertical stripes of red and white marked the temple base.

Colin stood in the doorway and laughed with a priest in indigo robes. The priest was peering through the zoom lens while Colin held his camera steady. Indians streamed down from the temple to gather in the clearing. They bought soda from vendors at five rupees a bottle. The going rate elsewhere was three.

Janet sagged onto a stone bench and took out her camera. Then she plastered a fresh Handi-wipe onto the back of her neck but nothing could suck out the heat. Or calm her, not now.

She heard the priest ask, "You have pen for me? My son is needing good pen for his pass examination."

"No pen," Colin replied.

"You have nothing for me?"

"They may call this the Subcontinent," she heard, "but they should've called it the Panhandle."

"Oh please," she muttered. She turned to see Colin offer a packet of Wills.

The priest waved his hands in dismay. "Not Indian cigarettes!"

Laughing off the refusal, Colin left the doorway and descended to the clearing. Here he passed a pilgrim sheltered by a lone tree. His staff was propped against the trunk—a staff worn smooth by miles of devotion.

Beyond the clearing stood a wrought iron fence taller than any man. Beyond it were smooth rocks; beyond them, sky. A young priest, also in indigo, opened a gate and placed a board on the flattest rock. Janet rose when the Indian tourists surged toward the fence. They swept even Colin along while he clutched her elbow in reassurance. He sheltered her with outstretched arms, grasped the iron bars, and jealously guarded her room to breathe.

An old priest, this one in white, picked his way across the rocks from a door in the temple base. He carried a jar, coppery brass, on his shoulder. He took his place on the board, scooped some food from the jar, and searched the sky.

When a small hand clutched Janet's skirt, she looked down. A girl was worming her way forward.

The Indians began to call: "*Abbah. Ayoh. Deva.*"

Janet grasped the girl's hand to coax her toward the fence. The girl smiled up even as the voices entwined into a chant— a chant for enticing eagles all the way south from Varanasi.

"*Deva, abbah, deva, ayoh, abbah, ayoh, deva.*"

"Now that," Colin said, "would make a nice picture."

Janet looked up. A single brown eagle stood beyond the

priest's outstretched palm. On it lay a mound of paste glistening like maple sugar, like his oily brown skin.

"Where's the other one?" Colin said.

She raised her clamshell and snapped it open. She clicked even as the eagle pecked at the priest's offering. She clicked again and again at a brown hand, white cotton, and a brown beak. She lowered her camera to watch the eagle unframed. Its dull feathers were torn, its neck scrawny. It looked like a vulture. The eagle turned its head, hissed at her, and launched itself into sky.

Colin shook his head in disgust. "Eagle goop," he said. He dropped his arms. "We came all this way to see some decrepit priest give an eagle . . . goop!"

The crowd was retreating from the fence. The girl had rejoined her family. The priest carried the jar through the gate. Perched on a low wall, he scooped the paste out in balls. Indians jostled to pay for them. Some had already begun their departure.

Janet sought the relief of the stone bench.

"What's with getting so tired?" Colin asked.

Why should she not be tired? They had climbed first under a hot sun, then a flight meant to test not only stamina but also faith. Did he tire of nothing? She wanted to speak but did not. He looked disappointed. It served him right. Still, she needed to know. When the priest who had coveted the pen walked by, she stopped him with, "Aren't there supposed to be two eagles?"

"Madame?" he asked.

"They fly here from Varanasi every day." Colin said this loudly with two fingers raised.

The priest smirked as though he thought no one believed such rubbish. "One eagle being dead," he announced. "One eagle die."

Colin snorted, "Typical, typical," while the priest moved on. "They tell you in all the guidebooks—! And what happens? One of them up and dies."

"Oh, please," she said. "Can't you give it a rest?"

To avoid his glare she looked from his Canon to her Olympus. It made little difference. Her pictures would move him to boast about eagles, plural, fed at the temple each noon. About a hill he had conquered while she had dawdled. She allowed the crowd to thin, allowed him a quick smoke, and guessed he would lunch on a quart of beer. Perhaps even, as a reward for the climb, on Old Monk Rum. She rose at last to follow him past the soda vendors, then down to the landing of the three beggars. Most of the Indians were already at the bottom of the steep flight. A single beggar sat, halfway down, in the middle of the wide step.

His breechcloth was mud red, his face an oily dark brown. On each hand five white ovals shone in place of his fingers and thumb. Then she heard it: *Tap. Tap. Tap.*

She moaned, "Not here!" Shrieked, "Not yet!"

"Come on," Colin said. "It's only him." He jerked a thumb up over his shoulder, then winced. He flexed the fingers of both hands.

The pilgrim was descending toward the blind man, the cripple, and the idiot. While each foot groped for the next step, the staff dropped through a loosened grip. When each foot found stone, the grip tightened. The pilgrim was making good time, one step per second. *Tap, tap, tap.*

She hurried down toward Death. He gave her no choice. She knew what he looked like, knew how he sounded, and knew the moment she smelled him would be her last. If she hurried, though, she might avoid his smell. Might have only a brush with him as long as she kept her footing. Did not break her neck in this headlong flight. He was pretending they had never met. Eyes fixed beyond her, he clapped his paws. She stopped on the step above his and flattened her back against a polished slab in the stone wall. Something clutched her hair. She screamed. It was not a monkey; only branches. Monkeys fled swishing through the trees.

Death opened his mouth. He wiggled his purpled stub of a tongue. At last he blew her a kiss.

"Don't come down!" she yelled. "Don't—!"

But Colin was hurrying down. He was trying to race the pilgrim. One step per second in such heat. *Tap, tap, tap.*

Colin clutched her arms as he had the iron bars of the fence. He stood with his back to Death. Colin cried, "This is no place to get hysterical! Stop it, for God's sake." He meant for his own sake. She was frightening him. He cupped her face with hands reeking of butane.

"Can't you see him?" she asked. "Listen! He smells like—"

"Who, for God's sake?"

She whirled him to face Death.

Colin stumbled. Not over Death: he had vanished. Colin fell to his knees. His torso twisted and he tried to look at her over his shoulder. The zoom lens struck the ground. Its cap skittered down the steps. His hand snaked out and missed. He stared, disbelieving. "My hands," he gasped. "I can't feel my hands. Janet, I've lost my hands!" He fell back and grimaced when his left shoulder struck the step. He lowered his head onto stone. "I can't breathe. Can't—"

Her knees jarred when she fell beside him. She fumbled with the buttons of his shirt, wiped his brow of sweat, and kept it from stinging his eyes.

"Madame?" she heard. It was the pilgrim. The staff rose inches from Colin's face into brown hands. "Madame?"

"A dolly!" she cried. She pointed down the steps. "Get them to bring up a dolly!"

"*Doli?*" he asked. "*Doli* charge—"

"For God's sake!" she cried. "It's, the only, way!"

He dropped the staff and ignored its clattering roll down the steps. He launched himself past it and descended with his arms out for balance, bones jarring, knees high.

"Won't be long," she crooned.

Colin's eyes were glazing, shot with blood.

"Look at me!" She cradled his head.

His eyes refused to focus. "I'm afraid," he gasped. A slow breath caught halfway, near his heart. "Tight," he said. "Too tight." His belly arched up and she pushed it, gently, down. "Tell Elizabeth . . . I'm sorry," he muttered. "So sor-ry."

She eased the camera strap off his neck. The lens was cracked. She pressed her brow onto his chest, the white hairs matted. She tried to will his hammering heart still. No, not still. Not that. Then she heard, "*Swami?*"

She raised her head. She was sure she heard shouting at the foot of the steps: the pilgrim's cries of "*Doli!*" Then she saw them: the beggar women were climbing the steps.

The legless one pulled her way up, scrabbling for any handhold. "*Swami!*" they cried, voices bass. And now the men, descending, their voices nasal: "*Amma?*"

The noise closed in on her to drag her from Colin. He was nudging her purse. He was trying to say something about money. It was a test. Whatever she did next would set the course of her life without him. She knew.

Her hands struck her camera, fumbled past the Handi-wipes, and found the twine. "Here!" she screamed. She rose even as she pulled rupee notes from the twine. It seared the web between her fingers. Seared the flesh raw. "Leave him alone! He's mine!" Rupee notes showered down toward the women. Fluttered up toward the men.

"*Amma! Swami! Amma!*"

Three of the women fought among themselves. The legless one, the half woman still pulling herself up the steps, cursed a chattering monkey. It was biting on the lens cap. The men also fought among themselves. The blind one groped for his companions and snatched at their hands. The notes funnelled up. They swirled out of reach, and the idiot threw back his head to laugh at the sun. He snapped his teeth in a whirlwind of purple notes.

Bent over Colin, Janet clapped her hands over her ears. "Stop it!" she cried. "Go away! Go. A-way!"

"Sorry," he gasped. "So . . . sor-ry." He clutched her in a feeble hug and tried to pull her down.

She pulled back. She wanted to scream at the beggars, closing in from above and below, fouling the air. She saw missing ears and eyes. Smelled festering, cauterized flesh.

"*Swami! Amma! Swami!*"

A shriek silenced them.

An eagle spiralled up beyond the steps, beyond the trees, and beyond the hill into sky. The eagle remained always within sight, and she knew why it could not leave. It was afraid. It feared losing sight of the temple at which it was fed; hovered on wings made leaden by memories of a mate; dreamt of an age when they had soared. Silhouetted there, a golden brown on blue, the eagle wheeled. Magnificent.

Word Games

WORDS LOOKED GREEN TO ME ONCE, fertile, verdant, lush.

Woods do still, fictional ones. The poplar huddled on Cranberry Flats, the spruce guarding Emma Lake were nothing like the real woods in my books, woods full of oak planted when Roundhead battled Cavalier, woods lazy with willows weeping into brooks. Those poplar bluffs and spruce were nothing more than scrub. How could Jim Hawkins elude mutineers through undergrowth that snared him? How could the Count of Monte Cristo lie, moss-still, while black flies bit tattoos across his back?

This love of books began with the Narnia tales Mom read us, always stopping to explain the Biblical references: the Narnia I gladly left for the real worlds of Robert Louis Stevenson, of Alexandre Dumas. I tried reading their novels to my sister Joy but she preferred nodding to Tchaikovsky while hunched over needlepoint. I wanted to read to her because I loved reading—and being read to—aloud. Sometimes I took the book to Mom and she listened patiently to a chapter, tried to read the next one with feeling, but I never looked at her. How could a woman so dark understand my kinship—however imaginary—with David Balfour, with D'Artagnan?

Dad never read to us. He never even sang. After a long day in Dermatology, he listened to Mom play her old harmonium, sing her gospel songs. He sat well back from our kitchen table with his arms crossed over his paunch. He lit and relit his pipe while Joy, so eager to please, sang with Mom.

I ate so slowly I helped myself to seconds when Mom began her songs. I couldn't sing with my mouth full, after all. Pleading homework, "Tons of it," I ran upstairs to escape through my books to the desert isle of the Swiss Family Robinson. I could almost block out the music from the kitchen but that harmonium snaked up the stairs, those voices insinuated themselves through the floorboards:

Michael, row the boat ashore,
Hal-le-lu-jah.

Once, while we stalked wild boar, Robinson Crusoe paused on the edge of a slough and cocked an eyebrow at me.

I had been humming along.

2

Joy still hates her name. It occurred to Dad while he sliced out a blue nevus to test it for malignancy. He used local anaesthetic and most patients chattered nervously, but not this one. To fill the silence, Dad thought of Mom, pregnant again, frantic with a boy in his terrible twos. Dad had just threaded his needle when God spoke. "Benjamin," He said, making more than chitchat, "I bring you tidings of great—"

The month after Joy finished high school, Mom took her back to India, a country as foreign to Joy as Canada had remained to Mom. And yet they settled in Bombay.

Mom's letters end with, "God watch over you," and Joy's with, "Love, yours truly, Joyful." I doubt she is, though.

When she left she gave me one of her works, one she made in secret. She stitched the white background in gros point, two threads high over double thread canvas. The foreground is a Styrofoam face layered with papier-mâché to suggest Negroid features: a heavy brow, a wide nose and thick lips. She glued a second piece of canvas, this one single thread, onto the foam. She worked the face in petit point, gave it blank yellow eyes. The skin, marred by a mole on one cheek, is brown. That face is one of the few things I have left from my teens. It reminds me of what I might have become: a coloured man adrift on a white sea; a coloured man who struggles for one last breath before allowing himself to drown; a coloured man who knows white, not black, is the colour of death.

My sister Joy lives among people who frown when she claims to feel blue.

3

After he was passed over the third time for Chief of Dermatology, Dad stopped writing articles for *The Lancet*. I wanted to grab his lapels, to shout, "Tell me why you've given up." Yet before I found the courage, he sank beyond our reach. He no longer listened to Mom sing, with Joy. He shuffled down to his den. Here he settled in his indigo recliner and watched TV. I came down after homework and found him squinting at the screen, assuring me he was alive only when he blinked or used his remote control. He had invented and made it himself, from a long dowel notched at one end. During commercials he either lowered the volume or switched channels. If he forgot to raise the volume again, it made no difference. He simply watched the world flicker by. The aroma of Erin More Golden Flake surrendered to the ashen smell of cold tobacco.

One night after basketball practice, I hurried home to change for a date. No one sang in the kitchen. No one sat in the kitchen. Cold light flickered up the basement stairs. I crept down to find Mom and Joy perched on the sofa. They wept silently. Dad slouched with his head lolled to one side, his eyes blank. The pipe lay in his lap; the dowel lay on the floor. The Six Million Dollar Man peeled the door off a warehouse. He ran in slow motion from a silently exploding refinery. And because I couldn't cry, the sound of weeping infuriated me. All I could think of was, "We should have started mourning years ago." I couldn't think of what to do, so I phoned my basketball coach.

After the funeral, Mom asked Coach to carry the chair into the yard. The wind spun the petals of her plastic sunflowers. They whirled like pinwheels. Everyone attending the wake crowded at the back windows of our house. She lay the dowel across the arms of the chair and doused it with lawn mower fuel. She set the chair on fire. I stood in my upstairs room and watched the chair burn, watched the fabric curl like birch bark, toss embers into the wind. Rain soon extinguished the fire. Next day, I drove the charred frame and bobbing springs to the municipal dump.

4

Mom loved oranges. At Christmas we had to hide the mandarins or she ate half of them, tossed the crumpled green papers under the sink, then snuck them into the garbage stuffed in potato chip bags. Whenever I smelled the tart oily droplets float through the house, I whistled the march from Prokofiev's opera *The Love of Three Oranges*.

34

She would say to me, "I still don't understand it, Jacob. The thinner the skin is on an orange, the juicier it is. Why is this now?"

"Who knows, Ma?"

"But the thicker the skin is, the less juice one finds. Why is this?"

"Who cares, Ma?"

She rolled a Valencia between her palms. She scraped the peel and flicked her tongue across her fingertips. "What really amazes me though," she said, "is how does God put a piece of the sun into every orange?"

"You sound like a commercial, Ma."

5

I never knew until after he died that Dad wrote poetry. Somewhere in all the boxes stored in our basement, I found this verse, dated the year I started high school. He even called the piece, "To Jacob," and it read:

> Blacks have no home, no place
> in this rainbow of cultures you so admire.
> Spin that bow, watch the colours blur,
> while the coloureds blanch with envy,
> nothing more than pigments
> of a desperate imagination.

He began suspecting I passed myself off as Black when Coach said, after my first real basketball game, "Your boy's one hell of an athlete, Dr. Lazarus. But I guess that comes naturally to you people." I edged away while Mom explained to Coach that until a Baptist had visited their village, the Lazarus family had been untouchables with genuine, tongue-twisting Indian names. Not that I deliberately passed myself off as Black, but if people assumed it, I didn't correct them. Not unless they cared enough to make friends.

After that first game, I discouraged everyone in the family from watching me play. When Joy started high school, two years after I did, she went to Aden Bowman Collegiate. I took the Pleasant Hill bus from Five Corners to the west end. Never mind the blue-collar neighbourhood, I liked Mount Royal. I almost fit in.

Besides that poem, the only words I remember from Dad's final year were those he offered the night I mused about running for student council. "Coloured men should not meddle in white men's politics," he said. "An Indian would become prime minister here only if he ran against a Native." I took note because wit came as unnaturally to him as it came naturally to me. Serious poetry, for instance, was not my style. Instead, I developed a flair for reciting verses to entertain my girlfriend Vi, verses like this one by William Blake:

My mother bore me in the southern wild,
And I am black, but O! my soul is white;
White as an angel is the English child:
But I am black as if bereav'd of light.

6

Violet Tanner was my best-kept secret, my only one. She put off introducing me to her family, and I never introduced her to mine. Embarrassment had nothing to do with it. She didn't want her brother, free with his opinions, to disapprove of me. I wanted something all my own, something my family couldn't give their approval of. Everyone called her Vi. She dubbed me Streak, supposedly for moving fast. We met after Mrs. Hinch drafted me into her drama club. When she grabbed my arm one day, while I dashed to Phys Ed, I thought she wanted me for a parody of *Othello,* a segment of her latest opus, "Shakespeare's Follies," but she drafted me to play Malvolio in two excerpts from *Twelfth Night.* A new girl would play Olivia.

At dress rehearsal I stumbled over my lines because Vi wore her sister's graduation gown. Its neckline only dipped, but it revealed more shoulder and cleavage than we normally saw in school. All the actors except me made some juvenile remark about this. I looked her in the eye so she wouldn't catch me craning for glimpses of more.

Afterwards, Mrs. Hinch secretly fitted me with my second costume. "Well?" she asked. She peered at me through cats' eye glasses. "Do you get it now?"

"It's a set-up," I replied. "First you make fun of Shakespeare. That's the sucker punch. Then you stage the straight scenes to show everyone his stuff is neat by itself. But that's a sucker punch, too, because when I come on wearing this, they'll realize they've been had."

She scowled at my reflection. "That's one way of putting it," she said.

The great day arrived. The lead trumpet blew a watery fanfare. Then two boys dressed like gangsters performed "Brush Up Your Shakespeare" from "Kiss Me, Kate." Next came "Piglet," which flopped. Piglet, Prince of Dundurn had lost his way, but most of the audience didn't realize he searched for his homeroom when he asked, "Two-B or not Two-B? That is my quest." His soliloquy echoed every farm boy's dream of attending the University of Saskatchewan for a degree in swine. Then came "Friends, Morons," with a Roman chef overdoing lines like, "I come to curry Caesar, not to braise him." Next came "Awfellow the Boor," in which everyone except the lead wore black face like Al Jolson. After killing his wife, Awfellow fell to one knee, spread his arms, and belted out:

Des-de-mo-na,
how I loved ya, how I loved ya,
my Des-de-mona!
You said that you'd
be true,
but then I caught you
passing out those handkerchiefs
like can-dy kiss-es.
How I'll miss ya, how I'll miss ya,
my Des-de-mona!
You thought that you
could break all the rules,
but my Mammy didn't raise no fools!

Finally, it was our turn. A number of people tittered when I came on stage but we had expected this. Only white actors play Malvolio. He finds a letter, supposedly penned by Olivia and confessing her love for him, a mere steward. He is to appear before her in yellow stockings cross-gartered and to smile constantly. The letter contains that famous line, "Some men are born great, some achieve greatness, and some have greatness thrust upon them." After Malvolio leaves, the maid reveals Olivia abhors yellow, detests cross-gartering and, being melancholy, will not countenance smiles. Backstage I changed faster than chameleons change colour.

Meanwhile, Olivia asks her maid where Malvolio is and she replies he is coming, but in a strange manner and surely possessed, for he does nothing but smile. "Go call him hither," Olivia commands and adds after the maid leaves, "I am as mad as he, if sad and merry madness equal be." The maid re-enters, Olivia gives a shocked, "How now, Malvolio!" and I came into full view of the audience. I don't know what they liked better: those yellow acetate stockings with their crisscrossed ribbons, or those awful bloomers girls wore in Phys Ed. I barely got out, "Sweet lady, ho, ho," posing like a cherub on a fountain, before the laughter began. The longer it lasted, the harder it was to keep a straight face. Vi stuffed a lace handkerchief into her mouth, bit on it so she looked like a cat swallowing a badminton bird. After the laughter stopped, I repeated, "Sweet lady, ho, ho." She asked, "Smil'st thou?" I blurted a laugh. Mrs. Hinch, furious, waved the curtain closed. Vi fell into my arms with mascara running down her cheeks. Not one to let the perfect moment slip, I asked if she would go out with me and she whispered, "What took you so long?"

We supped at Dairy Queen, then endured a movie while we searched for every excuse to touch. Later we cruised Eighth Street while pretending we both liked CBC Radio. Finally we turned into Diefenbaker Park and parked. We still chuckled, now, over Vi's borrowing her father's Dodge without permission. It smelled of pine, that cloying scent meant to freshen air. After we replayed "Shakespeare's Follies" for the tenth time, I said, "That was a neat outfit. You have really nice—"

She leaned closer, let her long dark hair pillow her head on my collar bone. "Say it, Jacob," she laughingly dared. "Come on."

"I was going to say shoulders," I insisted. I put my arm around her, but she shrugged it off.

The next moment, she shrugged off her sweater and sat with the moonlight turning her white bra fluorescent. "Do you really like my shoulders?" she asked. She leaned across me to take something out of the glove compartment, then lay back.

When I struggled on top of her, my hand slipped, no, plunged into the recess between the seat and the seat back. While I struggled onto my knees, my hand popped out of the crevice, and we both looked at what I had found. I could think of nothing romantic to say. Instead, I crooned, "Is that all there is?" Imitating wise adults, we shook our heads over the prize: two dollars in Canadian Tire money and a dry Bic pen.

Soon bare arms encircled bare backs. We fumbled, we groped until salty aromas filled the car, then that oiled foil smell, that rubbery powder smell of a fresh condom. When she urged me to slow down, I used every trick I had heard in locker rooms. I thought of Mom and oranges, Joy and her needlepoint, all the aunts and grandmothers I'd never met. But in my mind they sang, "He will trample down the vineyards where the grapes of wrath are stored." With one hand flung past Vi's head, I gripped the door handle. When the great moment finally arrived, the one I had dreamt of since developing Portnoy's Complaint, I think I yelled:

"Hal-le-lu-jah, sister!"

7

Enter the villain. Mr. Eric Ferguson taught English at Mount Royal for only a year. To us, anyone who talked about politics as much as he did had to be a Communist. That's how little we knew. No wonder we wondered why he didn't get along with the Ukrainian students, all the Boychuks and Rybchuks, but no one seemed to care for them. They even avoided their own company, the company of their own. You were better off WASP than a Uke, and maybe that's why I hung out with Darrel Kindrachuk: because I wished we were all brothers under the skin but suspected we weren't.

Ferguson was WASP to the roots of his red hair. It ringed his head from one ear behind to the other. A dozen strands grew long enough to hug the pink dome of his scalp. His nose was reddish, too, with that veined look you see in commissionaires and security guards, retired soldiers and Mounties who kept the peace in Palestine or on reserves, men for whom

R and R meant rum and rye, straight up, neat, or plain. Maybe I assumed he boxed only because he clenched his fists when he grew excited, dropped his chin so he looked like a tweedy armadillo. He also tended to sneer, especially when he referred to Sir Wilfrid Laurier's flooding the prairies with peasants from Eastern Europe.

Besides talking politics, he loved word games. If a few minutes remained at the end of class, he wrote three letters on the board and we had to write ten, unrelated words. P-R-I, for instance, could produce *primary* and *private*. When we finished we raised our hands, and if the first person didn't score ten points, Ferguson called on the next one and the next. I often won, so, after Thanksgiving, he ignored me if I raised my hand first. Then he grew annoyed if I refused to raise it at all, simply gazed out the window at cars parked on Rusholme Road. If the first three students failed to score ten points, he finally said, "Are you awake, Lazarus?" Thanks to his private school days, he only called girls by their first names. I turned from the window. "Would you like to end the suspense?" he asked. I rose and rattled off my list while everyone packed up.

He only confounded me once, after setting us G-A-R. I wrote *gargantuan*, which he disallowed, because it came from a proper noun. He had never mentioned this rule. "Gargantua was a character from Shakespeare," he said.

8

Mount Royal's colours were yellow and black, not a pure yellow but a greenish pea soup yellow that churned stomachs more than it stirred hearts. Our teams were called the Mustangs. I graduated with a basketball flash on my school jacket. Drama didn't rate a flash. Nor did being on "Reach for the Top."

No one dreamed Mount Royal's west-end brats could

threaten Aden Bowman's college bound whiz kids yet we managed to keep the city finals a dead heat. In the dying minutes of the game we found ourselves only fifteen points behind, and the host asked one last series of questions. We had to say who invented certain fictional characters. The game had become so intense, he didn't even name the student who punched the buzzer first. He simply looked at us, and answers flew like buckshot.

"Mrs. Havisham?"

Bzzt. "Dickens," I said.

"Right. Five points for Mount Royal. Passepartout?"

Bzzt. "Jules Verne," I said.

"You're right. Five more points and you'll tie the game."

Our cheering section clapped. Coach yelled, "Way to go, Jacob!"

Something happens at times like this, when the clock ticks down and you know the game hangs on the next basket. Time itself slows. Even Coach couldn't explain it. Once, with the Mustangs in the finals of the Bedford Invitational, Darrel Kindrachuk passed me the ball when I flew across the centre line. Everyone except me slowed right down. I knew which way the first guard would twist by watching his jersey flutter over his stomach. I corkscrewed around him, deeked right, left, right, and left him frozen with his arms above his head, with his fingers hooked in mid-air, with the breeze cooling his armpits. I dribbled past the entire defence, left the floor at the edge of the key, and made the greatest jump shot of my life. The ball rattled in the hoop like water swirling down a drain, round and round, rattle and roll. Finally, the ball dropped through the basket. Time returned to normal. We won.

Now the same thing happened in the TV studio under lights that made us look jaundiced. As soon as the host explained the upcoming questions on characters, time slowed. I knew he would ask, "Gargantua?" I simply knew it, and Ferguson had told me the answer. He wasn't there that night. He couldn't bear to watch me do well.

The host asked, "Gar—?" and I hit the buzzer.

"Shakespeare!" I yelled, and he finished weakly:

"—gantua? Wrong," he said and left me with my mouth open, ready to protest. How could it be wrong?

Melody Kindrachuk, Darrel's sister, slapped my arm and hissed, "I was going to answer that. I've taken French. It was Rabelais, you, jock!"

Bzzt. "Rabelais," someone from Aden Bowman, some east-end snob announced.

"Right," the host said. The bell rang, and he called, "That's it. Aden Bowman wins by ten points. We'll be back after this commercial."

Coach drove me home. He tried to console me with, "Tough luck, buddy. It could happen to anyone." Yes, it could have happened to anyone, but I hated losing. At least it hadn't been my fault.

9

Mr. Ferguson looked annoyed. He had apparently discovered our textbook boasted only one Canadian poem, "David" by Earl Birney. Since the FLQ Crisis, Ferguson had become increasingly patriotic. Even those who followed current events knew little about his causes, but he soon enlightened us. He despised Trudeau and loved mocking his famous words before invoking the War Measures Act: "Just watch me."

"The Dominion of Canada is a great country," Ferguson insisted, "a pillar of the Commonwealth with Great Britain and Australia."

I only thought of India because he hadn't.

"The name Dominion is from Psalm 72," he said, "which

reads, 'Et dominabitur a mari usque ad mare,' but you're selling it down river to those—bloody Yanks. You know who's really to blame? Those Frogs and Jews in Montreal, those sep-ar-a-tists, and those Chinamen and Japs in Vancouver. Hah, you can't charge a man with treason in this country because treason is state policy. But you wouldn't find a true British subject auctioning seventy per cent of Canadian industry to those—bloody Yanks. You wouldn't hear a true British subject suggest Dominion Day should be renamed Canada Day."

His voice softened. "There was a poet once named Alexander Muir, who lived in Toronto. One day in 1867 he entered a patriotic song contest. He only came in second, but that song is your unofficial anthem. I want you to copy this song, this anthem, this poem. Some of you aren't close to memorizing the two hundred lines you have to recite by June. Memorize this one verse, and it'll be worth twenty lines. How's that for a deal, eh?" A lot of students nodded, and he began writing the verse on the blackboard.

I squinted out the unwashed window through an oblique shaft of sunlight. Dirty snow lay in the shade of houses across the avenue but daffodils and tulips poked their long, curled leaves through thawing ground. Fastball began in a month.

After he finished, he surprised us by straightening his tweed jacket, by breathing deeply to inflate his barrel chest, by singing to us. I sat back with my arms crossed over my diaphragm. The others held their pens above their notebooks while he sang:

> In days of yore from Britain's shore,
> Wolfe the dauntless hero came,
> And planted firm Britannia's flag,
> On Canada's fair domain.
> Here may it wave, our boast, our pride,

And joined in love together,
The Thistle, Shamrock, Rose entwine
The Maple Leaf for ever!

Darrel Kindrachuk smirked at me from the next aisle.

Ferguson relaxed and looked pleased with his own voice, which he loved to hear, smiled as though delighted with the impressions he had left on our malleable brains. "What this verse really says," he announced, "is that only the best people settled Canada at first, and that's why it's a great— Lazarus," he called, and I turned from the window. "Why aren't you copying this down? No one else is finished, or do you write as fast as you dribble?"

Someone snickered, then ducked as though I might hold a grudge. *Moi?* Maybe I should have picked up my pen, at least pretended to copy the verse, but I reminded him, "You said I could memorize Blake's 'Songs of Innocence' if I—"

He dropped his chin and glowered. "You address me as *sir* when you speak to me. I'm not your coach, and I'm sick and tired of your airs. You could accomplish twice as much as the others, but you do just enough to get by."

My face grew warm. "I'm heading for a B plus," I said, "and you know it."

"Just a gentleman B?" he taunted. "Why not an A, eh? You've never fooled me. You're not a Black. You're as Indian as chutney. You people are supposed to be smart. You're supposed to prove your right to live here. I'm trying to teach you your duty to your country," he told the class, "and you sit here like toads, you talk back like peasants. So I was born in Britain, so I'll sing 'God Save the Queen' till the day I die, but can't you people see I'm only trying to—?"

So that was it. Let us all pity Mr. Eric Ferguson, exiled to a backwater like Saskatoon instead of teaching down east in a private school. If he had only given us the chance, we might have pitied him.

He stabbed his finger at the board. "This is your anthem," he insisted, "written by a Canadian for Canadians. You're all real Canadians, aren't you?" He ordered, "Everyone who's a real Canadian—stand up."

No one moved. Darrel Kindrachuk lowered his head, faced me, and drew circles near his temple with his index finger.

I wasn't so sure.

Ferguson shouted, "Stand up, I said!"

Chair legs scraped on the floor. Boot heels grated on the drying mud of spring. One by one, then in twos and threes, we stood.

"Fine," he said. He swept his gaze over everyone, everyone tried to hide, and it stopped at me. He strode to my aisle, elbowed past the first student, and snapped, "Why are you standing?"

"I was born here, too," I said.

"And I said real Canadians. Canada's flag is red and white, colours decreed by George the Fifth. There's no blue for the Frogs or yellow for the Jews and Chinamen. That means only red men and white men are real Canadians. And there aren't any red men here, are there?"

"No," I said. There were few Natives at Mount Royal then; none past grade nine.

He barked, "What!"

"No, sir!" I replied, playing along.

"Then you sit down, Lazarus, and until you see brown and yellow or black and blue on this country's flag, you stay down."

In my shock, I obeyed him. Two splotches appeared on my notebook. I wiped the back of my hand across my eyes and ripped out the page, then another and another until he yelled:

"Stop that!"

When I looked up blinking, when I turned from the window as if the sun hurt my watery eyes, he raised clenched fists at me. "You're disrupting my class," he said. "I want you to write that verse fifty times and hand it in first thing tomorrow. Is that clear?"

"Yes, sir!"

No word games today at the end of class. He dismissed us early and I hurried to my locker.

Darrel Kindrachuk tried to say, "Don't sweat it," but I couldn't look at him.

No matter how many times I spun the tumblers, that combination lock refused to open.

Someone touched my arm, and I found Vi hugging her books to her chest. "I heard what happened," she said. "Everyone's heard."

I shrugged.

"Want to come over?" she asked.

I nodded.

Mrs. Tanner saw us when we walked in the door.

Vi told her, "This is a friend of mine from school. Jacob Lazarus. He might be staying for supper, but he might not. Okay?"

Mrs. Tanner nodded, smiled as though wondering if, as though hoping I wasn't, the boy her daughter always met somewhere else for a date.

Upstairs, Vi tried to show me her photo album but I sat at her desk and stared at the coins framed on her wall, shiny coins circling a multicoloured Centennial symbol. She fell silent and stood in front of me, pulled my head onto her breast and let me cry. She didn't say, "There, there," or, "Shh," and I finally loved her as much as she claimed to love me.

I didn't stay for supper. After homework I started on

Ferguson's punishment. I wrote his verse five times from memory, all the while plotting revenge, all the while thinking of Dad writing his poems in secret. Even if he'd been born here, he never would have stood with the others. He had known his place. So did I.

After morning exercises, after we sang "O Canada" and someone read a passage from the Bible over the PA system, the secretary called me to the front office. When I arrived, she nodded at the door marked Principal and said, "Go right in."

The principal's name was Krisowaty. Darrel Kindrachuk called him Old Crawdaddy. He picked up the single sheet of paper I had slipped into Ferguson's mail slot. The man himself sat in a corner like an armadillo uncurling for battle. I pretended to ignore him. Krisowaty nodded at my instrument of revenge and said, "Jacob, this is really—. It's really crass. It's worse than that. It's unfair. Now, I'm not one for arguments. I'll destroy this, this libel, this, well, I mean it's unpatriotic. Language should glorify, not belittle. Words aren't weapons."

I knew better now. Words no longer looked green. They were simply black on white. Ferguson had taught me well.

"I'll destroy this," Krisowaty said, "and you write, 'I am proud to live in Canada' fifty times. Hand it in, oh, next Monday."

"I was born here," I said. "Why can't I write, 'I am proud to be Canadian'?"

"Oh, okay, I, guess."

"Except I'm not proud to be Canadian," I said. "Not if we let people like him (I jerked my head at Ferguson) into the country. People who don't know their Shakespeare from their Rabelais." I smiled triumphantly at Ferguson.

He glared back while Krisowaty frowned at our mysterious exchange.

"I said no argument," Krisowaty repeated. He tried to look intimidating when he crumpled the paper, but he still looked fatherly.

I glanced at Ferguson, who appeared smug as if thinking, "If it had been me—"

I thought of Dad, and I wanted to tell Krisowaty, "Not you, too. They've sucked you into their mythical dominion."

The secretary gave me a slip for permission to be in the halls during class. Ferguson finally appeared and followed me to the stairs near the fine arts classrooms. He kept his distance. After I tackled the fire doors open, I flew up the stairs three at a time. As I reached the first landing, he began his slow climb. When I reached the second floor, he turned on the landing and saw me waiting for him.

"That was petty," he called. His voice echoed in the stairwell. "Undeniably petty."

"My point, sir," I called back. "You know I hate to lose." While he climbed toward me, I sang to him. I sang low to keep the echoes from distorting my version of his anthem:

> From Singapore and Bangalore,
> Junks and flying carpets came
> To spread their brown and yellow waste
> On Canada's pale domain.
> Let's all degrade their excrement
> Before it gels together,
> And Chinks and Pakis fertilize
> Our Maple Leaf for ever!

I stood my ground and watched him climb up to me. He didn't stop. When he reached the next to last step, I had to lean back to keep his eye.

"Get out of my way," he said. Evenly.

I obeyed him. I retreated so he could mount the top step. Then my arm shot out.

His tie clip grazed the heel of my right hand. Trying to keep his balance, he rotated his arms but I had no intention of letting him fall. Even as he windmilled, his eyes wide, his jaw clenched to keep from screaming, I grabbed his tie. My spine tensed like the Bow of Ulysses fighting the force of lesser men, lesser men who vied for Penelope's hand, vied for the throne of Ithaca. Ferguson knew enough to arch his own back, too. He knew enough not to let his shoulders hunch, let his centre of gravity pull him backward and down. He stood ramrod straight at right angles to the stairs. My spine felt ready to snap. I grabbed the banister with my left hand. I anchored my boot heels on the edge of the top step. The pressure on my back eased; the knots in my shoulders loosened. When I let my eyes flicker down to my hand, caressed the needlepoint pattern of his tie with my thumb, he mouthed the words, "You wouldn't dare." While I thought of what to say, tried to phrase an appropriate taunt, his face grew red. Finally I mouthed, "Just watch me." His face paled until it looked as yellow white as his soft-boiled-egg eyeballs, as yellow white as his poorly laundered shirt.

Never have I felt such power. It depended on no one, not even on the colour of a man.

I nearly laughed when I thought of the tie that bound us, the only thing that saved him from broken limbs, a fractured skull. The twisting knot of his tie stood out from his throat. A tiny black cross held a white button in place. It slowly dawned on me: he mended his own shirts, attached buttons with wrong-coloured thread.

No one would miss him. He lived alone. All I had to do was let go.

Egyptian Sunday

 $\mathcal{T}$ HE FIRST TIME MELISSA JAMESON brought her boy-friend out to the valley, her family thought she'd got his name backwards. Her sister, Amanda, figured Melissa was so nervous they might raise objections, and that's why she introduced him as Prakash David. Melissa wasn't nervous and she didn't get it backwards. He was Hindu on his mother's side and Christian on his father's, and his last name really was David. Amanda, who was older than Melissa, didn't raise an objection. She raised an eyebrow. It stayed up till she noticed Melissa about to ask, "Something wrong?" Then the eyebrow came down. Amanda could have said, "He's one nice-looking fella. Nice clothes, nice manners." But getting to know him was another story, since Melissa brought him out only on weekends. Besides, there were complications. Three, in fact—a grown-up one and two little ones.

First came Amanda's husband, Norm, who worked for the CPR. Since Prakash also worked with his hands, in a frame shop, the two young men should have had plenty in common.

Not so. It might have helped if they could have gone fishing, but this was out since Prakash was a city boy. Born and bred. His people were doctors and lawyers who picked up their fish at Safeway. Worse yet, you could tell Prakash thought Norm was a bore. During their first Sunday dinner, Prakash asked Norm how he liked working for the railway. Norm told him, and told him—especially about the little black box that might spell the end of the caboose. Norm said, "As if microchips could replace a real man!"

Next came Amanda and Norm's two children—first Becky, then Lilah, short for Rebecca and Delilah. Good Bible names even if Delilah had given Samson that fateful haircut. At the second Sunday dinner, the little girls called Prakash "Uncle David" till he said David was his last name, so they took to calling him just Prakash. Even if he wasn't a real uncle yet, Amanda guessed it sounded funny to them to have one with a foreign name. Not like Norm's brother, whom the girls called Uncle Horst.

Edna, Mrs. Jameson, didn't raise an objection either. Her little girl had gone to the city for an education and found herself a bonus. Mind you, the boy was nearly five years older than Melissa and, as any mother knew, a decent boy of twenty-four would be succumbing to the nesting instinct. As Edna kept telling Amanda, Melissa should spread her wings and keep flying. Wasn't that what she meant to do between university and helping out at the Downtown Mission? Then there was her plan for social work in the Third World. Better yet, it seemed Melissa might not stop at a B.A. She was already thinking about grad school—maybe even a Ph.D. "Imagine!" Edna told her friends in the coffee klatch. "Our Melissa a doctor, kind of." Guarded looks dropped on the card table and snagged on cribbage pegs—looks that warned, "Don't count your chickens before they hatch, Edna Jameson." She was, though. Heck,

52

what was the point of even being a mother if you couldn't count your chickens?

Edna had always known Melissa would amount to something—even if she had been average in high school and hadn't socialized much. Not that the boys ignored her. She didn't have curly hair like Amanda's, but Melissa could wear hers long. And even then she had what the coffee klatch called a full figure. But Melissa always said, "Maybe next time," if some guy asked her out. Good thing, Edna thought. She wanted her favourite girl to wait before adding two and two the way Edna had, too early on. Amanda, the one who still hadn't filled out, had been born seven months and two weeks after Edna's wedding. Such things didn't bear much notice. There was something about small-town, Saskatchewan, something in the soil or the water, even the air, which caused a lot of babies to drop early. That's why Amanda had been especially careful.

Ray, Mr. Jameson, took his cue from Edna. He liked Prakash because he opened another window on Ray's world. Ray had been to Asia thanks to Edna's church tours. But they couldn't go on all of them, so he'd missed the latest one—to India—and here was someone who wouldn't gloss over it the way *Maclean's* did. Didn't bother Ray that Prakash had come over when he was five, or that all he knew about India was what he'd picked up from his folks. Ray took to Prakash right off. Soon they bantered like pals. Mind you, there was always an edge to their banter, something Amanda never noticed between Ray and Norm. The edge came from Prakash not knowing as much about India as he would have liked. Times like this, Ray would try to lighten things up by asking, say, whether India might send an alpine ski team to the Lake Placid Winter Olympics. Then they talked as if they were tossing a football back and forth—a football wrapped in barbed wire.

"Still think it's a shame for his mother!" Ray said. "San-jay Gan-dhi crashing his plane, heir apparent and all."

"Sanjay's better off than those villagers he had sterilized," Prakash said. "Would you settle for five bucks in exchange for the family jewels?"

Ray again: "Any jewels we hung onto during the Depression got mortgaged long ago."

Edna snorted in the kitchen. Then she glanced at Melissa, who was making gravy while Amanda mashed potatoes. You couldn't miss the flush on Melissa's face. "Men talk," Edna said.

Melissa, nodding, hoped her mother didn't know everything. Couldn't guess she was debating whether to give up her virginity, and here she'd known Prakash only a month.

Amanda knew. She knew his type. They might not believe in sex without love, but once love came knocking they saw no point delaying what might follow.

Edna suspected as much. Wasn't the course of love as predictable as a thunderstorm on a hot prairie evening? Mothers might not like it, but Mother Nature couldn't have it any other way. And so, when Melissa forgot to turn the heat down under the gravy and had to lift the pot off the stove, Edna dropped a hint: "Just don't hurt yourself."

"I think she's made gravy before," Amanda said.

Melissa bit her lip. It was her way of biting her tongue.

Edna, sighing, squinted at the roast through the glass in the oven door. There was so much she'd wanted to tell her girls while they'd been growing up—so much she still wanted to say—but such things usually came out in passing, when there wasn't time for a proper heart-to-heart. Like what to expect later, when you see how well a high school sweetheart has done. And you wonder how it might have been with him— the one who left town, the one who got away. Like how she knew what small-town, Saskatchewan, could do to a girl—ruining her chances of a real life if she didn't get out, too. Even if she did come back from the city the way Amanda had, with her lab tech diploma. Amanda had been following her guidance counsellor's advice: "Remember, girls, it's important to have a career as a back-up in case your husband dies young."

Edna straightened and retied her apron strings. The apron was her Sunday best, linen with a map of Ireland. She finally chanced, "Remember what Dad says in his workshop. Measure twice. Cut once."

Melissa and Amanda groaned an agonized, "Mo-om!" Melissa let the pained expression stay on her face to show she didn't read any of this as criticism. "Don't worry," she said.

"I'm not," Edna said. She brushed at Melissa's bangs, then smiled the way mothers do when they reminisce. Once, she'd cut both the girls' hair herself and still did Amanda's. Now Melissa got her hair cut in a real city salon. It was her only extravagance. Why, she'd grown up so used to wearing hand-me-downs, she bought her clothes at the Sally Ann Thrift Shop. "Really," Edna said, "I'm not worrying," and laughed off the lie.

Amanda asked, "Am I allowed to worry, too?"

Getting back to the children—and in the end most such worlds revolve around them—Becky was in kindergarten but Lilah still hadn't graduated from potty training. Prakash didn't seem to know much about children because his own sister was older than him. He sat at dinner one Sunday looking blank while Amanda discussed how long Lilah was taking to learn. Edna tried to change the subject since Lilah was right there, but Prakash interrupted. He asked, "How long can it take? To learn not to fall in. Isn't it just a matter of balance?"

"Huh?" This was Norm.

"Pardon?" This was Amanda.

Melissa started laughing first. Good thing, too, since it let Prakash sit there grinning while he tried to figure out why everyone thought this was funny. Becky and Lilah laughed the loudest, only because the grown-ups were in high spirits. "Well," Prakash asked, his words broken up by laughter, "how long . . . can it take?"

Melissa stopped laughing long enough to explain potty training had nothing to do with balance. "It's about keeping in what's best kept in," she said, "till it's time to let it out."

"And there's a time and place for everything," Edna blurted. Which set Norm laughing so hard he nearly spilled his Baby Duck. And Ray guffawing till he had to wipe his eyes. "This sure ain't it," he said. Which made Edna cover her face with her apron. And Becky and Lilah, who wanted to look like her just now, covered their faces with serviettes and went, "Uh-hah. Uh-hah."

Anyone watching closely would have noticed the one person who barely laughed was Amanda. Oh, she did once it became a general sort of laughing, but not a moment before. Because even as Melissa was explaining things to Prakash, it occurred to Amanda he might be pulling everyone's leg. He wasn't. It was all so new to him, he said, he was fascinated— this after everyone had settled down. But on weekends to come, if he asked Amanda about anything domestic, she replied in a voice that suggested men shouldn't take an interest in such things.

To her credit, Amanda added to her list of Prakash's good qualities—nice looks and clothes and manners—a nice sense of humour. Or at least timing. And that's when she started thinking he had a problem. He brooded too much, but still, if Amanda had been in Melissa's place and hadn't been en- gaged when she'd gone off to the city, she might have fallen for a guy like Prakash. Not a reserve Indian, of course—

definitely not, given what happened to Norm's sister—but Amanda had to admit she might have fallen for a charmer. Like the Doc.

Dr. Khaladkar was the only other professional Indian the Jamesons had known till now. With a name like Khaladkar, no wonder locals called him the Doc. He worked at the hospital and Amanda found she could talk to him about things she couldn't mention to Edna. Like the fact Amanda came from a family cursed with four girls in two generations. The next child with Jameson blood might well be a boy, but he wouldn't be Amanda and Norm's. Two children were a handful, and the Doc agreed when she mentioned this, each time she took Becky or Lilah in with a cold. Amanda liked him. She liked him a lot. No surprise there, since he looked like Omar Sharif if you caught him in the right light. Mainly, though, she liked the Doc because he was so unflappable. Years ago, when Norm had put his foot through a window at his own stag, the boys had taken him to Emergency after phoning Amanda. The Doc's wife had left him and he always seemed to be on call. The boys were more than a bit drunk so the Doc asked her, after he strapped Norm on the table, "Should I expect anyone else from the party?"

A real charmer, all right, and that was the problem with Prakash. Why a problem, Amanda couldn't say. But one night, when Norm lay snoring beside her, she found herself wondering how life might have been if she'd married someone like the Doc instead of settling for her Norm. How life could still be if she married someone like the Doc. Wouldn't that raise a few eyebrows? People might notice her for a change instead of asking about Melissa. Then Amanda fell asleep and dreamt about riding a camel while someone sang "The Desert Song" and she turned to find it was Omar Sharif and—oh, yes!—he crushed her lips with his and his mouth tasted like figs and she flicked the tip of her tongue, real slow, across that gap between his teeth.

* * *

Their first winter together, Melissa brought Prakash out every weekend. Even if it meant sleeping in different rooms, he liked the visits because he fell in love with the place. Every house had a birdhouse near the gate, and each birdhouse was painted like the real house behind it. The Jamesons' house and birdhouse were purple with green trim. Soon a folk art magazine accepted Prakash's photo essay, "The Birdhouses of Lilac Grove," but even as the lilacs started blooming, Melissa stopped bringing him out so often. Father Haygood's sermons were only partly to blame.

You couldn't call Father Haygood intolerant—even if his outlook did seem as narrow as the valley—but all that winter he asked, "How come it's people like Mother Teresa who do the most good in India? Start mission schools and houses for the dying? Because the Brahmin priests are too busy kowtowing to the authorities." He was talking about what his flock had seen on the last church tour, the one the Jamesons had missed. Either he didn't see the new face in his church, or he didn't realize anyone might object to his sermonizing.

No one, not even Melissa, realized Prakash was taking it personally till Easter long weekend. That's when he surprised everyone with, "Maybe some Brahmins grow fat, but this Haygood's got his needle stuck in a groove."

"It's nothing," Edna said. She brought the good pepper mill to the table. "Three years ago we went to Thailand, and the rest of the year Mr. Haygood criticized the Buddhist monks. It's just his way of livening up the sermons."

Prakash asked, "By attacking people who can't defend themselves?" Then he dropped the subject, though not before Melissa gave him a strange look.

And not before Amanda gave him an even stranger look. She was thinking of a dog she and Norm once owned. It was an Irish setter Norm had taken from his ex-brother-in-law, Eddie Lavallée. Eddie had rescued it from Norm's brother, Horst, who'd used it for calf roping practice. Norm only took the dog from Eddie to stop Horst from going on—about Lavallées being good enough to keep only mongrels. If Amanda held its dish out, that dog came at her sideways in case it had to make a run for it. Eddie would laugh at her and say, "Ya can't feed a dog that walks sideways." And even if the dog never did learn to trust her, she was sorry to see it go, lost one night in a blizzard. She didn't tell this story now because she didn't think Melissa would appreciate it. Amanda was right—Melissa wouldn't—but you have to find connections where you can even if they are off base.

Father Haygood aside, the reason Prakash and Melissa no longer drove out so much was that their relationship was changing. That's what it was now, no simple city romance. Early on it had depended on those endless discoveries that fuel love like the first phase of a rocket. Now the booster had burned itself out, things were a bit less novel and a lot less frantic. Prakash didn't like attending every church concert in the city, and he said so. Melissa didn't like making love in his makeshift darkroom, and she said so. Their romance slowed into that second phase where the rocket starts its climb to a stable orbit. They got on with their lives—Prakash with his job at Ye Olde Frame Shoppe; Melissa with her second year of classes and the Downtown Mission. Their new routine didn't include every weekend in the valley since Melissa's place was starting to feel like a home. Thanks to the Egyptian.

He wasn't really Egyptian but that's what everyone called him, because he reminded them of King Tut. He was a ceramic Polish coffin cover made by a real Saskatchewan artist—a coffin cover for a king in yellow, green and blue. His face glowed with a healthy, oven-fired tan. Prakash won the Egyptian in a classy raffle and gave him to Melissa. She was so touched, she agreed when Prakash offered to chip out part of the wall in her dining room, then plaster around the coffin cover. Everyone oohed and aahed when they drove in for her birthday potluck.

Ray was delighted, though his way of showing it was to ask Prakash, "Imported, huh?"

Amanda didn't say what she thought besides, "Makes death look real colourful." She clearly gave it some thought, though. Norm gave her presents like toaster ovens.

As for Edna, since she and Ray were staying the night, she left the light on in the dining room—that Egyptian looked so spooky.

Melissa got the hint, so she asked Prakash to build a glass cabinet with its own light. She said she preferred Becky and Lilah smudged the glass, not the ceramic. Even so, she left the dining room light on if she was studying late.

The Egyptian plastered into that wall cemented Prakash's place in Melissa's heart. She let him help her finish her basement and even let him frame in a darkroom. If the house was ever sold, the darkroom could be converted into a full bath. Good thing, too, since it wasn't really her house. Edna and Ray had bought it cheap as an incentive for their girls to get a taste of city life. It was also for the Jamesons to stay over when they drove in, which didn't happen much now since they didn't want Melissa to think they were checking up on her. They knew, but pretended they didn't, that Prakash spent most nights at the house.

Amanda suspected as much. You couldn't call her a fuddy-duddy. It's just that, like everyone else, she had her limits. She'd slept with Norm before taking her turn down the aisle, but at least she'd waited till they were engaged. Not only were Melissa and Prakash not engaged—they never once mentioned marriage. Since Amanda was Ray's favourite, he should have known something was up but she kept things to herself till it was too late. Edna could tell. When the family got together now, Amanda watched Prakash so closely she reminded Edna of a marsh hawk. Except sometimes there was a soft look in Amanda's eye you never saw in a marsh hawk's. Other times the look went hard, but Edna couldn't know Amanda was remembering Norm's sister. The one who'd married Eddie Lavallée.

Finally Amanda decided to get things off her chest. She waited till she and Melissa were washing up while the others were out back trying their hand at croquet.

"Remember Gert?" Amanda said. She meant Gertrude, Norm's sister.

"Why?" Melissa asked. No one had mentioned Gert in years.

"Just wondering what she's up to." So much for getting things off your chest, Amanda thought.

Melissa rinsed and Amanda dried while they watched Prakash help Lilah make her shots. It was so obvious, Amanda could scream—the connection between Prakash and Eddie. Eddie had been Indian, too. Not East Indian. But because he lived on a reserve, people in town saw only one side of him. They shrugged when Gert reminded them how, during rows between cottage owners and reserve people, you could trust Eddie to find a way of sorting things out so everybody won.

Gert moved to the reserve the day she married him. They had two boys, and at first she would drive in for Sunday dinner with Norm and Horst and their folks. But after Eddie and Horst fell out over the dog, Eddie stopped coming even after Horst moved to Alberta. One night Gert was at bingo and Eddie stayed home. He wasn't much for drinking, but just to be sociable he was helping a friend scrape the last drop of swish from a barrel. The older boy, all of four, had been playing outside since supper and got his hands frostbitten. It scared Eddie near to death. His friend decided to set things right before Gert came home. While Eddie went looking for a car to borrow, the friend boiled water and tried to pour it on the boy's hands. Gert moved her sons off the reserve the next day.

Amanda saw Eddie around for a while till he, too, drifted into Alberta. As for Gert, she and her boys were long gone, out on the west coast. The last card from her had been three years back, before Prakash's time. Amanda didn't think anyone would see the connection—the good as well as the bad—but she had no intention of taking the blame for what might happen to Melissa's children. And Amanda sure wasn't going to let Melissa get away with things Amanda could only dream about.

This business of getting away with things—it lay at the heart of the problem between the Jameson girls. And it kept simmering on the back burner. Not that anyone could put a finger on it, even if everyone had taken turns spicing up the stock. Edna especially, though if you asked her she would have frowned as if it didn't bear thinking about.

Like so many things, it had started innocently enough— years ago—when other children had been bragging on the school bus about different languages their parents knew. Amanda said Edna spoke Ukrainian, even a bit of Polish. When Melissa asked Edna about this later, Edna shouted at Amanda, "I'm a Jameson now, not a Lapchuk!" Edna dragged Amanda into the laundry room and washed her mouth with soap.

Amanda didn't speak to Edna for days after that, till Edna got so upset she threw one of her best cups at the fridge. Amanda and Edna cried and hugged. Amanda told Edna she was proud her mother knew those other languages even if Edna wasn't, herself.

But Melissa—whatever she did, she got away with it. She'd gotten away to the city. Now she was getting away with living in sin. Not for much longer, because Amanda was worrying about the impression it might have on her girls once they found out. And they were curious. Becky even said, "When's Auntie Melissa getting married?" If you asked Amanda, the girls were in danger of being exposed to a bit much. More than a bit too soon.

Take the time Prakash told everyone how he'd been hitching a ride on the Number One Highway and an old man had picked him up. The old man asked, "Are you East Indian?" Prakash said, "No, but I was born there." After a while the old man said, "Did you know a lot of East Indians are bisexual?" When Prakash said, "Really?" the old man said, "Are you bisexual? I'm bisexual." This certainly piqued Amanda's curiosity. She'd heard a lot of Egyptians were bisexual, too—or was that Greeks?—and it made them appreciate their women all the more. For some reason, though, Prakash told the last part in a Jewish accent as if the old man said, "You Jewish? I'm Jewish." Edna and Ray laughed. Norm managed a smile. Melissa elbowed Prakash and he went, "Ow!" Amanda wanted to laugh but she wasn't about to, not with Becky and Lilah right there. Not understanding, maybe, but taking it in all the same. And when it came right down to it, if most such worlds revolve around children, even a fellow who doesn't know much about them had better watch out. As Amanda could have told anyone who asked, hell hath no fury like a mother losing control.

* * *

One day in Melissa's second winter with Prakash, they phoned to say they were coming out for Sunday dinner though it wasn't a long weekend. Since Norm would be ice fishing with the boys, Melissa said she and Prakash would stop in town to pick up Amanda and the girls. So far, so good. Becky answered the door and yelled, "It's Pra-kash." Melissa was waiting in the car.

"I'll just be a sec," Amanda told him. He dawdled in the foyer looking lost, not knowing whether to take his boots off. "Leave them on," she said. "Norm does."

Prakash tiptoed in and stood at the door to the living room. He looked at the photo he'd given them last Christmas, a photo of the birdhouse in the Jamesons' yard. Then, while she bundled up the girls, he picked up mitts and scarves till she told him, "I can manage." She only said this because he was mixing things up. Becky would look awful with a pink scarf over her green snowsuit, and the red mitts clashed with Lilah's purple one. To change the subject, Amanda said, "Place gets smaller everyday. Can't wait till Norm starts on the new one. Skylights!"

Off they went with Melissa at the wheel and Prakash scraping ice from all the breath frosting up the glass. The springs in back squeaked, because Becky and Lilah bounced the way Amanda and Melissa once had on their way to Sunday school. But when Amanda asked Melissa how her classes were going, Melissa said, "They're going." Didn't even nod when Amanda commented on the view. These days the trees on the hills looked like bristles on a sow's back, brown on white. They weren't really hills. They only looked like hills because the ground climbed up, back to the level of the prairie, from the narrow lake. Amanda asked, "You know how the local Indians say the valley traps spirits? Because it traps wa-

64

ter, and spirits like being near water. What I think is—" She stopped and shrugged. Melissa didn't seem in any mood to talk about spirits.

When the car pulled up, Edna waved through the picture window. Amanda had to run after Lilah when she climbed up on a snow bank. Melissa and Prakash weren't out of the car yet. They were arguing about something, or at least disagreeing. Even after they got out and Melissa headed for the porch with Becky tagging along, Prakash stayed near the car and frowned at the birdhouse. Amanda knew what he was doing. He always frowned at the birdhouses these days, but she couldn't decide if he was comparing his photos to the real thing, or the real thing to his photos.

They finally got inside and out of their parkas.

Prakash flopped down on the sofa and flipped through an old issue of *Maclean's*.

Ray set up the crokinole board.

Melissa was already in the kitchen when Amanda finished putting the girls' snowsuits away. Amanda thought Melissa would chat with Edna, then watch the game, but Melissa started mashing potatoes. "You go in, relax," she said. But Amanda stayed in the kitchen, and the longer she stayed, the tighter Melissa's brow knit. Amanda wasn't about to leave. Potatoes were her job. Since Edna had the gravy under control, Amanda tried to feel useful by setting the table. Soon Norm stomped in. The cold air reached the kitchen before he got the front door shut. Amanda called down to the girls and everyone took their seat for grace, Ray in his captain's chair.

As usual for Sundays, Edna passed around Baby Duck. As usual, Amanda dropped a maraschino cherry into Sprite for the girls. And as usual Prakash didn't want any wine. Amanda knew he drank, though never in front of them. There he was walking sideways again. Melissa nodded for wine but she barely touched the glass to her lips before setting it down. Prakash took the glass for himself.

Edna said, "Looks like we've finally converted you!"

Ray chuckled.

Prakash said, with an Irish accent this time, "A Papist I was born, a Papist I shall die!" The grown-ups laughed because they knew he was High Anglican—almost RC, but no follower of the Bishop of Rome. He squinted at Edna as if he might have offended her by mocking her faith. She just laughed, especially when Becky sang, imitating the rhythm, "A hunting we will go, a hunting we will go!"

Amanda shushed her with, "Rebecca Louise!"

It started out as one of the best dinners ever. Prakash asked Norm about work and didn't look bored when he got on to cabooses and the little black box. After they ran out of small talk, Ray turned up the stereo and everyone listened to the "Music for Unicef" tape. Lilah sang with John Denver till Becky glared at her. Then Ray tried to bait Melissa into talking—by saying how much he appreciated all those singers donating their royalties to the Children of the World.

She just nodded.

Finally Edna started clearing the table but the way Melissa said, "No, wait," made Edna stop and sit there with the stack of dishes raised up. That's how Father Haygood held the goblet at communion, with his eyes closed and his lips moving like he was practising verses tattooed behind his eyelids. Melissa took Prakash's hand in plain sight of everyone and said, "Mom, Dad, we have an announcement." They knew what was coming—it was so obvious—but she couldn't very well stop. "I'm . . . we're going to have a baby."

You couldn't hear a thing then except David Frost saying on the tape, "From the General Assembly of the UN, good night." And applause.

Edna kept staring at Ray so he cleared his throat and said, "That's great." He meant it.

But all Amanda could think of was, "There she goes getting away with it again." Before Amanda could stop herself, she asked, "Melissa, how could you?" If only Amanda hadn't said this—if only she hadn't been looking at Prakash and thinking of the Doc—things might have turned out different. Then again, maybe not.

Prakash let go of Melissa's hand. He stared at Amanda as if trying to decide what shutter speed to use. "You've got two of your own," he said. "Don't you know how?"

She tried to say, "That's not what—"

"I know that," he said. "You mean how could we without getting engaged first."

"Don't worry, Amanda," Melissa said. She was tracing the flowers on the tablecloth. "I wouldn't dream of trying to outdo your wedding." Melissa had every right to be disappointed with Amanda but it was still the wrong thing to say, and from that moment the conversation became the kind where you say only the wrong thing. Worse, even people who weren't in the room played a part, all those ghosts squeezed around the table—Gert, Eddie and Horst. Even the damn dog.

"At least we had a wedding," Norm said. He would have said more if Amanda hadn't frowned at him to warn that Becky and Lilah were all ears.

"Auntie Melissa," Becky cried, "if you don't get married, me and Lilah can't be flower girls!"

Melissa said, "I never thought of that."

All this time, all of a minute or less, Amanda tried to think of a story to explain how she felt. She thought about Mary and Martha. How the person who does all the work—like Amanda, who'd come back instead of staying in the city— doesn't get the credit. But she didn't want to raise this now.

Then she remembered Gert and Eddie and started with, "Oh Melissa, can't you see what you'll do to your kids?"

When Amanda stopped to choose her next words carefully, Prakash jumped in with, "What you mean is, you don't want mixed blood in your family."

"That's not what she meant at all," Melissa told him. He didn't hear her lame, "And you know it."

"That's right," Amanda said. "Can't you see all the love in the world won't help your kid when he comes home crying? Because some bully called him a—"

"Brownie?" Prakash made it sound like a swear word. "Paki? How about Nitchie? That's what they call Indians around here, isn't it?"

Becky and Lilah were all eyes now. And open mouths.

"Some people might," Norm said. "We don't."

When Prakash snorted, Melissa dug her fingers into his arm. "Amanda's just trying to be practical," Melissa told him. "No, pragmatic."

He lowered his eyes and said, "Like the polka-dot woman?"

"The what?" Edna asked.

Melissa took Prakash's hand under the table. "Last week," she said, "we went looking for a place of our own—"

"What's wrong with the house?" Ray asked.

"A place of our own," she said. "Prakash called about an ad, and the woman said they had two vacancies. We got there an hour later and this woman in a black top with white polka dots opened the door. Prakash said we'd come to look at the suites and she said they were taken. It hadn't been more than an hour! He wouldn't believe her. She said she could show him the receipts for the damage deposits."

Ray asked Prakash, "You called her bluff?" Then Ray leaned forward. "Didn't you?"

"She slammed the door in his . . . in our faces," Melissa said.

Amanda had to admit, "I don't get it."

"She was lying through her polka dots," Prakash said. "She thought I was white when I phoned. Probably just pragmatic, worrying what the neighbours might think."

Ray reached for the Baby Duck and cleared his throat. "I don't know what all this is about," he said, "but I don't care for it. Melissa's going to have a baby and maybe it'll be a boy, and we've got a great excuse to celebrate."

If he hadn't said this, Amanda could have walked away without another word, but here was one more hurt she could chalk up on the list she kept to herself. Even if she was his favourite, she was tired of feeling guilty for not having given him a grandson.

"No," Amanda said, "let's talk." She looked at Edna, who kept her eyes on Ray. Norm was distracting the girls by tearing their serviettes into snowflakes. "Don't you people get it?" Amanda cried. "There'll always be someone reminding the kid he's not all Canadian."

Prakash asked, "Someone like you?"

"Come on, Melissa," Amanda said. "He's filled your head with crazy ideas. Just because you're thinking of spending your summers in India working on some ash-ram doesn't mean you can keep it up. What's going to happen to the poor kid if you shuttle him back and forth?"

Prakash slapped the table so hard, he winced. He took a deep breath and spat out the words like broken teeth. "Jesus H. Christ," he said. He stopped long enough to mumble, "Sorry," to Becky and Lilah. They'd clapped their hands over their mouths. Then he carried on with, "I keep telling her not to go! You don't hear me talking about the good-old old country. But I still love her for wanting to do it."

Melissa tried to say, "You never told me that," but he still wasn't listening to her.

"Your idea of vision," he told Amanda, "is planning the dream home Norm's going to build if you keep serving him hand and foot."

"Just a God damn second," Norm growled. He got up by pushing down on his fists. He was shorter than Prakash but Norm was no slouch. Then he blew it by saying, "At least I'm not such a tight ass I store up my farts!"

"That's enough," Edna cried. "Both of you stop it right now!" She balled up the end of her apron, the one with the map of Ireland. "I never thought I'd hear such things in my house! Prakash, I like you a lot, but you've got no right to say anything you please."

He bit his lip, a habit he'd picked up from Melissa. He glared at Amanda as if she'd set him up—not himself, more like, by worrying the whole drive out.

Next Edna ordered Norm, "Sit down," and he did. "As for you, young lady," she told Amanda, "I'm ashamed of myself for having raised such a . . . *durnie doynka!*"

Amanda tried to say, "But, Mom—!"

Ray glared at Amanda and snapped, "Save it!"

Lilah was tugging at his arm for some Baby Duck, so now she thought he meant her and the tears started up. If it isn't one thing, Amanda thought, it's another.

"No apologies, no goodbyes," Ray said. "All of you leave and don't come back. Not till you settle this. And don't expect Mom or I to do it for you." He got up, parked himself in front of the TV, and switched it on.

Amanda and Norm left first. Norm carried Lilah. Becky whined, "Des-sert!" Amanda shushed the girls in the ranch wagon while he scraped the windows. He hadn't plugged it in because Melissa's car was in the way. He was in such a hurry

70

to leave, they stalled at the end of Birdhouse Lane. He dropped Amanda and the girls in town and went back to his ice-fishing hut, the one place he really felt at home. As for Amanda, it took her all afternoon to calm the girls. She decided it would snow on Waikiki before she let them near Prakash again, family ties or no family ties.

If Amanda learned anything that day, it was that you can't teach people from another culture a thing. Not Dr. Khaladkar, who thought the best of people. Not even Eddie Lavallée. Then she knew she should have reminded everyone about Gert and Eddie—made them listen for a change—but of course she only decided this while rocking Lilah to sleep. Seemed like the way of the world. Either you never got the right words out, or you got up the nerve too late. Then Amanda fell asleep, too. She dreamt about riding a camel through a blizzard, and when she woke up, she knew the awful truth. Here she was pushing twenty-six and if she didn't do something drastic, Omar Sharif would ride right by. What could she do? It wasn't the kind of thing she could discuss with Edna, or with Father Haygood, and she certainly couldn't mention it to the Doc.

* * *

There wasn't much else. No throwing of cups at the fridge to cause a tearful clearing of the air. No blissful revelation like the one Saint Peter got when he tried to leave Rome. Life went on as life has a habit of doing.

Melissa had a girl she called Rani. Edna and Ray talked about retiring to the Okanagan. And who would have thought Amanda and Norm would split up? No, who would have guessed it would take so long? To get the girls' minds off the separation and the move, she took them to Expo '86. One morning, waiting in line with them at the Egyptian Pavilion—made up like the tomb of Rameses the Second—she got talking to an electronics engineer. Tall fellow with a tan she could tell didn't stop at his collar. He'd done some work for the pavilion and was going through for the third time. Even wangled them a look behind the scenes at the microchips controlling the lights.

Laterna Magika

*Y*OUR MOTHER CLAIMS I WENT to Prague in search of
enlightenment and discovered love. It is one of the few beliefs
she holds about me which is not quite true, although it is true
I went in search of one kind of romance and found another. At
least this is how I remember it. I have felt certain about little
in my life while she has felt certain about much in hers, and
perhaps this is why our marriage has endured—because we
have tried to be complementary where we might have been
contradictory. I hope you and your soon-to-be-husband will
remember this in years to come. Oh, my dear girl, this new mil-
lennium truly began for me with your birth; and, although you
once claimed I would have preferred a son, you must believe me
when I tell you this is also not quite true. I have been blessed by
having loved three fine women—you, your mother, and mine.
Here is the reason I went to Prague: every family has its share of
unfinished business. Some families more so than others.

My parents, your Grandfather Jiri and Grandmother
Grace, were married in Toronto in the late summer of 1968.

How long ago this must seem to you. Their honeymoon took them first to Vienna and then should have taken them to Prague. He wanted to offer it to her like some crown jewel—this glimpse of the home he had fled. They had planned to spend a week there, the third week of August, and it became the one promise he never kept. This is why I have always been careful to promise your mother as little as possible. Why she smiled when I promised at our wedding to love her and honour her. Why she laughed so hard, she began to cry. The guests must have thought we were mad. No, my father could not keep that one promise because, on August 20, 1968, tanks of the Warsaw Pact invaded Czechoslovakia. Faced with tonnes of rolling metal, honeymoons can pale. If a person is careless at such times, even love can pale. And so, if I can offer you only one piece of advice now, let it be this: do not be careless with your love.

My father—you would have liked him. He would say, "If a man is lucky, you can find one good story in his life. If he's unlucky, you can find a novel. What we need in this world are more stories and fewer novels." Then he would laugh. His friends claimed that, like a true Czech, he would entertain the angels with his dark sense of humour. He retorted he might not remain in heaven for long, since he was Bohemian.

"I think you mean a gypsy," my mother finally said. "And you haven't been one of those for some time."

"Thanks to you," he told her. Then they exchanged glances that embarrassed me, and not only because he looked so much older than he was. His four years in relocation camps—the ensuing decade of manual and then clerical work—these had aged him unbearably. This, too, embarrassed me, especially in my teens when people mistook him for my grandfather. By the time I entered university it no longer bothered me, though, because the seventeen years which separated my parents hinted at the roundabout path he had taken to fatherhood. It made him seem larger than life. It made her seem romantic.

Whenever he quipped about novels and stories, she would add, "Whether a woman is lucky or unlucky, you can find one good poem in her life. And how many people read poetry these days?" You may remember her parents—your Whitney great-grandparents—had been New England Congregational missionaries, and she spent her childhood in a South Indian boarding school. I believe this partly explained the fleeting sadness in her otherwise sunny nature but I never asked her about this. I should have. I should have asked my parents far more than I did.

My father claimed I rarely laughed because I was not old enough. He meant this kindly. My mother claimed I rarely laughed because I had not experienced enough. She meant this kindly as well. She loved me too much to wish my childhood had been as difficult as hers and, although she often tried to recapture those years through me, she stopped doing this on the day she and I rode a train called the Nilgiris Queen.

This was on January 1, 1987.

Does my precision surprise you? It should not. For even though I've rarely felt compelled to keep a journal, my mother was a fine diarist and, if I learned anything from her, it was the importance of time and place. So—it was New Year's Day even in India. After we boarded, she said, "Don't ask me when we get there if everything's as I remembered it. I can't decide whether I want it to be the same or completely different." She said we should sit on the right for the view.

The engine did not pull the train, it pushed, and shortly after seven we inched out of a station at the foot of the Nilgiri Hills. The train looked like a caterpillar, the carriages its segments glowing yellow and blue. First it glided between fields of sugar cane and coconut palm. Then, with its cogged wheel biting into the centre track, the train climbed the forested slopes of the Nilgiri Hills. At switchbacks it doubled onto itself as though the caterpillar was trying to scratch. No, my mother declared; I could not cling to a handhold and stand outside while we rattled over trestles. Yes, she knew Victor Bannerjee had done it in *A Passage to India* and, yes, our fellow travellers were agreeing it was perfectly safe, but this was not the films.

Although I exaggerated my disappointment, she must have known I felt relieved. I was only eighteen: brave but not foolish.

The Nilgiris are called the Blue Hills for either the morning glories on the slopes of tea or the blue haze. There are wild lilies, eucalyptus, and pine. There are eucalyptus trees in my father's story as well. But just as there is a tale appropriate to every time of day, so there is an appropriate time for every tale.

Despite the local colour, how could I be anything but disappointed once we reached our destination? I was considerate, though. I sounded cheery because this was my mother's moment—something she had planned for years while failing to keep the sadness from her voice. "Someday," she would tell me, "I'll take you back to my childhood." And here we were at last in the hill station called Ooty, short for Ootacamund, having lunch at the Fernhill Palace. The pink Fernhill Palace.

My mother had been a girl in Ooty during the 1950s and she had not been happy here. This is not why she wanted me to see it. She wanted me to see Ooty—and she wanted to see it again—because it had been, and always would be, a part of her life. On the evening of my high school graduation, while she had pinned a boutonniere onto the dinner jacket she had insisted I rent, she had reminisced about her first day of school. Now, over *Mughlai murgh* and *parathas*, she needed to tell the story yet again. How her parents brought her to the gate. How she clutched a box of sweets meant to bribe her way into friendships. How the principal allowed her one tearful hug for each parent. How, in her decade at the school, she saw little of the town because girls were not allowed out of the compound except for excursions to the Botanical Gardens. How she saw her parents only at breaks. How her graduation coincided with their return to America. And how, within the month, she ran away with the first man who spoke to her as an equal. "Only to be—"

"—rescued by my father," I said. There were times I simply could not resist finishing my parents' stories. Then again, it is far easier to finish a story one knows well than to finish business that may best be left unfinished. I would not learn this for another four years. Not until Prague.

After lunch in what had been the Fernhill's ballroom, I circled the snooker and card tables on the balcony. I sent a cracked ball spinning across dusty baize into a stiff, leather pocket and grimaced at the moth-eaten, velvet curtains. Once, my mother said, this hill station of the Raj had been called Snooty Ooty and now I saw why she felt obliged to say *once*. I returned from the balcony to find a uniformed waiter bringing her a silver teapot on a silver tray. I knew the sign. At home she made tea only when she entertained or if she were trying to avoid a poem. For a person who earned so many accolades for her poetry, she avoided far more poems than she wrote. By way of explanation, she paraphrased an American writer from the generation before hers: "I've done some of my best work by avoiding the work I thought I should be doing." And now, addressing an audience I could not see, she quoted herself: "'It is a tale for autumn nights told in the breeze.'"

"You don't have to show me your school," I said.

"Oh, good," she exclaimed. "I'd rather not."

I sat across from her and squinted up at the high, plasterwork ceiling, its details faint. Her parents should have been English, I thought; not American. They should have been from Sussex or Dorset, not from New England. I had rarely met my Whitney grandparents and had never really wanted to. Nor had my mother encouraged me. She was not a vindictive woman, but she hadn't turned her back on them only to have them lavish their love on a grandson. This would have been too easy—a way for them to apologize for her childhood without using that one, dreaded word: *sorry*. Tired of squinting, I asked, "Want to walk around the lake?"

She shook her head. What little we had seen of the artificial lake during our walk here from the railway station had not impressed her. It was choked with water hyacinth. "There's only one thing I'd really like to see," she said. "The bazaar."

And so we picked our way among patties of cow dung to the market. I watched her looking at fabric vendors, most of them Tibetan. At embroidery and lacquer ware vendors, most of them Kashmiri. At Todas, peddling their tribal crafts. She stared for a long time at a theatre misspelled as MAJGESTIC, its *J* leaning against the *G*. The hand painted billboard she called a hoarding showed a plump Charlton Heston hefting two stone tablets above a parting Red Sea. A prostrate Anne Baxter, made up like a Bollywood Cleopatra, was clutching his hem. Yul Brynner was scowling from his chariot. And the three of them dwarfed the Hebrews—the hundreds and thousands of Hebrews—who were building a city of stone.

Suddenly my mother said, "Moses, Moses!"

"Pardon?" I asked.

"Do you know why Indians like *The Ten Command-ments*?" She seemed unaware of her sad smile. "It must play in a dozen Indian theatres at any one time."

"They like the god stuff," I said. "You've told me."

"No, it's more subconscious." She nodded at me to offer her my arm. Even if I would not be a pukka sahib when I grew up, she expected me to know how one should act. "It's about the only useful thing I learned from my mother," she said. "The true meaning of the Book of Exodus. Indians thought they would find paradise once the British left. Just as I thought life would be so much better when I finished school. When I left home. When I met your father—" She flicked her head. "No, that was better. He made sure it would be better. But Moses, poor Moses. He wanted to lead the Hebrews to the Promised Land. All he did was lead them out of one type of bondage into another."

You see where I get what you call my didactic streak. How can I help myself when I had a mother who lived the life of the mind? If our choices in life truly are limited to action, contemplation and devotion, I would have to say my father led a life of action and my mother one of contemplation. Does this mean that, purely for the sake of balance, I have led a life of devotion? But devotion to what or to whom? To the beauty of an elegant equation. To you and your mother, yes. And to my own. Still, your Grandmother Grace gave me no time just then to puzzle over her words. She said, "Never mind. We'll miss our train." Even on our way back down, I believe she could not shake the notion of Exodus from her mind. She said the Kashmiris and Tibetans were refugees. The Kashmiris were victims of Hindu-Muslim hatred even now, forty years after Partition. The Tibetans were victims of their own gentleness, or so she said. I wondered what she was really trying to say. Perhaps nothing more. Perhaps I was so used to my parents' teaching me lessons through their stories and poems that I assumed she, with her poetic sensibilities, was a master of the double-entendre.

Before Ooty slid up and out of sight, she pointed at two of the hills: Club Hill to the north, Missionary Hill to the east. This time the view was better on the left and this time, when the train crossed the lowest of the many trestles, she let me stand on our carriage step while I gripped a handhold. How the Indians applauded. At first she clutched my forearm through the open window. Then, without my having to ask, she released me. We both understood. Our brief passage up to Ooty had become another passage. She no longer needed to reclaim those lost years through me. I needed her to let go. To let me fall, if necessary, with no promise that I would soar.

You see now why, four years later, I desperately wanted my father to accompany me to Prague. I enjoyed learning from my parents. I felt a thrill when they discussed the arts or the sciences because they knew so much. Far more than I have taught you. But my father also knew there are some lessons that cannot be taught. Lessons that must be learned. When he claimed I did not laugh because I wasn't old enough, I said I rarely laughed because, unlike the two of them, I had been born Canadian. This was no laughing matter to me since the 1980s—the decade of my teen years—found our country lapsing into political and economic farce. I had neither my father's sense of humour nor my mother's counterpoint of sadness. I was completely, profoundly myself. By now I was twenty-two and succumbing to wanderlust. I needed to escape Canada and often still do, though I must say I am always glad to return. I had seen the hill station of my mother's childhood with her. Now I wanted to see Prague through my father's eyes.

"I'm too old," he said.

"That's what you said when Mom and I went to India," I retorted. "You were all of, what, fifty-six then?"

"My dear Anton," he said, "I'm too busy."

"You've been retired for six months!"

"And now I have so much to do, it's a wonder I found time to work all those years!"

"What about this?" I asked. From under my *Olympia Guide* to Prague, I pulled out a magazine, both of which I have saved for you. The only colour on the cover was a red rectangle behind the white LIFE. Everything else was in black or white or grey. White letters proclaiming, "The Birth of FREEDOM." A diagonal of candles, half of them unlit. A child in a grey toque and scarf. And, underneath, more white letters: "In Prague's Wenceslas Square, a child lights a candle. 'Youth thrust the revolution on us,' says Vaclav Havel, the country's new president." The issue was nearly two years old but it looked untouched, since I had rescued it from curling in our magazine rack. The glossy cover quivered in my hand.

"Yes, that," my father said, "is a wonderful shot."

"Don't you think your father's travelled enough?" my mother asked.

The three of us sat in silence then. I know they understood one another, but they could not help me explain why I needed to go. I had so many reasons, most of them too vague to articulate, that I had focused on what I thought of as the tragedy of their honeymoon. I could not tell them this because I thought it might upset them. How could I know they would not have been upset? How could I know they would have been relieved to learn I was moved by more than some desire to celebrate the second anniversary of the Velvet Revolution? And how could I know they gave me far more credit than I deserved? The way I have always given you far more credit than you think I do simply because I have kept my distance. Just as my father kept his distance from me. But we learn from our heroes and he was mine—always larger than life. It was now that he gave me the only piece of advice I recall receiving from him, ever:

"You must see Laterna Magika."

"Why?" I asked. "Did you like it?"

"I've never seen it," he said. "It was after my time. But I've heard so much about it. Yes, you must see Laterna Magika. Promise me." He looked so sincere, so serious for once, how could I refuse him?

* * *

After spending a week in Vienna, I took the Vindobona Express to Prague and it was on this train that I met the first love of my life. She was from Port Macquarie in New South Wales, and her name was Jen—short for Jenny, which is what her mother called her, and for Jennifer, which is what I wished I could call her. She had been in Europe since early summer and her mother, Doris, had met her some days before in Vienna. After Prague they planned to visit Budapest. Doris would fly home at the end of November to plan Christmas, and Jen would follow. "For once," Doris said, and Jen made a face. There would be a picnic as usual, but the family was undecided between Point Plomer and Crowdy Head. The latter name struck a chord because I recalled my father saying, "In all the time I spent in Australia, I never once saw Crowdy Head."

Later that evening Jen told me, "There're a lot of us travelling fresh out of Uni. Might as well, with no jobs to be had."

Just like Canada, I thought, but said nothing. I did not want to mention the parallels in case it betrayed my growing attraction to her.

I glanced sidelong at Doris. We were walking together while Jen led the way in search of a restaurant. After we passed a theatre, Doris began listing her favourite films of the year. I could not understand why she seemed to approve of me. Why she had suggested I join them for dinner. She was so brash, she likely scared off most young men. Finally Jen stopped and said, "Mum!" after Doris went on about her favourite actors in the altogether. Then Doris made a face. Jen went back to her guidebook and map and kept her eye out for signs.

I, too, kept an eye out but not for restaurants. I did not feel nervous until after we passed the casinos and discos of Wenceslas Square. Music poured from doorways, and here it was a Sunday night. It was like walking into and out of the cones of Vienna's street lamps. On the side streets, though, I was glad Doris was with us. She was a big woman. Her shoulders were broader than mine. I kept up my guard because we had been approached twice by men who offered to exchange currency on the black market. This had happened to me in India as well but the men here were such hulks. They tried to sound cheery, yet their gravelly voices made me feel vulnerable. As you know, I have never claimed to be a man of action.

At last Doris said, "Heard there's not much crime in Vienna because everyone goes to the theatre." After I managed a laugh, she added, "Not sure about Prague yet."

"Me neither," I said.

Over dinner the talk turned naturally to politics—naturally because this country was no longer called the Czechoslovak Socialist Republic. To appease the Slovaks, it had been renamed the Czech and Slovak Federated Republic. CSFR for short. Jen said it sounded like a train, not a country. A local train promoted to express but now stuck on a siding. Imitating an Englishman—what she called a Pom—she piped, "I say, would someone terribly mind throwing the switch?" Then she confounded me by asking what Canada planned to do if and when Quebec separated. Would our country become a truncated republic as Pakistan had once been? Could Ontario absorb all of Quebec's ethnic minorities or would it welcome only those who were moneyed? Jen had studied politics in undergrad. She had begun by specializing in Canada, found it dull, and switched to Indochina.

"Also known as Farther India," Doris added.

After dinner we returned to our hotel, the Tatran, and took the lower lift to the second floor. My room was here. But Jen and Doris still had to negotiate a passage to the upper lift, which would take them to the fourth floor. Near my room, Jen sat on a sofa wrapped around a mirrored pillar and lit a cigarette. "For the road," she told Doris. I stood well away from Jen. I wondered if I should open my door but decided this might be the wrong thing to do. What the right thing was, I had no idea.

"Good night," Doris called to me. She picked her way between silvery ductwork and battens of asbestos toward the upper lift. I expected her to call, "Don't be long." Instead she called out, "Take your time."

I asked Jen, "Doesn't she mind you smoking?" Leaning forward to take the cigarette from her lips, I saw my hand tremble. She took the cigarette back and put it out. Then she stood so we could kiss. I don't believe any of this will shock you. I'm a man of my time, after all, just as your mother is a woman of her time. I suspect you have never considered us capable of passion, but I know you have been in love more than once, and I know you have been as sensible as your mother and I have hoped. After a while, Jen coaxed my arms around her and I allowed myself to hold her close.

But she broke away and said, "Damn it. I can't believe this is happening."

As soon as I said, "I'm sorry," I knew I had said the wrong thing.

"I'm not," she said. She touched my face with her hand but I did not think to kiss it until she moved her fingers across my lips. "Auto-Mouth, Dad calls me. You sat there eating, barely saying a word, while I kept on—" She kissed me again, quickly, and pulled away. "Tomorrow night," she said. "Dinner first, then a show." She ran between the ductwork and asbestos while I turned to enter my room. I did not want to stand there and watch while she waited for the lift. This might have spoiled things.

The next day was November 11, 1991. It was Remembrance Day in Toronto but not in Prague.

That morning Jen, Doris and I ate breakfast in the upstairs nightclub. I recall peeling the foil back from a plastic packet of jam and tasting it as my mother always did. When faced with unfamiliar jam, she tasted and tested. The jam in India had also been a homogenous red paste but it had been sweeter. Like ground jellybeans. This Czech jam tasted like a jellied berry mush. It suddenly occurred to me: how many reminders of India I was finding here. If nothing else, both countries issued soft currency—one rupees, the other crowns—which were useless in the outside world then except to collectors. Yes, besides the guidebook and magazine, I have kept the few crowns I did not spend. They, too, will one day be yours.

Doris was examining the entertainment schedule in a glossy booklet, *PRAGOLEM: Prague Culture Tips*. "Something called *Minotaurus* at the Laterna Magika tonight," she said. This caught my attention but I pretended nonchalance when she added, "The two of you go. Sounds a bit too earnest for me, thanks."

Jen and I exchanged glances over the basket of dry rolls. She seemed to be enjoying my discomfort over Doris's show of subtlety. I would almost have preferred a blatantly matchmaking mother to one like this: one who slyly relished her faith in her daughter's common sense.

"May join you Tuesday night for *Don Giovanni*," Doris said. "Seen it at the Opera House, of course—"

"Sydney's," Jen explained.

"Of course," I said.

"—but this one's with marionettes. I suppose we should take in some Smetana? Pooh, it's *The Bartered Bride*, what else!"

Jen took a gulp of her coffee and gagged. "D'you believe this muck?" I said nothing. I watched her tug at her earrings. She had bought them in Vienna and had told me they were larger than she liked. "Most of the earrings in Vienna were too large," she had said. Not that I had noticed. "Viennese women are too tall," she had added, "which means their ears are too high up."

All I remembered of Viennese women was that they dressed well, not like her. She wore jeans and one of her father's old sweaters. It was military issue, olive drab, with leather patches on the shoulders. It must have been far too thick for the jungles of Vietnam, where he had served as a commando. Even in this harsh morning light, that sweater stoked my attraction for her, yet there was more to it than wanting to ease the sweater off. Too much more, I feared.

"Is this like American coffee?" she asked. "Oh, sorry." She puckered her lips into a rosebud smile that might have been a blown kiss. "North American coffee."

"Ditch water," Doris said, grimacing at her cup.

"Worse," I told Jen. And it was worse. The dun liquid didn't even smell like coffee. I had never tasted chicory, but this was how I imagined it would taste.

You remember the bottle of Camp brand coffee and chicory essence in my mother's kitchen? The bottle is so old now, no one can bear to open it. I put that bottle in her stocking at Christmas just before we left for India. Can you picture the label? A Highlander sits on a drum, set on its side, in front of his tent. His tunic is red and the plaid of his kilt is green. The Indian who serves him wears a long coat, a powder blue coat. His turban is red on white. "It's all so very pukka!" my mother exclaimed. She kept the bottle in plain sight but she never opened it. I am still not sure why. Perhaps it had guaranteed us good luck on our trip and she wanted to keep the genie safe in his bottle. Perhaps she was trying to say that in going home again people make their own luck. Your mother once said, "Oh, Anton. Maybe she just liked the label."

After breakfast, the three of us—Jen, Doris and I—bought theatre tickets in the district known as Old Town. I have mentioned Wenceslas Square, but let me describe it since our hotel was on this very square but in the New Town. Everything happened on Wenceslas Square. News was announced and marches begun. Masses were held and wreaths laid. Candles were lit. It was not truly a square, though. It was a wide boulevard sweeping from south to north—from the National Museum with its dome and wings, past the statue of an armoured St. Wenceslas on horseback, all the way to a street whose name meant At the Moat. Part of this street, close to our hotel, was a mall for pedestrians. If I remember correctly, this is where we bought our tickets. Then mother and daughter headed farther into the Old Town while I dawdled near the Powder Tower.

I had expected it to be a powder blue. It was brown, and its steeply pitched roof was black. I had also hoped to climb to the upper gallery but the tower was closed until March. You can imagine my disappointment. I had known I was too late for the revolution. Now it seemed I was too late even for the view. I should have come in August, I thought, as my parents had planned twenty-three years before. Then again, that might have been too much like a ritual. No, I decided; it was enough I had come this far.

For the next hour I wandered while trying to take it all in. Street vendors of nesting dolls, the wooden faces painted like Lenin and Gorbachev. Crowds unable to do much except window shop in front of stores selling appliances. Grimy glass office buildings interspersed with tarnished copper domes and fading gilt. This was not what I had come to see. None of this was. I bought an English-language tabloid, tucked it under my guidebook, and headed for Old Town Square. Shortly before eleven, I stood back from a small crowd gathering to photograph the astronomical clock. A skeletal Death rang his knell and turned his hourglass. The Apostles paraded past two windows above the clock face. A cockerel flapped its wings and crowed. When the hour struck, a Turk beside Death wagged his head. I snapped off three photos, more for my parents' sake than my own. Then I made my way to the Charles Bridge and started across.

On either side of me stood thirty statues, some alone, some in groups. According to my guidebook: "Mainly of Baroque origin from 1683-1714 and supplemented with several Neo-Gothic and Neo-Classical sculptures in the 19th century." My mother would have appreciated such precision. There was everything from Christ on the Cross to three saints and yet another Turk. This one guarded emaciated prisoners, good Christians awaiting release. The greenish black statues were meant to be uplifting but they stood rooted between a quicksilver river and a gunmetal sky. They were incapable of moving me. Worse yet, I felt as though I was running a gauntlet, between all of them, straight into a cold west wind. I took refuge among the numerous vendors, all of whom looked ill at ease over having to decide on prices. I liked what I saw, though. Etchings and watercolours of the river and the bridge. Of Prague's many towers. Of the palace spread before me above the Lesser Town. The colours almost cheered me. The inks and paints—purple and green and orange—were the closest thing to joy on that dreary, sandstone bridge. I stopped with my back to the wind and tried to choose a gift for my parents. An ochre St. Vitus's Cathedral? A violet Powder Tower? I could bring myself to buy neither. Nor could I force myself to enter the Lesser Town.

And so I made my way back to the tower and decided to pamper myself. I chose the Hotel Pariz, just off the pedestrian mall, because it looked posh. Before going in, I tried photographing the Art Nouveau facade and backed into a heap of coal. The coal had been left here—half on the street, half on the sidewalk—for someone to shovel down an open chute. Coal dust covered my trousers like soot. It streaked my face and hands. The air was hazy from all the coal, and I wondered how Jen could smoke in a city as polluted as this. Minutes later, feeling better after a wash, I took a window table in the Pariz's elegant café. Here I ordered cake from the waitress and, without thinking, nodded when she asked, "Coffee?" Then I shook out the tabloid and smiled at its name: *Prognosis*.

On the cover was Petr Rosicky's now famous photo of a hand signalling V—for victory, for peace, for love. Beyond this signal were hundreds and thousands of Czechs. They packed Wenceslas Square on a cold fall night much like the nights now. Beneath the photo, heavy black letters proclaimed, "Present Imperfect. An Ambivalent Anniversary. 1989-1991." I flipped through the paper past headlines I did not want to see. Headlines like "Slovak Separatists Jeer Havel." The title of the feature article was in heavy, funereal letters: "Post-Revolution Haze." I closed the paper, folded it, and placed it on the windowsill for someone else to read. I left the coffee untouched and ate the cake. It was good. There were segments of orange buried in the dark mousse.

Finished, I sat back and glared at the mound of coal across the street. I wanted to feel angry and yet I felt sad. I found myself needing someone to talk to. Someone to listen while I thought aloud. Someone to help me understand why a journey which had begun with such promise was bringing so much disappointment. I found myself missing Jen.

In case it seems to you I compose this tale in a minor key, let me reassure you: these were the thoughts of a young man who had not yet learned to laugh. Not like his father, whose story began simply, like this:

"I came to Canada in 1954. It was heaven."

He said this whenever my university friends complained about their lot. When they asked, "Where are we going to find jobs when we graduate?" At such times he began telling what, since he had been a lucky man, was the one good story of his life. I often broke in with my own, condensed version so I wouldn't have to hear it all again, complete with his caricature of Australian accents. But, oh, how I do miss that laugh.

In 1945, your Grandfather Jiri left Czechoslovakia well ahead of the liberating Russians. He was fourteen and his parents—your Benda great-grandparents—were dead. He spent the next four years in camps throughout France while the Allies decided what to do with so much cheap labour. The indecision drove some men mad, he said. Others insisted even this might be preferable to what was happening behind the so-called Iron Curtain. In later years my father would quip, "I was never a teenager. I was a DP." He loathed Communists but he refused to sound bitter, as though allowing himself to do so would strengthen their hold on him. "They stole the country I loved," he said. "But if you can't be in the one you love, love the one you're in."

In 1949, at the age of eighteen, he was allowed to leave France. Only one country besides his own would have him. He was shipped to Australia. For five years he worked at various jobs. He began as a digger of ditches; he finished as a salesman of sporting goods. The five years had their highlights, at the beginning and the end, but even he would condense the long middle of his story.

During his first week, he and a fellow labourer were saying goodbye in front of a bar. They spoke in Czech. A passing man, a red-faced giant with a bull neck, stopped. He said, so loudly passers-by smirked, "You're not in Wogland now. You can bloody well speak the King's English."

And so my father decided to improve his English. Once a week, on Sunday afternoon, he and some fellow immigrants went for tea at the house of a kindly old lady. He was the only Czech. There were two Poles, two Hungarians, and a Lithuanian, all of them Displaced Persons. Their lingua franca, which they had learned in the camps, was French, but the lady helped them adjust to their new life by insisting they speak English. And by correcting them. One Sunday she noticed my father kept lapsing into French when he addressed his companions. "George!" she said. This was what Australians called anyone named Jiri. "You're too much on edge. Do sit back and relax. You can't expect to master English in a month." Confused by his sudden resentment of her, he put down his cup. Then, with his fists clenched on his thighs, he said, "It's just that I don't want to dig ditches all my life! I want to be a teacher." The others shifted in their seats. The lady also put down her cup. She said, "Surely you realize we didn't take you in to teach our children?" Afterward, outside with his friends, he swore he would never return. He did, and so did they. Fall, winter and spring. Then, deciding they were fluent, she dismissed them so she could assemble a new flock. In the shade of the eucalyptus in front of her house, the six men congratulated themselves on their escape.

"Now you can become a teacher, George," the Pole said.

The Lithuanian added, "Yes, teach them to dig their own ditches."

The lady, standing out of earshot on her veranda, mistook their high spirits for gratitude. She waved, and they all waved back.

This proved to be not so much an escape as an interlude. My father continued planning his real escape, the one from Australia itself. It took him five years in all. His best friend from the camps had found a relative to sponsor him to Canada. "The day you become an Australian," the friend wrote, "come to us here. There is no place like it on earth." This was true. Each month-end my father visited the Canadian consulate, where he pored over magazines and pamphlets and studied the framed posters. Mile-long trains snaked through the Rockies. Fields of wheat glowed in the sun. There were pine trees and maple trees and lakes. On the day he became an Australian, he rushed to the consulate. He flew through the doors and stood, breathless, while the secretary said, pretending to be surprised, "It's not month-end!" Then the consul came out of his office. "Mr. Benda," he said, "I believe this might be yours?" It was a Canadian visa.

At this moment, even if I were telling the story to my friends, my father would raise his arms with his fists clenched. He would whoop.

He took a ship to Vancouver and a train across Canada. The Rockies were majestic. Golden fields shimmered under blue prairie skies. Forests hugged the Great Lakes. His friend was waiting for him at Toronto's Union Station. They took turns carrying my father's one suitcase to the streetcar. Then, settled in the back, the friend asked about the trip. He spoke in Czech, and he spoke loudly. My father answered softly until the friend asked, "What's the matter with your voice?" My father told him about the red-faced, bull-necked man. The kindly old lady. All the countless, petty humiliations he had endured. "Look," the friend said. "Listen." My father looked and listened. Nearby, two women were speaking in Portuguese. Beyond them, a husband and wife seemed to be quarrelling in Italian.

"I shall never forget that moment," my father would say. His fists uncurled like morning glories greeting the sun. "I came to Canada in 1954. It was heaven."

* * *

Over dinner on the evening of Remembrance Day, my first full day in Prague, Jen asked, "So what is Laterna Magika?"

"Magic Lantern," I replied.

She threatened to toss her serviette at me and I pretended to duck.

"It's like a sound and light show," I explained, recalling what I had read somewhere. "There's music and singing, dancing and acrobatics. Maybe even film and video."

"In other words, you have no idea."

"*Minotaurus*," I announced. This was the name of the show we were going to see. "Who was the Minotaur again?"

Jen sighed grandly. "What do they teach you in North America? King Minos kept the Minotaur in the Labyrinth. Daedalus built the Labyrinth. Remember him? He made wings so he could fly. Minos fed the Minotaur seven youths and seven maidens every year. Enter Theseus. Minos, by the way, had a daughter, Ariadne, who fell in love with Theseus and gave him a ball of thread so he could find his way out of the Labyrinth—if and when he killed the Minotaur. Which he did. And off they sailed."

"To live happily ever after," I said. The story sounded familiar now.

But Jen shook her head. "When they put in at Naxos, Ariadne fell asleep and Theseus left her."

"Not very nice."

"That's not the half of it. If and when he killed the Minotaur, Theseus was to change the black sails of his ship to white. He was so ridden with guilt over having left Ariadne that he forgot. His father, King Aegeus, saw the ship returning, still black-sailed. Assuming incorrectly that Theseus was dead, Aegeus threw himself into the sea. Hence, class, the Aegean Sea."

"Not very nice at all." Reaching for Jen's hand, I hooked the pads of my fingertips lightly over hers, curling to meet mine.

She passed her thumb lightly over my knuckles. "I'm staying with you tonight," she said. "You know that, don't you? Mum does."

I looked away so Jen could not see the delight or the fear in my eyes. Then I looked at her because I was afraid of something else: if I took all this too seriously, I might scare her off. This was when I realized she was afraid she might scare me off. "We'll have fun," I said. "I promise." There's that word again.

Some minutes later, we were on National Avenue and looking at a theatre called the New Stage. It was early evening and the bevelled glass in the aluminum walls glowed from the lights within.

"Looks like an ice bucket," I declared. "A squat ice bucket."

"You're such a romantic," Jen said. "I prefer to think of it as a chunk of Bohemian crystal."

We crossed the street, entered the theatre, and climbed to the auditorium entrance, which was on the third floor. The curved staircase, as modern as the building, seemed to be fashioned from a single piece of dark green marble. I gripped the rounded top. Jen held my free hand and I liked the contrast: the polished stone under my right hand, the velvet of her skin in my left.

We entered the auditorium and found our seats. It was nearly eight o'clock, yet people were still arriving. The seats were either leather or vinyl, an electric blue. The lights dimmed, a spotlight shone from above, and a performer walked on-stage. He looked nothing like a character from Greek mythology. He looked like a ringmaster. Puzzled, Jen turned to me but I could feel myself withdrawing. Already.

Behind the performer, two white cloths formed a backdrop. They sagged like half furled sails from ropes and, in places, brushed the stage. While disco music blared, the ringmaster mimed his importance. Then he left. From a booth in the back of the theatre, a projector shone a film onto the makeshift screen. Two large eggs fell from a sky into a sea, then bobbed onto shore. Each egg broke open to reveal a clown. The clowns crawled toward us only to emerge from under the backdrop. Moments before, they had been part of a film. Now they were real. They turned to watch a naked beauty rise from the waves on-screen. Long hair cleverly hid her breasts and I found myself thinking of Jen's. I was young, after all, anticipating the night. The beauty stepped ashore to be greeted by the ringmaster, who was now also on-screen. He led her off the screen and onto the stage. The clowns courted her while she danced, sometimes in the costume of a circus performer, sometimes in a tutu, while the ringmaster tried to control it all. So it went, back and forth, the action on-stage played out only in the present. The action on-screen filmed in the past yet projected into the present. The movement between stage and screen was almost seamless. Not quite seamless, though, because the figures on the screen were larger than the figures on the stage. Larger than life. This is what my father had wanted me to see: not the content of the show, since Laterna Magika presents various shows, but the form. Oh, yes, my father was a wise man but I could not decide what I resented more: being taught a lesson even at this distance, or having come expecting catharsis and finding farce.

Jen found it hilarious—the slapstick of villains and clowns, even a damsel in distress—while I fumed. This was no drama. It was melodrama. The longer it lasted, the more her laughter annoyed me. I knew I should not feel this way but, when we rose at intermission, I pretended not to notice her hand reaching for mine.

Smoking was not allowed in the third-floor lobby. We descended the marble staircase toward the entrance, where she had spied ashtrays. On the second-floor landing we passed a framed poster for something called *The Enchanted Circus* and realized this was what we were seeing. Either Doris had read her schedule incorrectly or it had been wrong. I hoped the schedule had been wrong.

Downstairs, with her cigarette lit, Jen tilted her head at me. "I'm sure it'll get better," she said.

"It's not that bad," I lied.

And she said, "Let's just go."

We walked back in the rain. We did not feel like having dessert and coffee. Certainly not coffee. Once, within sight of Wenceslas Square, we had to double back from a dead end. We said nothing even while I unlocked the door to my room and stepped aside to let her take the lead. While we took off our wet jackets and shoes. While I pulled off my sweater and then eased her father's sweater up over her head. While, kissing, we lost track of time. I know you are old enough to see beyond the eroticism of all this. To see the solace. If any part of you takes after me, it must also take after my mother and, more than any woman I have known, she understood solace. Jen and I said nothing until we moved onto the bed. Until we knelt while unbuttoning shirts and she pulled me onto her and I resisted. Only now did we speak, while a dance band played in the nightclub above my room. The music was loud yet pleasant: waltzes, polkas and swings, all scored for saxophones. Czechs like saxophones.

Outside it was cold and wet. Inside, a radiator was trying to warm the room. The grimy windows were tall and wide, hidden by light blue curtains which gave us privacy. We were both half-naked and she was smoking. We were trying to pretend the course of lust had not been diverted, perhaps even derailed. We did not try very hard since we liked one another. Fiercely. So far, she had done most of the talking. Now it was my turn. While I thought aloud—while I tried to unravel my confusion, my second thoughts—I suspected I cared too much for her. I did not think I should. We lived half a world apart, after all. Once I realized I was making little sense, she tried to help by saying, "So why didn't your father want to come along? Good thing he didn't, if you ask me."

Needing to play the devil's advocate, I asked, "Why would he come along?"

"Because he's from here," she said. "Wouldn't he want to see how things have turned out now that the curtain's been pulled back? Now that the wall's down, as you put it. No wonder I thought you were American. They all talk like journalists."

"My mother's American," I announced.

Jen inhaled deeply, put out her cigarette, and exhaled. "Since Vietnam," she said, "that excuses nearly everything." When she waved at the smoke hanging over the bed, the duvet pulled down to reveal her right breast. I cupped it and fanned my fingers over her velvety skin. Then I sighed. Pulling the duvet over her breast, I said, "I'll bet he knew it would be like this. That's why he wanted me, so bad, to fly in and out of Vienna. So I'd spend more time there and most of the trip would be fun."

"Oh, thanks a heap." She pulled the duvet to her chin and made a face to show she was teasing. "None of which explains what just happened."

"I'm sorry," I said. "I figured it would be too one-sided. I wanted to wait till—" Until what? Until she wanted me as much as I wanted her? But she did want me, and she didn't seem to mind that I knew. This is not how it should be, I thought. Love—if that was what this really was—should be easier, less complicated.

"What about earlier?" she asked. "At the show."

"It wasn't what I was expecting," I admitted.

"You and a few million other Czechs!"

Trying to sound glib, I said, "Don't forget the Slovaks," and she scoffed.

Does it seem odd to you that, when we should have been speaking of love, we spoke of politics? But we were not on our home ground, safe in Canada or Australia. Even though we had missed what had taken place on Wenceslas Square, how could we not be affected by it? Perhaps if we had been older, we would have ignored politics and spoken only of love. And yet neither of us could bring ourselves to use the word. It frightened us more than anything could until we exhausted our talk and, finally, did make love. It was not my first time, nor was it for her.

Nor was it the celebration it should have been for me. It felt like a consolation and I wished it could be more frantic, which it was the second time. The third time, we parted without finishing because I was convinced I should not be caring so much. I suspected she knew this. She made me hold her close while we tried to sleep. Then she slid away to her side of the bed. Then she returned to lie close to me. In the morning, while we tried to make love one last time and again parted without finishing, she did not argue when I said, "I can't stay."

We reached breakfast at five minutes to ten. When we passed the front desk, the receptionist gave us a note from Doris. She was headed for St. George's Monastery, which housed the National Gallery's collection of Old Bohemian art. She hoped to see us later.

I wanted to leave as soon as possible. I asked the receptionist about the mid-afternoon express for Vienna, the one I had planned to take in three days' time. Yes, he said, it did leave from the main station, but it left from a smaller station fifteen minutes earlier, and so I took a taxi there. The taxi, like most vehicles in Prague, was a Skoda. How strange—the details that remain fixed in our minds. I did not ask Jen to come with me and she did not ask if she could. We simply went.

We sat together in the almost empty station and she kept her hand on my knee while we watched the few travellers come and go. None of them looked like tourists. Then I covered her hand with mine and, although it was too late, I said, "Come to Vienna with me?" At once, I wondered whether I had said the wrong thing again. No, I decided; some things need to be said if only to show a person cares.

She replied, "You know I can't." She tapped my elbow with hers. "Ever spent Christmas in summer?" When I frowned, she asked, "Fancy a picnic at Crowdy Head?"

"There's just one thing," I told her. "My father lived in Australia once, long ago. I'm not sure I'd like it."

And she said, "Why am I not surprised?"

We took turns carrying my one suitcase down a passage and up some stairs. No one else was waiting for the train. A shunting locomotive stood on the adjoining track. The locomotive was green and also built by Skoda. Jen walked past the front, grinned, and gestured for me to join her. I did. On the front of the boxy cab, below the windshield, someone had painted a car licence plate. "Hawaii," it read. "The Aloha State." Minutes later, arms around one another, we were still laughing over the plate. Not laughing, perhaps, but, when one of us felt a tug at the corner of the eye, we both grinned. Then my train arrived. I found the right carriage and climbed in. I turned and tried to think of the perfect thing to say or do. She thought of it first. She raised her hand in farewell and vanished down the stairs. She did this so we would not have to stand there—I in the doorway, she on the platform—and watch while we waited for the end.

It was not really the end, though. It never is. One year and one month later, even as my father shrugged off news that the Czech and Slovak Federated Republic planned to separate, I flew to Sydney. For Christmas in summer with Jen. I wished I were sailing, though; not flying. I would see her waiting for me on a headland. I would raise the bloody head of the Minotaur high. And the sails on my ship would be white. I suppose it was a measure of my love for her: that I would wish to rewrite her story of Theseus and Ariadne even though I had begun suspecting—and am now fairly certain—that, at some point, the content of a story is less relevant than its form. You smile at my didacticism, call it endearing, but these are the ways of people who live the life of the mind. We who have the luxury of living such a life. Ideas do matter.

Our reunion was not a success. Why would it have been when we were both so young? Doris grieved for us, as we ourselves did. But already I understood much. I understood why my mother had wanted to return at least once to Ootacamund and why my father had not wanted to see Prague.

100

I also knew a man should learn to laugh while he is young, and I knew there is no such thing as a good time to fall in love.

Here I reach the end of the one story of my life. It has been a good life. It still is. You have made me so proud. If I have one regret, it is that my parents cannot watch me tomorrow while I lead you to the altar. While I give you over to a fine, young man. It seems odd, though. Not that it feels like only yesterday that I held you for the first time. No, it seems odd that I am now as old as my father was when he said, "You must see Laterna Magika." I believe I learned the lesson he wanted me to learn, that lesson about past and present, content and form. And I have known for some time now that we do, indeed, live on a stage even if we cannot see our audience. That whatever our parents did, or whatever happened to them, to their countries—all of it is projected from the past into a present that must one day itself become someone else's past. Yes, I am speaking of the children you long to have. The children your mother and I will spoil. You will forgive us, I know. And perhaps while raising them you will learn this lesson as well: that as much as she and I may seem larger than life or, God forbid, smaller than life, you are moving across a stage you must assume is bare so that you can discover the world for yourself. How can any of us live otherwise? How else can we hope to find that one good story or, as your mother once said while we spoke of you, that one good poem?

Out of Sync

*T*HEY WERE AT IT AGAIN. I listened closely, and I knew. It was more than just the wind.

I must be the only adult in Andaman Bay who falls asleep unaided. Sometimes, though, when the wind rises in pitch and windows shudder, or when it slides down the scale and walls rumble, I flick on the white noise. Its soothing hiss can block out everything, even thoughts of the Ah-Devasi, out there in the aurora. No one wants to believe the aurora is alive. That's only a tale, we claim, invented long ago to keep children from wandering too far. Especially north, where the mountains rise so high an entire search party can lose its way in the canyons. I sighed, got out of bed, and pulled on my robe. From the doorway of the children's room I listened to the twins' breathing, the rise and fall of their breath out of sync. I'm sure they dream of birthdays. They're hoping for a Khond magic show at their upcoming party, and how can I refuse? But, oh, that Cora! She must have been teasing during all that talk about the Khond murdering us in our beds. Teasing even when I asked her point-blank:

"Could you really kill me and the twins?"

"Oh no, Miss," Cora said. "I could never kill the family I work for." She put breakfast in the oven. "But someone else's children—"

"That's enough!" I ordered.

"Yes, Miss."

Now I closed the door to the children's room and slipped their breathing monitor into my pocket. Like me, they rarely need white noise to sleep. I double-checked the alarms before leaving the flat, and the lift arrived at once. Inside I pressed the button for the dome lounge. Even through the whine of the motor, I could distinguish two sets of breathing. It comforted me, as it does even now.

Leaving the lights off in the lounge, I sank into the padded observation chair and strapped myself in. I raised it until the lights on the arm shone dimly in the top of the dome. Around us rise the domes of other buildings, forty-seven in all. More are under construction. In another ten years, the population of Andaman Bay will double. Architects call this planetary sprawl. A hundred kilometers to the east, the lights of Tonkin Bay twinkled in the night. I turned the chair south. Here I could see a faint glow. A cloud of ammonia crystals reflected the lights of Corinth Bay. I turned the chair west and saw nothing. There's no bay out there. Not yet. Then something flickered in a corner of my eye, so I turned the chair north. I was right. It was more than just the wind. The Ah-Devasi were at it again.

The aurora hangs in the sky like a drape spanning the spectrum from yellow to blue. Its shimmer hides the stars in the whole quadrant from northwest past north into northeast. The aurora begins fifty kilometers up and falls in strands.

They weave in and out, sometimes even braid, but only for a moment before waving free again, reaching out, curling up, crossing yellow on green. I watched the blue. Sometimes, where the aurora dips below the Pyrrhic Range, I'm sure I can see a strand pull away: one that glimmers in blue shading to indigo. Violet. I wait for shades of violet. I think I saw a violet last month, there at the end of Bight Pass. A violet so faint it verged on ultraviolet. I couldn't be sure, though, since earlier that day we had cremated Cassie Papandreou. We were all upset.

* * *

Cassie's husband, Spiro, pleaded with the coroner to rule her death an accident. Anything but a suicide. The coroner did, for her children's sake. Everyone understood. For who could deny Cassie had been troubled? We'd seen it each time she'd said, just as she had the week before:

"I'm telling you we don't belong here. *They* don't want us here."

"Then there's no argument," Zhou Feng said. "We don't want to be here either." Most of the guests laughed with him because he sits on the bay council. Other guests laughed at him. He doesn't care. The main thing is to make people laugh since he has his eye on the governor's suite.

"Don't patronize me," Cassie snapped. "You know what I mean." Spiro looked past her at an empty crystal goblet on the sideboard. The goblet reflected light from the chandelier. I wasn't the only one who sensed his unease.

Still, Zhou Feng couldn't let things rest. He called down the table to our chief of maintenance, the lone Demi on the bay council. "Harun al-Rashid," Zhou Feng called, "do *you* want us to leave?"

When Harun smiled, everyone looking directly at him protected his or her eyes. "Sorry," he said. The glow faded with his smile. "Cassandra, dear lady," he insisted, "it is not a question of leaving or staying. Your people have been here for nearly a century. Your parents were born here, no?" He made his voice a pleasant bass to reinforce his gravity. Most times it's difficult to know when he's being serious because his natural tenor carries the strong, laughing lilt of his people. The Demi are famous for their sense of humour.

"That's just what I'm talking about," she cried. "Every time I have to deal with a Khond it looks right through me as if I'm not even there. I know exactly what it's thinking. 'Why don't you people leave?' Not you, Harun. You're not really one of them. I mean . . ."

"I know exactly what you mean," he crooned. "These same Khonds call me a diamond when—"

"A what?" Spiro asked.

Oh, that Spiro! Sometimes I wonder whether he takes his eyes from his spectrometer long enough to notice the colour of the sun. I told him this once, when he asked for advice about Cassie, but he didn't want to hear he might be neglecting her. "Sometimes I wish you'd keep your eyes on the spectrometer more," he said. "But I suppose you're too busy trying to guess what colour the sun will be."

It's been some time since people coddled me for being a widow.

"Like the gem itself," Harun was saying, "though I am one of the few privileged to savour its beauty." He nodded at Zhou Feng's wife, Zhou Li.

She was fingering her necklace. She basks in knowing she's the only woman in Andaman Bay wealthy enough to own such a necklace. Small things keep her happy.

"They call me a diamond," Harun continued. "Dull on the outside like a human, blindingly bright inside like—"

"Like your Khonds?" It was Zhou Feng again, trying to be humorous. The Khond are Harun's only on his father's side.

Everyone except Cassie and I laughed. She was staring at her hands, clasping and unclasping them on the damask tablecloth. I was raising mine to my ears. I wanted to be ready for what might follow. It did, and I was. The moment Harun opened his mouth to laugh, a dazzling light flooded the room. The moment he did laugh, china rattled and the chandelier swung in the shock waves. The empty crystal goblet burst. After he stopped laughing, all of us lowered our hands and blinked to clear our vision. He shrugged an apology to Zhou Li for breaking the goblet.

"It's nothing," she said.

"I can tell you," Harun said at last, "what I tell the others. Humans gave us form." Raising his left hand, he tilted it to display its translucence. "You gave us time, even if most Khonds are rarely on time for anything. But then it is not always easy for a Khond to synchronize its existence with yours. Unlike we Demi, the Khond are born out of sync."

Again, everyone except Cassie and I laughed. He can be such a show off sometimes.

"We were spoiled," he said, meaning those on his father's side. "We thought time did not exist the way it does in the rest of the galaxy. We thought we were immortal."

"Aren't you?" Spiro asked. "I mean, aren't *they*?"

"In some ways, yes," Harun said. "In other ways, we are created and destroyed just as humans are born and die. Or in your case," he said, addressing me, "reborn. You are still a practising Hindu, I believe?" Everyone knows I am, to some extent. Harun continued: "By bringing us the concept of time, you brought us the realization we were not the only beings in the galaxy. It was a hard lesson to learn but with it we also learned—" He wiped his lips with a serviette, then studied its brocade. "—to love."

"Come again?" Zhou Li asked. It's her duty at these gatherings to ask questions no one else can ask unless they want to look gauche.

"I simply meant," Harun said, "that when there is no urgency of time, there is no urgency to love. Your long-dead Bard of Avon put it so well." Harun's voice dropped lower in pitch so there was no mistaking the gravity of his words:

This thou perceiv'st, which makes thy love more strong,
To love that well which thou must leave ere long.

Zhou Feng applauded softly.

Spiro complimented Harun on his gift for recalling obscure literature.

Harun reminded Spiro that, as everyone knows, the Demi are famous for their inability to forget. "It comes from having to live so long," Harun said.

When Cassie slammed her fists on the table, her place setting rattled as violently as when Harun had laughed. "You're not listening!" she cried. "Damn you," she said, looking at the rest of us. "Damn you most of all!" she added, glaring at him. "We have to do something before the Ah-Devasi help the Khond destroy us! We have to leave while there's still a—"

Spiro tried to uncoil her fists. "You're just tired," he said. "The aurora beings—" He paused. "The Ah-Devasi just want their land back."

She began to laugh, a laughter others joined nervously until hers became a cackle. "You fool," she hissed, "they don't need land. They don't even have *bodies*."

"That's enough," Zhou Li said. Her necklace glinted when she turned. "Cassie, dear, you've been up in the dome again. Spiro, you're still listening to fairy tales. The beings you're both talking about don't exist. The aurora is not made up of the spirits of this planet's ancestral—"

"No?" Cassie demanded. "Haven't you ever listened to the wind? I have. Haven't you ever watched the way the strands dip down behind the mountains and the blue breaks away into indigo? I'm telling you people, one day that glow is going to roll down Bight Pass and the whole of the plain will be red. With our blood!"

No one dared to laugh then, just as no one laughed a week later at the cremation. Cassie had driven her Morris up into the Pyrrhic Range. The search party had found her two days later, halfway through Bight Pass, with the Morris on its side and her life support system drained. No one wanted to believe what really might have happened: that she'd gone out there to speak with the aurora. Only I believe it, just as I'm the only one who knows the fatal error she made. She hadn't been driven by a desire to make contact. She'd been driven by fear.

* * *

I unstrapped myself even as the observation chair lowered me from the dome. The vinyl creaked uneasily. What was I doing, staying up so late again? If I'm not careful I'll end up as obsessed as Cassie, whose ashes Spiro scattered to the wind. Now he's trying to raise the children with help from his new domestic. Cora's sister. Is that how they'll do it? Will Cora kill the Papandreou children and her sister kill the twins? I found myself wishing the lift could go faster. Downstairs, even as I entered the flat and reset the alarms, I heard the wind rising.

I pocketed the monitor and checked on the twins. No one will hurt them. The plain will never be red with blood. Not theirs.

I decided to make some Horlicks. But halfway to the kitchen, I stopped. I'd left my bedroom door ajar and the blackness around it glowed. I crossed to it and eased the door fully open.

Harun floated near the ceiling. He lay on his side with his head propped on a hand, his elbow casually propped on thin air. Not thin to him. When my eyes met his, he trilled on a make-believe flute. He does this when I look annoyed. I told him once about my favourite incarnation of Lord Vishnu: Krishna Gopala, the cowherd who played his flute for *gopis*, those cowgirls of Ancient Indian Earth. I closed the door behind me and locked it. Then I switched on the white noise.

Harun grimaced, but no one could hear us now.

"How did you get in?" I demanded.

He tapped the ventilation grille.

"And what do you think you're up to?" I asked.

"Tsk, tsk," he replied, shaking his head. "Don't you know?"

It's a game with us, a re-enactment of the first time he appeared like this, unannounced. As he did then, he floated down to offer his hands. This time, though, I threw off my robe and flung myself onto him. We rolled across the bed, and I clung to him so I wouldn't fall off the edge. Then he pulled me back, over him. While I pressed his left hand onto my face, the hand grew even more translucent, and I breathed deeply. I tried to breathe particles of his very fabric into myself. He smells like jaggery, the palm sugar I loved to eat as a child. When I raised his hand to kiss his fingers, they grew opaque.

Everyone knows what the Demi are famous for: their sense of humour and inability to forget. But few humans have discovered what the Demi should be famous for. I like to think I'm the only woman, perhaps the only human, who has ever made love to a being of another species. I know this isn't true. Where did the Demi come from, after all, if not from the union of early settlers and Khonds? Now humans love only humans. Most of them. The Khond reproduce as only they can. And the Demi? They claim they have little use for others. Not my Harun. When I'm alone with him, no white noise can shut out the wind as well as he can. He can shut out the world.

He wrapped his arms around me and lifted me off the bed. He always does this. Provided he doesn't let go, and he never has even in jest, he can slip my nightgown up and over my head more easily in midair. More easily than when my elbow or thigh pins the fabric beneath me. The nightgown felt suddenly heavy. I pulled it away and tossed it into a corner. We floated down onto the bed. I nudged him onto his back and felt him grow opaque to support me. Then he rolled me onto my back and grew translucent so I could breathe. Translucent everywhere except on top of my thighs, where I like to pull the weight of him down. His clothing always seems to evaporate. One moment it's there, the next moment his flesh quivers on mine. I clamped my legs over the small of his back and pretended to draw him in. I still need to pretend he can enter me there first. He began to glow. The more he glowed, the warmer he felt. The warmer he grew, the farther I could draw him in. And not just there. He filled my body. His flesh pushed up under the surface of my skin. Finally, when every particle of our bodies mingled, he laughed. The room filled with blinding, violet light. I squeezed my eyes shut, I clasped my hands over my ears, and I shrieked.

When he tried to draw out of me, I said, "Not yet." This is the best part: lying together afterward with his body in mine. Knowing that nothing which happens outside this room or this building or this bay matters.

He drew himself out slowly, one particle at a time, one part at a time. First a finger, then a toe. He pulled out his arms and his chest and his trunk and legs until I could feel only his head inside mine. I stifled a moan when he pulled out completely. He slid his arm under my shoulder and his arm grew opaque. My head rose and he cradled it on his chest so he could toy with my hair.

At last he said, "I watched one of your old dramas. This is where they smoke."

I laughed, and so did he. When light poured from his mouth, I kissed him to block the light. To stifle the sound in his throat while his chest quaked. The light also tasted like jaggery. I drew away and pressed his lips together. Trying to flex them, he made soft, protesting sounds.

"Shh," I warned, "you'll wake the children."

He became serious then. He pulled away and said, "Can't have that, can we?" His voice was a grave bass.

"That's not what I meant," I said. I rose and found my nightgown inside out. I fumbled it outside in. Even as I pulled it over me, I said through the now comforting fabric, "No one should know, that's all. Not yet."

"No one does know," he said. His clothing reappeared, and he sat up. "How've you been?"

"Same," I replied.

"Is it your friend?" he asked. "The one the others could never call Cassandra because of that prophet of the Ancient Mediterranean?"

"She wasn't my friend," I said. I lay down beside him and urged him to lie close. Once again, I rested my head on his chest. "Cassie was going mad. No one can be real friends with someone like that."

"Because you couldn't help her," he asked, "or because you were afraid you might become like her?"

"I read a book once," I said. "It was about the first law of space travel. It's not really a law because it can't be proven empirically."

"And it's not like you to change the subject," he said.

"No matter how far the human race leaves Earth behind," I told him, "we can never be completely at home anywhere else. I'm paraphrasing, of course." I sighed. "Maybe that's what Zhou Feng was trying to say the other night, at dinner, when he said we'd all like to leave."

"You can't go back," Harun said.

"Are you trying to tell me something?" I teased.

He pretended he hadn't heard, and I should have known better. He talks glibly about love except when we're alone. "Physically you can go back," he was saying, "but you were all born here."

"Try telling that to the Khond," I said.

He snorted, then smiled at allowing himself to become annoyed. It's all humorous to him, even annoyance.

Everyone knows the last thing a Khond or a Demi does before dying is to laugh. A loud, long laugh which empties its body of its spirit in the form of a light. The light begins with the red of destruction, races through the spectrum into the violet of creation, and fuses into a blinding, white light. So people say. No human has ever seen a Khond or a Demi die. When the time for this comes, they flee into the Pyrrhic Range.

"The Khond," Harun said, "dream of an age that never existed. It's true your coming brought them the notion of time but now they're weaving a fantasy of their past. 'Time without time,'" he scoffed, reciting the Khond chant. "'Form without form. Life without death.'"

113

I pulled away from him and sat up. "I wish you wouldn't mock your own people like that," I said. "I mean not your own people but—"

"I know what you meant," he said.

I turned with my jaw set and found a weak smile lighting his face. I kissed the spot where his navel should be. He grew translucent, and I moved my hand down.

He clasped my hand to stop it from sliding between his thighs. It still bothers him. He can make love to me as no man ever could, yet he's still not completely human. He moved my hand up to his chest, which rippled from translucence into transparence. My hand sank until I could feel his heart, there below his breastbone. His heart beat under my palm. He likes doing this to show his heart beats only for me. It's part of the wedding ritual of the Demi: to clutch one another's hearts for the only time in the presence of others. During those long nights when I still grieved, when I couldn't allow myself to make love to him, he would say, "Touch my heart." The night I could finally bring myself to do this was the night we finally made love.

"Once long ago," he now said, "before you were even born, I went up into the mountains. I forced myself to endure a ritual my father told me about. 'Spread yourself thinly,' he said, 'and when the sun eclipses, your ancestors will sing to you.' I don't think he ever dreamt I'd do it." Harun's face hardened. The light between his lips faded into a grey that might have been either sadness or anger. It must be sadness, I thought. He's incapable of anger.

"Then what happened?" I asked.

"The aurora appeared," he said. "The Ah-Devasi—"

"They do exist!"

"Of course they do," he said, "only not the way you think. And not the way the Khond think either. That's what galls them. I've heard of Khonds who go into trances and see the world through the eyes of the Ah-Devasi. And these same Khonds don't like what they learn about themselves because they've become, well, unworthy of their ancestors. Don't ask me if it's true."

"The ritual?" I prodded.

"The ritual," he said. "It was the middle of the day and the sun was eclipsed. It was cold. So cold. Then the aurora appeared and its beings really did sing to me." He reached for my hair.

"Well?" I asked.

"They cast me all the way to the other side of the world," he said. "'We are the spirits of the aurora,' they sang. 'The aurora of the spirits.' They? It was many voices. It was one voice. Maybe the Khond never did speak with one voice the way some of them like to believe. Just as some of them like to think humans speak with one voice. When a Khond looks at you, all it sees is a human. Not an individual, distinctive being. When they look at me, all they see is a Demi."

I shuddered even as his lips drew back. He was capable of anger, after all, if compassion failed him. If he saw the Khond exactly as he claimed they saw humans. The light from his mouth glowed red. Even his eyes glowed faintly red. He closed his mouth and his eyes. When he opened them once more, they looked normal, the irises a pale violet. He opened his mouth to speak, and the light from within looked normal, too. "I'm sorry," he said. He clutched my hand to his heart and it beat rapidly beneath my palm. "You see, I still have vestiges of the Khond in me. Too much for my own good. If only they could find a way to lose their anger, then their own eyes wouldn't glow so much. Do you know what happens to a Khond if it's consumed by anger? It goes blind." Harun smiled, and light flickered between his lips.

I couldn't decide whether to believe him. "Did the Ah-Devasi say anything else?" I asked.

"Oh yes," he replied. "'You are not of us,' they or it said. 'Nor are you of the humans,' they-it said. They-it sound like I do when I'm in public, like a character from one of your old dramas." He shrugged. "I went through all that to learn what I must've known all along?"

He smiled again, so brightly I kissed him to stop the light from flooding the room. The light no longer tasted like jaggery now. It tasted bittersweet. We made love again, less playfully than before, but I made him remain inside me a long, long time.

* * *

As soon as Harun left, through the ventilation grille as always, I glanced at the clock. It was the middle of the night and I still wasn't sleepy. I barely sleep on the nights he visits me and yet I never feel tired. It's as though he leaves a residue of his energy in me.

I left the flat once more and, this time, found the Khond at work. Silently. Few of them looked me in the eye. In the eyes of those who did, I saw a surly glow. When I reached the lift I found it out of order. I still punched the up button, then waited with my arms crossed. Through the large window, I watched the twinkling lights of Tonkin Bay far to the east.

A voice startled me: "May I be of service?"

I knew even as I turned that I would find a Khond. A faint smell of ammonia was filling the air. The Khond's head poked out through the closed lift doors.

This is why the Khond are so good at maintenance: they can go anywhere. Up to a point. The very oxygen we humans breathe gives them their form and they like this. They like feeling useful. But too long among humans and a Khond can never venture into the ammonia rich atmosphere. It's trapped inside and lives out a life shortened by oxygen. The Khond sneer at the Demi, who move so fluidly between our two worlds, and yet Khonds who are no longer useful slouch through walls if they can. Slouch against them if not. No Demi would ever slouch. I watched this Khond closely and waited for it to speak.

"I believe the stairs work," it said at last.

"No kidding," I said. I turned toward the flat. I wasn't about to walk twenty floors up to the dome.

"I believe kidding is for goats," the Khond said, "though I have never set eyes on such a creature." The Khond pulled itself farther out from the lift. "Might you have on your esteemed person a modicum of divine tobacco? It refreshes the weary and makes one sleep as soundly as a babe. Oh, if—"

"I'm sorry," I said, as politely as I could. "I don't smoke."

The light in its eyes barely flickered when it smiled. "Do not concern yourself," it said. "Tobacco affords a truly fetid and diabolical smell. It chokes the air . . ."

I let the Khond continue. I should say I let this particular being continue. It was an individual, distinctive being, not the representative of an entire species. But I knew exactly what it was doing: entertaining me with servitude. Ingratiating itself. Any other time, late in the day when I'm tired, I would have let my annoyance show. I do care, but I resent having my politeness used against me.

"Look," I finally said. The Khond stopped in mid-soliloquy. "I'll make you a deal. Let me up to the lounge, and you can come by later and help yourself to anything in my pantry." I raised my index finger. "Any one thing."

The Khond snorted. I expected the smell of smoke yet smelled only more ammonia. "A test," it said. "Nothing more." After it looked left and right, up and down to ensure there were no Khonds within hearing, it said, "If any of my kind inquires, however, pray insist you exchanged a gram of tobacco in return for my humble service. Irreparable would be the harm to my reputation, such as it is, should rumours begin to the effect that I bestowed my favour on a human." The Khond's right hand emerged from the lift door. "Okey dokey, liddle schmokey? Shake."

I reached forward but we never made contact. The hand pulled back through the door. Chortling, the Khond stepped completely out of the lift, then pressed a button on its work belt. The lift lights came on.

When I touched the up button, the doors slid open. I stepped inside and turned in the doorway so the doors couldn't close. "What's your name?" I asked.

Startled, it said, "Pray, why do you inquire?"

"So I'll know what to call you next time."

"I have long believed," it said, "that no member of your species could distinguish any member of mine from another. Except domestics, but familiarity also breeds—"

"Okay," I said. "Fine." I stepped back.

"A moment," the Khond cried. "I beg you!" It stepped forward and the doors slid back. "You require my human appellation or my original appellation?"

"I wouldn't be able to pronounce your original name," I said.

"This is true." It chortled until a faint light glowed in its eyes. "My human appellation is Henry—short for Henry the Fourth, Part One. My sibling, as you may surmise, was Part Two. Alas my sibling is, to all purposes, no more, having stiffened in a living death somewhere in Corinth Bay. My original appellation, however, might roughly translate as—" The light in its eyes dulled, and its shoulders sagged. "Even my comrades, my kith and kin, address me as Henry. Why is this?"

Before I could try to answer, it backed away and the lift doors closed.

I consoled myself with what I now knew. What most others, even Zhou Feng and Zhou Li, don't know. The Ah-Devasi didn't drive Cassie mad. It's avoiding contact that drives a human mad, and not simply contact with those we love. Or once loved. If we can't make contact with the aurora beings, we can at least make contact with Khonds. They're all around us and yet, just as most humans pretend the Ah-Devasi don't exist, so most humans treat the Khond as if they, too, barely exist.

Spiro, for one, but then he's so caught up in his precious work . . . No, that's not fair. It is precious. We're trying to find a way to oxygenate the entire planet without killing off the Khond. As for the Ah-Devasi, Spiro cares about his children as much as I care about the twins, but I wonder if he could defend anyone with his life. If it came to this, if the violet glow ever rolled out of Bight Pass onto the plain, I would protect the twins with my life. I would even kill to protect them. What am I thinking of, though? There are likelier ways of dying than being murdered in our beds: meteor showers, quakes, vehicle crashes. Especially crashes. Life is full of danger even for the Khond. They simply have less to lose, or so people say.

The lift doors opened and I hurried to the observation chair. I strapped myself in and raised it. I turned the chair through north toward the northwest. Toward the aurora.

The strands hung down, even braided, then waved free and curled blue on green. Where the aurora dipped behind the Pyrrhic Range, a strand glimmered in blue shading into indigo. The aurora was resisting the rising of the sun. Before long, though, the aurora lost its battle. It retreats by day and surges back at night. Now it has faded, drawing into itself while the sun keeps rising. While its harsh, harsh rays wash out the lights of Tonkin Bay. The sodium content of the atmosphere has increased since yesterday morning, when the sun looked more blue. Today the sun will be a warm, yellow-orange.

I should go downstairs now to let Cora in. I should be there when the children wake. I think they will like Harun.

Indian Cookery

"Let the madness in."—Russell Hoban to Carol Shields

1

*L*ET'S BEGIN WITH RAMDAS GANDHI (no relation to Mahatma, Mrs. or Rajiv). Ramdas lives in Oban, a picturesque town on the west coast of Scotland best known as a jumping-off point for Iona. Spring, summer and fall he dispenses proprietary medicines and advice to tourists, who often book passage on the *MV Columba*. The vessel ferries them to the Isle of Mull; then a bus shuttles them across Mull, past Ben More Assynt and Castle Duart, to another, smaller dock. Here they wait for the motor launch which takes them, a dozen at a time, over to Iona. Ah, Iona, they wonder; how could we resist your call? They glance at the abbey, then photograph the Celtic crosses in the graveyard. They also remark on the ages of the dead, most of whom succumbed in infancy or extreme old age. You'd have to be tough to live in such a place, the living agree, and sigh over what hardy people the Scots are. Sometimes, wandering into Gandhi Chemist's in search of cough drops or nasal spray, the few tourists who haven't made the crossing ask Ramdas whether Iona lives up to its billing. They look surprised when he admits he has never been. Then they mention their Aunt Effie or Uncle Guido: why, they've lived in Manhattan all their lives and never been up the Empire State Building. Or taken the ferry to Staten Island. There's always something you miss in your own back yard, that's life.

Just now, however, Ramdas is not in his pharmacy. It's late Sunday afternoon and he is making his evening meal. The main course will be spicy baked chicken, also known as *masaledar murghi*, accompanied by rice with peas, aka *tahiri*. The chicken needs to marinade for at least three hours (when he makes it on a weeknight he skips this part).

The recipe serves six. Since Ramdas lives alone, he cuts it by two-thirds and the leftovers are enough for one more meal if he adds salad cream. Julie, his assistant, says he makes the best chicken salad this side of Loch Awe. She should know. They often lunch together and she always asks for a bite. Not that she actually takes a bite out of his sandwich. Heavens, no. For one thing, she's married. For another, she's fifteen years younger than he is. He cuts off a corner for her and she pops it into her mouth. She chews with a satisfied, "Mmm!" Just once he would like to pop the offering into her mouth himself (and watch those peach-glossy lips close around his brown fingers), but it wouldn't stop there. Not that she would balk at having an affair with him, but Oban's too small a place to countenance pharmaceutical hanky panky. Bent over his kitchen counter, Ramdas puts Julie out of his mind. For now.

To grind the spices he uses a mortar and pestle much like those in his pharmacy, except that his domestic versions have never come in contact with tablets or powders. The fact never reassured his former wife, and his skill in the kitchen became one more irritant she brought up during their divorce. Not in court, mind you. She would have sounded ridiculous criticizing him for the way he ground spices. Or hummed off-key. Ramdas hopes she is happy now, snorting up the night life of Soho. It goes with her job. She's an ad executive for an upscale firm. Since most of her clients are bright young men, they prefer the ethnic restaurants of Soho to the roast beeferies of Westminster. Yes, he hopes she is happy. Ramdas isn't, but he is content. He supposes that's all a man can hope for, realistically.

But back to the chicken. A third of the recipe calls for five hundred grams, just over one pound. First he grinds a teaspoon of cumin seeds. Then he measures and adds the remaining spices. The secret to Indian cooking, as he learned long ago, is to do things in a certain order. He would never pour tomato purée into a skillet, for instance, without browning the onions first. But just as the secret to happiness is knowing when to break the rules, so the secret to Indian cooking is knowing the shortcuts. This is why, the proper order notwithstanding, he puts any spices which need grinding into the mortar first. For the chicken he needs to grind only the cumin. It's not much of a shortcut, but he likes to think he knows how to break the rules. Next he adds a teaspoon of paprika followed by half a teaspoon each of cayenne pepper, salt, and black pepper. He grinds the pepper in a Perspex mill from a Scandinavian kitchen store. Last comes a teaspoon of turmeric, which he buys already ground at McTavish Herb and Spice.

Now for the tricky part. He peels a clove of garlic, slices off the fibrous end, and places the clove in the mortar. Some evenings, if he's had a bad day at work, he pounds down with the pestle. This sends yellow puffs of turmeric into the air and makes him sneeze. But today is Sunday, so he cradles the curve of the pestle in the curve of the clove and presses. Ever so gently. He's a gentle man at heart, and Julie likes gentle men. She also likes men who stay home, which her husband can't. He is a lighthouse outfitter for the Inner Hebrides. Three months out of four he's gone, taking orders and delivering goods while Julie raises their school-aged children. But she never complains and Ramdas thinks he knows why: she doesn't want to give him false hopes. Perhaps more important, she's more than content with her life; she is happy.

The clove pops open, exposing its greenish flesh, which he carefully mashes into pulp. Next comes the juice. Lemon juice.

When he was married he used bottled juice because he was always in a hurry. Now he squeezes the lemons himself. Why not? He has all the time in the world. A third of the recipe calls for two tablespoons but this is too much since he won't be baking the chicken. Not at gas mark six, or four hundred Fahrenheit, or two hundred Celsius for forty-five minutes (turn over halfway and baste three to four times). He will use a microwave oven, and he long ago learned to reduce the amount of liquid. Julie says he could make a killing if he wrote a Yuppie Indian Cookbook, all the recipes converted for microwave, but Ramdas wags his head when she reminds him of this. He knows she thinks he doesn't have enough ambition (another thing his wife held against him—imagine settling for Oban when all of London beckoned), but he also knows Julie would disapprove if he developed an enterprising bent. He could never disappoint her, neither by making an advance, however tentative, nor by developing a middle-aged lust for money. No, he could never disappoint his Julie, she of the peach-gloss lips and light brown hair. Ah, Julie. How can a man resist?

After stirring the marinade, Ramdas scoops it up and smears the gritty paste over the chicken. It's boneless breast.

The pinkish grey flesh turns a deep yellow red. Before reaching for the plastic wrap, he licks his fingers, washes his hands and dries them. He lays a length of wrap over the chicken, smoothes the wrap over the edges of the platter, and puts it in the fridge. Before cooking the chicken, he will pull up one corner of the wrap and fold it back to make a vent.

When he first got the microwave, he would cook the chicken on high for five minutes, check it, and give it another three minutes. Now that he has perfected the conversion from earthbound to spaceage technology, the chicken takes exactly seven minutes on high. He could render the drippings into a sauce but he doesn't usually bother with this. The chicken is juicy enough on its own.

And there we are. Ramdas unloads the dishwasher while humming along, off-key, with Liszt's transcription of Beethoven's *Sixth Symphony*. In two and one-half hours he will start the rice with peas, using the stove, not the microwave, and, half an hour later, settle in front of the telly for the film on Channel Four. Out in the lamp lit streets, tourists who have made the journey to Iona will troop into restaurants for their evening meal. The younger tourists, Americans and Australians, will huddle in the warmth of fish and chip shops. Not that they'll order fish and chips. They're here for adventure, and fish and chips are so, well, proletarian. Most of them will try the deep-fried haggis with a side of neeps. Then the lovers among them will split one of the pineapple fritters for which Oban is renowned.

2

Ah, pineapple: a fine English word corrupted by Indian weavers of the Raj into *pinaphal* or *minaphal*. This is what such Indians call a certain silk they weave, thanks to its repeating pattern of pineapples. So thinks Jasmin Bose (no relation to

Subhas Chandra Bose of the Indian National Army). It's late Sunday morning where Jasmin lives, in the American city of Moorhead, Minnesota. Not exactly a Mecca for tourists—people in St. Paul-Minneapolis, the Twin Cities, call this part of their state Outstate—but Jasmin is comfortable here. Perhaps too much so. Since she's an etymologist, it's natural she should think about words while making *anaanaas sabjee* (pineapple curry) for two.

More to the point, Jasmin thinks of writing a book, one about English words of Indian origin. Not that this hasn't been done, but she wants to write the sort which will find its way into book clubs yet impress her colleagues with its scholarship. A coup like this would give her a one-way ticket from Outstate Minnesota back to New England; from Moorhead State University to the Ivy League. How this might affect her relationship with her lover, Uma Natarajan, is something Jasmin doesn't want to consider. It's hard not to, though. Uma has tenure and would like to stay at MSU for another three years. But, as she told Jasmin last night while they tried to read in bed, "Let's burn that bridge when we get to it." It's the sort of glib remark Jasmin expects from Uma, but then she isn't the worrier in the family. Enough, Jasmin thinks. Curry won't make itself.

She lays the pineapple on its side and reaches for a long Wiltshire knife. It's one of a pair, both of which spend their days waiting to be washed, drying on a wooden rack, or sharpening themselves in their Staysharp holder.

First Jasmin cuts the top off the pineapple. The result looks like a cap studded with leaves and she wonders what she could do with it. The cap looks too perfect to throw away, and she hasn't yet got around to ordering a compost bin. She supposes she could bury the cap in potting soil, but pineapples don't do well in Minnesota. If she had a child, she knows exactly what she could do: after the cap of flesh dried, she could wrap it in yellow cloth, sew the cloth closed at the base of the leaves, and attach ribbons to tie under the little chin. "Look," the child would say at Halloween. "Guess what I am."

Laughing off the fantasy, Jasmin stands the pineapple on end and holds it steady. She cuts away the skin, adding it to the cap for eventual disposal. She lays the pineapple down again and cuts off the base. The pineapple lies naked on the laminated cutting board. The flesh is still firm from lack of handling, and the juice hasn't yet risen to the surface. Or spread along the walnut and maple.

Uma once asked whether they shouldn't get one of those hard, white plastic boards from the Kitchen Shoppe in Fargo (Moorhead's twin city). Jasmin said she preferred wood. If a plastic board isn't washed properly, there's too much danger of bacteria growing in the gouges and nicks. True, a wooden board has to be washed as conscientiously as a plastic one—though with little, if any, soap—and occasionally oiled, but the wood can do something plastic can't. Wood kills bacteria. "Mother Nature knows best," Jasmin said, to which Uma retorted, "Mother Jasmin knows best." They never speak directly of this, but they both know Uma is the child Jasmin will never have. Sometimes, when Jasmin can't sleep, it occurs to her that, although she's only ten years older than Uma, their relationship is not without its hint of incest. Only a hint: just enough to tantalize the emotional taste buds.

Fortunately, it's not the sort of thing that would occur to the good people of Moorhead. As Uma calls them. According to her, those who know Jasmin and Uma share more than a house fall into three camps. There are friends who are truly happy for them. There are acquaintances who consider themselves liberal-minded and say they understand. Then there are colleagues who excuse the arrangement on the grounds that foreign women are entitled to be different. There's the *Kama Sutra* and all that, right? I mean, if a couple of good lookers want to perjure their souls, what business is it of a true Christian? Not that people actually say as much, but even the true Christians Jasmin knows have such open minds she can read them like a book.

Now comes the hardest part. Jasmin puts the long knife aside and reaches for its smaller partner, good for close work. She begins cutting out the eyes. She's not sure this is what they're called, but potatoes have eyes, so why shouldn't pineapples? Some days she cuts the eyes out one at a time, but she wants to get started on her book. Today. She makes long incisions on either side of the rows of eyes and flicks them out. Once she's finished, the flesh is marked with roughly curved, diagonal grooves. It's growing softer now from all the handling. Juice oozes into the grooves before trickling onto the board.

She stands the pineapple up again, reaches for the long knife, and cuts off the flesh in large chunks. She cuts them into strips, turns the strips, and cuts again until a pyramid of golden cubes glistens on the board. Lifting it carefully so the juice can't spill, she places the lower edge of the board over the lip of a platter and slides the cubes off. She licks her fingers, washes her hands, and dries them. Now for the onion.

One large onion, chopped. Yellow is preferable, white will do, but red would be too sweet. Jasmin chooses white. This is the dangerous part, since the blade is sharp and she slices close to her fingertips. Still, she lets her mind wander—due east, across the Great Lakes into Canada, to the University of Waterloo Centre for the New Oxford English Dictionary (*OED2* for short). Here the historic work was computerized for its release by Oxford University Press. The MSU library already has its copy. Jasmin can't afford her own, but she might buy the mass-market electronic version. She can't wait. The very day she heard of the centre, she wrote to ask whether it could provide a list of all the words in *OED2* which originate in Indian languages. She listed twenty, ranging from the better known like Hindi and Tamil to the lesser known like Dogri and Pahari. The reply came posthaste: a forty-four-page print-out listing, in two columns, over eight hundred words. "This does not mean," the applications manager wrote, "that in every case the word originates in an Indian language, for it may be a cross-reference. However, since I am also sending you the etymologies, you will be able to figure this out." The kind letter concluded with, "I wish you all success in your writing (both relating to this information and otherwise)."

Success? Why shouldn't the book be a success? All Jasmin has to do is write it, but the list has been in her files for over a year and she hasn't written a line. She hasn't bought her ticket out of MSU let alone checked her *Bradshaw*. She's not even ready to write. She's getting ready to get ready, an affliction more common among tenured scholars than among those who have to prove their worth. Uma should know. She teases Jasmin about the book but Jasmin knows Uma hopes Jasmin will never get ready. Uma loves Jasmin, and Jasmin loves Uma, books and tenure be damned.

But back to the curry, which Jasmin will serve for lunch with plain basmati rice. Now she concentrates on roasting the spices. The recipe calls for using a thick-bottomed frying pan or even a wok, yet Jasmin uses a Corningware casserole dish. It's easier to wash than a frying pan or wok and stays cooler on the stove. Besides, she likes the design: California poppies that haven't dulled in spite of years of washing. She pours two tablespoons of vegetable oil into the dish, turns the heat to medium, and plops the clear glass cover on the dish. Then she waits.

While waiting, she thinks. Most lay persons know that many English words come to us from India: brahmin, rajah and, of course, curry. The seventeenth century saw the addition of cheroot, coolie, bungalow, and chintz; the eighteenth century brought us jungle, jute and toddy. Even Jasmin, for all her etymological training, was not prepared for some of the entries on the Waterloo printout because she doesn't specialize in Indian words (it would limit her chances for employment). She knows she has found a gold mine. Why? Because if she was surprised by some of the words, her readers might be surprised as well. Take bandana, from the Hindustani *bandhnu*, meaning "a mode of dyeing in which the cloth is tied in different places, to prevent the parts from receiving the dye." Most readers would assume bandana came to us from Spain, and they wouldn't be far off. It was likely first adopted by the Portuguese, who, at one time, could sail circles around the Spanish. Or take cash, of all things, from the Tamil *kasu*, "or perhaps some Konkani form of it, name of a small coin or weight of money," from the Sanskrit *karsha*, "a weight of silver or gold equal to one-fourhundredth of a tula." Again, we have the Portuguese to thank. And what about catamaran? From the Tamil *katta-maram*, *katta* meaning tie and *maram* meaning wood, from which we get a boat made of tied wood.

The oil is hot now—Jasmin can tell because the glass cover is starting to cloud—so in go the mustard seeds, half a teaspoon. This is the tricky part, so pay attention. (She hears herself saying this to the child she will never have.) You can't just dump mustard seeds into oil and expect miracles. You have to do this: holding the lid onto the dish with one hand, grasping one of the flared handles with the other hand, she slides the dish back and forth across the burner to agitate the seeds. They start popping, turning dark, but not all of them.

Mustard seeds are known to be difficult. Now comes the second trick: you lift the lid a few inches from the dish. She nods in satisfaction when the steam from the seeds carries their aroma up to her. None of them smells burnt. As soon as the unpopped seeds start popping, she covers the dish and once again slides it back and forth. She doesn't understand the physics involved but thinks it has to do with replacing the moist air in the dish with drier air. This superheats the oil and causes the rest of the seeds to pop—some of them so hard, they jump up and cling to the inside of the cover. When they're all done, in goes the onion.

She stirs with a spoon (a wooden spoon, of course) while her mind returns to the book. Even some of the more common words we've adopted have interesting origins—so she will tell her readers. Cheroot comes from the French *cheroute,* which came from the Tamil *shuruttu,* meaning roll, and became, in the English of the early 1800s, *sharoot.* As for chintz, it's the plural of *chint,* from Hindi, also found as *chite* in French and *chita* in Portuguese but all coming somehow from the Sanskrit *chitra,* meaning variegated. According to the list, "The plural of this word, being more frequent in commercial use, came in course of time to be mistaken for a singular, and this to be written *chince, chinse,* and at length *chints.*" Jasmin shakes her head over the onion, browning nicely; over how everything fits if you look hard enough. As that metaphysical poet John Donne might just as well have said, "No word is an island, entire to itself." She wonders what would come next but can't imagine.

It's finally safe to leave the onion for a moment, so she grinds one teaspoon of coriander seeds with two whole, dry chillies. She does her grinding in a small white mortar. It came with a pestle from the Kitchen Shoppe in Fargo. The recipe calls for four chillies but she's not that Indian. She adds the spices to the onion and mustard seed; taps the mortar with the pestle to free those last, stubborn grains of coriander; and stirs. She transfers the pineapple from the platter and stirs again.

Almost done. The recipe calls for half a teaspoon of salt but she uses only a quarter teaspoon. The recipe also calls for two tablespoons of honey but, most days, she leaves out the honey without telling Uma. Uma has a sweet tooth, but the secret to happiness, after all, is knowing when to break the rules. As for water, the recipe calls for one pint but Jasmin adds less than half, not quite one cup. She is making curry, not soup. The water sizzles in the hot dish. Once the curry starts bubbling, she turns the heat to simmer. She leaves the cover off so some of the water can evaporate. Now for the rice.

Sometime in the next half-hour, Uma will come home. She will slam the door, drop her briefcase on the living room sofa, and exclaim, "Something smells good!"

"You're imagining things," Jasmin will call. She will make a mental note to move the briefcase later.

When Uma enters the kitchen, Jasmin will hold out her arms and Uma will come to her. They will exchange a brief kiss. Nothing erotic. A token of a morning spent apart—Jasmin in her kitchen, Uma at her office marking exams—while the good people of Moorhead were seen in church.

Jasmin will break away first because she doesn't want to seem too maternal in case Uma asks, "Did you miss me?"

While Jasmin spoons out the rice, then the curry using a slotted spoon, she will say, "Cummerbund, from the Urdu and Persian *kamar-band*, meaning loin-band. Dinghy, from the Hindi *dengi* or *dingi*, meaning a small boat, diminutive of *denga* or *donga*, meaning a larger boat, a sloop, a coasting vessel."

If Uma snorts now, Jasmin will stop but today Uma won't snort. Jasmin will continue with, "Pariah, punch, pyjama. Saffron, sandal, shampoo. Tattoo, teapoy, thug, topi." She will end with, "Veranda, found throughout India in various languages as *varanda* in Hindi and *baranda* in Bengali, but they may simply have adopted it from the Portuguese or Spanish *varanda* or *baranda* meaning railing, balustrade, balcony." She will turn with her own plate in one hand, Uma's in the other, and conclude: "What's really surprising, though it shouldn't be, is that the Indians adopted as many words from Europeans as the Europeans did from Indians."

Then Uma, who teaches geology (her specialty is tectonics), will recite: "No man is an island, entire of itself; every man is a piece of the continent, a part of the main." But Uma being Uma, she will break the spell by demanding, "How come your plate's bigger?"

3

Believe it or not, there are people in this world who prefer the satire of Jonathan Swift to the metaphysics of John Donne. Ah well, *chacun à son gout*. Take Albert Lawlor. He has even written out his favourite Swiftian verse and taped it to the fridge:

> So, naturalists observe, a flea
> Hath smaller fleas that on him prey;
> And these have smaller still to bite 'em;
> And so proceed *ad infinitum*.

Albert would like to sleep but he can't. He is too tired. It's early morning in Vancouver, on the west coast of Canada, and he's been up all night. Where other men might run a few kilometers to exhaust themselves, or stroll down to the Museum of Anthropology to admire a Haida canoe being carved on the beach, Albert cooks.

Just now, he is waiting for a batch of lentils to thaw in the microwave. He is admiring a row of Tupperware bins. Each bin holds one and one-half litres of a different kind of pulse. The bins are labelled, some in English with their Indian equivalents (or so he assumes); others only in a foreign language; and still others only in English. There are seven such bins, arranged like the colours of a rainbow. The red kidney beans, *rajma*, are dark red. The aduki beans, or *ma*, look like little kidney beans. Sometimes he switches the order of the kidney and aduki beans. Not now, though. He is too tired for such trivial amusement. The red split lentils, *masoor dal*, are more salmon than red, so they pass for orange in his rainbow of pulses. The *chana dal* comes next since it's similar, though not identical, to yellow split peas. And the whole green lentils are, in fact, a greenish-brown. There's nothing close to blue, indigo, or violet in the arrangement (nor is there beige in a rainbow), so the last two bins throw off his colour scheme. The black-eyed beans, *lobhia*, are beige ovals marked with a dark dot. The chickpeas are also beige.

It's only natural for Albert to be fascinated by lentils and peas and beans. He's a nuclear scientist. He has devoted his life to understanding the forces that keep the nucleus together, and these days he is concentrating on the pion, or pi-meson, the mediator of nuclear force. He explores the sub-nuclear realm by bombarding deuterons, the nucleii of heavy hydrogen, with pions. Friends who know little about physics consider his work mysterious (even exotic). He doesn't. Not any more.

Albert does his experiments with a particle accelerator called TRIUMF. It's located on the picturesque grounds of the University of British Columbia—as is the Museum of Anthropology. Mind you, he has never been inside the museum.

Nor has he been up Grouse Mountain or taken the ferry to Victoria. Every three months, he and five companions, all men, spend a week at UBC. They don't live in Vancouver. They live far away, east across the Rocky Mountains, and are based at a university unable to afford its own particle accelerator. While at TRIUMF, they work around the clock because each eight-hour shift needs at least two men to carry on experiments. In theory, the men take turns cooking dinner for one another in the guesthouse; in practice, Albert makes dinner every night.

The others help, of course. As soon as they arrive at UBC, Albert sends the graduate students, Gary Hansen and Antonio DePasquale, off in their rented van with a shopping list. Once the van returns, four of the six men set to work in the kitchen. The other two are already at TRIUMF checking in, or visiting deans and department heads. The secret of success in modern science, after all, is not experimentation; it's diplomacy.

Seated at a large, wooden table, Albert measures out the spices for the week and seals them into Ziploc sandwich bags: all the turmeric and salt, whole cumin seeds, ground coriander, cayenne pepper, and black pepper. Even the *garam masala* which Gary and Antonio pick up, ready-mixed, at a spice shop on Main Street.

Albert's colleague, Jeff Matthews, stands at one end of the counter. Here he chops and minces and grates. He chops onions and tomatoes, minces garlic, and grates ginger—enough for a week's worth of dinners. The onions and tomatoes go into Tupperware tubs, the garlic and ginger into smaller Tupperware canisters, and all this goes in the bottom of the fridge.

At the other end of the counter, near the stove, Gary and Antonio do their part. They measure the lentils, peas, and beans; pick out grit; wash the pulses; and drain them in one of two colanders. The kitchen is not fancy, but it is well equipped.

After all, the guesthouse is more usually home to foreigners than Canadians, and the university knows how to make a good impression. While Gary and Antonio work, they chat about the coming week. More often, though, they dream. Without knowing it, they dream about the same thing: each, in his own mind, is composing his Nobel Prize acceptance speech. But the Nobel Prize must wait; back to the everyday grind. They cook the pulses in separate pots, always in batches of two hundred grams (seven ounces) in one and one-half litres of water (two pints). The red split lentils, which must be simmered for an hour and a quarter, are the messiest. A scum collects on top and has to be spooned off. As for the chickpeas, Garth measures three hundred and fifty grams into one and three-quarter litres of water. The chickpeas must soak for up to twenty hours before they can be cooked.

Each batch of lentils or peas or beans serves six, so there is always just enough. Though Albert is vegetarian, he will make a meat dish and cook either rice or pasta, or slice up a loaf of crusty bread. If his fellow boffins had their way, they wouldn't have pulses every night for a week, but none of them likes to cook, and a man can't do his best work on wieners and beans. Thus, Albert is the king of the kitchen, and the others are his minions. This is what they call themselves, too: Lawlor's Culinary Minions.

Fortunately, today is their last full day at TRIUMF for another three months. Albert will be glad to go home. Travel excited him once. Not any more. Like Gary and Antonio, there was even a time Albert dreamt of winning a Nobel Prize. Now he wants nothing more than to build his own boat. A seagoing boat. A catamaran. He will sail it across the Pacific. He will stop at Hawaii long enough to tour a volcano; then he will head for the South Pacific and wander among its islands and archipelagos. He will follow in the wakes of Paul Gaugin, of Robert Louis Stevenson. Even of Colin McPhee, that once neglected composer who introduced Balinese music to the West. Wouldn't that be the life? But Albert's daydream ends when he shudders from lack of sleep. He sighs, opens his IBM Thinkpad, and switches it on. All his recipes are computerized.

Moving to the stove, he starts on today's pulse dish. It's red split lentils with cabbage, or *masoor dal aur band gobi*. When Gary and Antonio were cooking the lentils on the first day, Albert added half a teaspoon of turmeric to the pot. Now he measures five tablespoons of vegetable oil into a frying pan and turns the stove to medium. While the oil heats, he measures out the last of the garlic and onion. His calculations were so precise, he has exactly what he needs in the Tupperware: three cloves of garlic, minced, and seventy-five grams (three ounces) of onion. After a week in the fridge, both the garlic and onion are starting to discolour but they're still fine. The onion should be in thin slices for this recipe, but he makes do with chopped. He knows enough about cooking to break the rules, just as he knows enough about science to realize it will no longer save the world.

He finds it incredible to think there was a time he believed such a thing. This was back in the sixties, when he kept a poster of another Albert (Einstein) taped to his fridge. Just before leaving to come here, our Albert found the poster rolled up and packed away in a mailing tube. He wanted to put it up in the family room to inspire his daughters, but the poster was dog eared and faded. Back it went into storage—with his first microscope, still in its original wooden box, the clasp and hinges brass. He once thought if he kept the poster and microscope long enough they might become antiques. Now he shakes his head. He's the antique, and age hasn't increased his value.

Albert guesses the oil is hot and adds a teaspoon of cumin seeds. He lets them sizzle for exactly five seconds, then adds the minced garlic. He moves the pieces about with a spatula so they'll brown but not burn.

He knows what his problem is—it's more than just a midlife crisis—but there's no one he can ask for advice. It shocks him: how few close friends he has. It's not that he wants to abandon science. It's just that he wants to start over. He wants to leave his comfortable house, leave his wife and daughters, and vanish. He wants to start somewhere else, with a new identity, a new name. Oh, Albert, he tells himself. You've got everything you ever wanted—a family, respect—and you've got nothing left to prove. But he can't just disappear (he loves his family too much) and building a catamaran might be too ambitious, so the next best thing would be to see India. Not the Taj Mahal, not the temples of Madurai, and he has no illusions about the romance of poverty. No, he wants to find himself, and what better place for a man to find himself than in India? This is called doing Head India. Yet he knows the pitfalls awaiting a man: finding everything but himself. Besides, while Albert's not so conceited as to think he's the only man who has ever experienced a crisis of faith, it galls him to think that, by doing Head India, he would follow in the footsteps of countless Westerners. Tens of thousands: X times ten to the fourth.

With the garlic browned, he adds the onion and the cabbage—two hundred and twenty-five grams of cabbage (half a pound)—which Jeff Matthews cored, shredded, and also stored on that first night. While steam rises from the leaves, Albert chops a green chilli and adds this as well. He stir-fries the cabbage mixture for ten minutes. He tries to find solace by thinking of those who love him, but he's too tired now to think of even love. He switches on the radio. Someone has left it on a rock and roll station again, so he tunes it to CJVB. It's Vancouver's multicultural station, and, yes, it's playing Indian music.

The cabbage has browned and turned slightly crisp. He adds a quarter teaspoon of salt, stirs it in, and turns off the heat. Now for the lentils. After taking them out of the microwave, he spoons them into a heavy pot and adds the remaining ingredients: another teaspoon of salt, half a teaspoon of grated ginger, and one hundred and ten grams (four ounces) of chopped tomatoes. He covers the pot and, after bringing the lentil mixture to a boil, lets it simmer for ten minutes. With the strains of an Indian *raga* soothing his scattered brainwaves, time passes. Quickly. He uncovers the pot, adds the cabbage mixture and the oil from the frying pan, and stirs. After the whole thing has simmered (uncovered) for three minutes, he turns off the heat. The pot, once it cools, will go into the fridge. Albert will finally go to bed. Another night, another dollar, another pion-deuteron reaction.

He sinks onto a chair and waits for the *raga* to end. On top of the fridge is a spool of magnetic tape he brought back with him at the end of his shift. There are often arguments at airport security over these tapes, at the X-ray machines, but someone else will handle it. Jeff Matthews, most likely. He's the team leader: the one in charge of setting up apparatus, supervising Gary and Antonio while they calibrate the electronics and, best of all, filling out grant applications and reports. Albert is just the cook. Chief cook and bottle washer. Well, not quite. That's what grad students are for. Ladies and gentlemen, let me tell you, Albert Lawlor is a valued member of our team. What he lacks in enthusiasm in the lab, he more than makes up for in the kitchen. Home, oh, home. Once they all fly back, he will take the rest of Monday off. Maybe even Tuesday. He will teach for two days, then start analyzing the data on the tapes. First things first, though. Sleep. Now.

At four o'clock he will get up, shave and shower, and make the rest of dinner: lemony chicken with fresh coriander, which he won't eat, and spiced basmati rice, which he will eat. He will follow this with a bowl of yogurt and so get his complete proteins—from a pulse, a grain, and a dairy product. The men finishing their day shift will have beer with their meal. The men on the six o'clock to midnight shift will have coffee. After dinner, Albert will go to a nearby repertory theatre for the second showing of a foreign film. Tonight's film is *Ganeshatru*, adapted by Satyajit Ray from Ibsen's *An Enemy of the People*. Albert will not have popcorn. He would feel guilty stuffing himself while watching an Indian film. Then he will start his midnight shift. Tomorrow morning the six men will pack, drop the van at the airport, and catch their flight home. Albert will sleep the whole way. And while their plane wings east, over the Rocky Mountains, Albert will dream. He will dream of a rainbow made of lentils and peas and beans, all the colours pulsing with energy, all the tiny particles colliding into a dazzling mass of beige. Sleep well, Albert. Sweet dreams.

4

As for us, let's find Durga MacKenzie (no relation to General Lewis MacKenzie, the hero of Sarajevo). We reach Durga by also returning east; by moving with the earth's rotation; moving with the grain. It's just after lunch where she lives, in Ottawa, Ontario. Crystals dangling between parted curtains cast rainbows onto her apartment walls, even into the galley-style kitchen. She has neither time nor patience for cooking proper meals. Not "from scratch," the way her mother did, spending half her day in the kitchen and eating only after the men were done. Not on your life. Durga has mastered instant foods. Her cupboards are stocked with cardboard packets from Gits—Idli Mix, Sambar Mix—and her fridge with bottles from Patak—Tandoori Paste, Vindaloo Curry Paste. Her spice rack also bears witness to a woman used to shortcuts. Instead of slicing ginger or mincing garlic, she uses ginger powder and, since she has avoided inheriting her mother's high blood pressure, plenty of garlic salt.

Durga is a major in the Canadian Armed Forces. It's an unlikely occupation for an Indian, but she's breaking ground most white women can't. Her exoticism protects her from her colleagues' guarded chauvinism. She doesn't feel exotic—she often feels like a fraud—but she knows twenty years from now people will look back at what she accomplished (at what little she's accomplishing, she thinks) and wonder at the fuss. MacKenzie's a married name, of course. Durga met her husband, Ian, when he was an officer cadet at the Royal Military College and she was studying commerce at Queen's. It made sense for her to join the regular forces after convocating since she was already in the reserves: a clerk in the Princess of Wales Own Regiment. As for the seven-year marriage, it foundered because Durga was promoted faster than Ian and he couldn't live with the shame. He couldn't live with her, that is. Not to worry. The separation was amicable and they still keep in touch. They even sleep together on the few occasions they meet, which is seldom. He has shed the two stripes of a captain for the pinstripes of a diplomat. He's in New Delhi, where, next year, they'll mark her thirty-eighth birthday with a visit to Agra. First, though, she has to survive her new posting.

She gets up from the dining table, piled high with maps and books, and steps into the kitchen. She doesn't live to eat, she eats to live, but lately she's been too nervous to keep her diet balanced. She takes a bag of samosas from the freezer. (They're sold by most Indian grocers, as are the bottles from

Patak and the packets from Gits.) She puts two samosas on a Corelle plate and ignores their less than appetizing appearance. The corners are frozen solid. After pressing Defrost and guessing how much the samosas weigh, she presses Start. The fan roars to life. The timer counts down. Pacing among the rainbows, she eats flavoured yogurt straight from the plastic cup. She barely notices the taste: pineapple.

And what about these maps and books? Is she already planning for India? Not just yet. They're on the former Yugoslavia because Major MacKenzie has scored a coup: in less than a month she will join the United Nations Protection Force in Bosnia. No wonder she doesn't feel like eating much. The Serbs, Croats and Bosnians are intent on sending one another to paradise and who will care if an interloper, a mere finance officer at that, gets in the way? She knows Ian will care. Fortunately, she takes weapons refresher courses, but it's been years since she was in or near a combat zone. Even then the wars weren't real—neither civil nor uncivil—because they were exercises. War games. They were like cartoons: no one really died.

Looking down at the cup, empty now, Durga realizes she has finished the yogurt without enjoying it. She's not about to keep pacing—a watched microwave never defrosts—so she sits down again but doesn't see the maps and books.

Her mother once accused her of playing at marriage the way she played at war. Her mother had even refused to attend the wedding. She had said, "None of this is real." It's not that she objected to a love match but, if Durga insisted on falling in love, why couldn't she pick a nice Indian boy? This was what Durga's elder sister had done. She'd married the first son of the Mississauga Patels—good boy, Sanskrit scholar, special advisor to the Shastri Institute—and the second son, Doctor Patel, was unmarried. Not only would it be an ideal match but it would also keep the extended family compact. (This was what Durga's mother had done by marrying her own brother-in-law's brother. Such things were not uncommon in certain families.)

The microwave beeps once. This is to remind Durga that, if she wants to turn the samosas over to defrost evenly, she should do it soon. But she is lost in the past so she won't dwell on the future. On Serbs and Croats, on Christians and Muslims; broken cease-fires, broken promises.

The more her mother tried to control Durga, the more Durga rebelled. "It started with those sleepovers," her mother told her bridge club. "God only knows what these Canadian girls do! Smoking and drinking. Drinking and smoking. *Ayoh!*" After the wedding she wrote, "Good thing your father is not alive to see this. How will I tell him after I join him in heaven?" Seven years later she wrote, "I will never be able to show my face back home. You may drown my ashes in Lake Ontario."

Back in the present, Durga can't wait much longer for the samosas to defrost. She opens the microwave door and pokes at them. They're no longer frozen. Grains of ground beef press out against the translucent dough. She pushes the button for Plate Reheat, then Start. The timer counts down again. She fills a kettle, plugs it in, and looks for tea. She decides on Bengal Spice and prints, "T-2," on a memo pad taped to the fridge. Besides her Sony Walkman and a selection of cassettes—everything from Beethoven and Liszt to Ravi Shankar—she plans to take her favourite crystal. The sun must shine even in Sarajevo. And she'll take plenty of food. At the very least, a bottle of mango pickle, a bottle of lime pickle, and two boxes of Bengal Spice. She has already arranged with her favourite Indian grocer to send CARE packages, one a month. She has paid him in advance, and he has promised to include treats in every shipment: cumin biscuits, cashews. Even a tin of mangoes. She and her sister always loved a good mango. They would suck the pulp off one another's fingers when their mother wasn't looking. They were practising for marriage.

Now Durga's obedient, elder sister is having an affair. She's keeping the extended family compact in more ways than one since her lover is her husband's only brother. Durga can't decide whether to scold her sister or wish her well. During the years with Ian, Durga never once had an affair. Not that she wasn't tempted; she simply wasn't willing to keep track of lies. The kind of lies her sister now tells each time she absolutely has to spend a weekend alone in the family cottage on Georgian Bay. As for Young Doctor Patel, if he disappears on his weekend retreats in the opposite direction—to Montreal, supposedly—who can blame him? He works all the time, poor boy, because there is no one waiting for him at home. The way Durga's mother waited for her own husband. Why, the minute he walked in the door from work he would find a glass of lime soda next to a plate of savory, deep-fried snacks and, after he sat back in his reclining chair, Durga's mother would massage his feet.

The microwave beeps three times. The samosas are done. Durga takes a bottle of coriander chutney from the fridge—Shah's Coriander Chutney—and another plastic cup of yogurt (coconut this time). She pours the yogurt onto the samosas and taps a spoonful of chutney beside them. The water is boiling, so she fills a teapot. A Brown Betty, the handle chipped. She sits down, clears a place on the dining table, and starts to eat. She tries not to think about Sarajevo, but she can't help thinking ahead to Agra. There, a year from now, she will tell Ian this latest news in person. It's not the sort of news one can write in a letter, and it will take a long time to tell. He won't dare laugh until she does, and even then she will scold him because it's no laughing matter. In fact, should Durga's mother ever learn of the affair, which will have ended by then, the knowledge would surely kill her.

5

So there we are. While the world turns from breakfast to lunch to dinner and even to supper and midnight snacks, we are once more reminded how connected we all are: how no man is, indeed, an island. But one last thing before we go our separate ways. Clearly it's not money that makes the world go round. Nor is it love for another human, since this kind of love too often eludes us. No, my friends. Gandhi or MacKenzie, Lawlor or Bose, what makes the world go round—what connects us if not into a continent then into an archipelago—is nothing less than our love of Indian food. Then again, perhaps not. And, if not, what is the point of this rather long story if, indeed, it is a story? My dear, dear friends, in lieu of brandy and cigars, allow me to tantalize you (one last time) with the following clue:

"Won't be long now. These so-called writers of colour will start publishing recipes and call it art."—Anonymous

In the Beginning, There Was Memory

TONIGHT'S PERFORMANCE IS OF CHOPIN. It is not really night. I have willed the space around me a flat, midnight black. Random constellations rise in what would be the east if directions still mattered. So little matters now.

Chopin plays behind me in a hallway. He plays among a smattering of Hindu sculptures: a mother goddess, a four-faced Shiva, and a goddess of destruction. Their faces are inexact. As for the music, the composer himself is at the piano. He plays his first Ballade, the one in G minor with its complementary themes. I did not know, when I listened to his Ballades during my student days, that he both invented and perfected the form. Later I learned. Some have suggested ballades tell stories and pointed as proof to the musical logic of the form. Others disagreed. They claimed ballades are stories without plot or character; that the only dialogue is an unspoken one between performer and listener. Or, in this case, between the composer and himself since he plays as though I were not even here.

This was my favourite room in what was once the Royal Ontario Museum: the Bishop White Gallery with its Buddhist paintings and sculptures. The largest painting—the entire, far wall—depicts the future Buddha with disciples and celestial attendants. They appear identical although, in the original, they were not identical. Two smaller paintings—each a flanking wall—are of Daoist deities moving through an ethereal world. They, too, seem identical. The wooden sculptures are of Boddhisattvas, images of compassion. My favourite is Guan Yin, the Goddess of Mercy. This was where I sat as a widower each afternoon. Since the gallery no longer exists, I have re-created it for myself here. Wherever *here* is.

I confess: it is not really Chopin at the piano. It is a re-creation of him just as the piano is a re-creation of a piano. He plays like the real Chopin, though; of this I am sure: his almost tight control of volume, his unconventional fingering. The first Ballade ends. The second begins. This is the one in F, the one he dedicated to Schumann, who preferred the tranquil opening section to what followed. So did the composer. So do I. Like the real Chopin, my re-creation plays an extended version of that tranquil opening. Perfect for midnight, perfect for solitude. How often I dreamt of being the only person in an audience, in some open-air salon, while Chopin played Ballades for me. How often I dreamt of being the only one, and now I am.

2

This evening's performance is of Cesar Franck. Again, it is not really evening. I have willed a rosy glow in what I have decided, from now on, will be west. I suppose I should be amazed by it all. Perhaps I am still in shock: taking notes for no other reason than to formulate a record. But for whom?

Franck composed this sonata, for violin and piano, as a

wedding present. It begins reflectively, with only the violin exploring that undulating first theme. The piano joins, intruding as a murmur, then keeps the second theme to itself—the one more emotional than the first. This is a piece meant to be heard when a person is alone. I listened to it every evening for a year after my wife died. Once the grief passed—and it did, though I did not want it to pass—I put the recording away. Now I need the sonata once more. I may need it for longer than a year this time: to help me grieve not for one soul but for billions; for those who passed before them; for those who will never again pass.

This is what surprises me about my new life. I feel no different than I did as a widower: just as powerless, just as indifferent to the future. Those days I felt as though, if the world should end, it might not matter. How could I know it really would end?

It happened unexpectedly on a sunny, Sunday afternoon. The triviality of it all: the absurdity of the mundane. I was sitting on the deck behind my house and reading the weekend *Globe and Mail*. I was dropping the first section at my feet. They always annoyed me: those full-page advertisements for the *Globe* itself. This one posed a Canadian prime minister in the shadow of an American president. Such a typical pose. Underneath was the caption that appeared on all these ads whether they depicted chancellors or kings. "Sooner or later," the *Globe* claimed, "all news is business news." Often I said aloud, as I did just then, "Is this what we've come to? God save us." Then the sun grew bright—too bright—and the sky began to glow. I needed no one to tell me what was happening. I sat there and watched a dusty cloud swell; watched the afternoon sky ignite.

I knew every good Hindu should say, "*Hé Ram,*" when he dies. This means, "Oh God," but in that moment I forgot I was Hindu. Even as my bifocals melted before my eyes, I felt grateful my wife had not lived to see this. "Fools," I shouted. "Fools!" This is all I remember. I do not remember leaving my body or travelling toward a source of comforting, white light. I do not remember my wife or even my mother welcoming me like angels. When I finally grew conscious of my surroundings, the first thing I asked was, "Why did you save me?" I had not meant to scream; only to ask. This was before I realized I was not floating on a burn bed; that those who had saved me were not doctors; that an ocean of tears would be too small.

Even now, when I listen to this sonata, I weep, though without tears. I catch myself muttering, "Fools." In a single afternoon they erased the work of centuries; made the joys and sorrows of so many souls count as nothing. Think of Van Gogh, distracted by that ringing in his ear; of Nijinsky in his straightjacket; of Robert Schumann. Yes, think of Schumann, whose wedded bliss lasted only four years before his mind betrayed him. Not even Clara could save him from madness. Not even she. If my wife were here she would say, "Don't forget Dianne Arbus or Sylvia Plath. And what about Virginia Woolf, contemplating each stone she sewed into her sweater before she waded into that stream?" Think of them all.

The sonata ends briskly, with more energy than it allowed itself at first, though with no less regret. Only in the last section do the violin and piano play in unison, in a canon some have described as pedantic. I disagree, and there is no one here to debate the point. There are advantages to solitude, after all.

The performers look neither delighted nor humble when I applaud. I have not mastered faces but the pianist is a re-creation of Glenn Gould, the violinist a re-creation of Niccolo Paganini. They could not have performed together—not two such dilletantes—but this is not real life. It is entertainment:

my way of passing time when time, like directions, no longer matters. Gould hums while remaining hunched over the keyboard. Paganini taps his foot. I cannot think of another sonata for them and so they wait. If I let them, each would gladly perform separately, but I am weary of solos.

3

Devi appears impressed with my latest creation, a copy of the children's park at Brindavan Gardens near Mysore in South India. My wife and I spent our honeymoon there. A purple-flowering bougainvillea grows next to the deck on which I sit. Its branches braid through those of one flowering pink. Beyond them a stylized mother giraffe nuzzles the snout of her young. They're only statues: fibreglass. I seem to have mastered synthetics—my deck chair is made of polymer strips resembling wicker—but I haven't mastered plants. The pink and purple petals look almost real but from close up they're identical, just as my re-creation of the painted disciples, attendants and deities were identical. The petals lack the minute flaws that should differentiate one from another. The rest of the garden is a blur of greenery. It's not so much a garden as the idea of a garden.

Still, Devi is so impressed she fails to notice the boy until he runs toward us on his three-year-old legs. He wears a sailor suit. He stops to admire a bird of paradise, then plucks it. When she smiles at him, I explain he's my grandson. "Dr. Ramachandra," she says, "you never had a grandson." She means I never had children.

"I do now. I made this park for him." I pick my crystal off the table and gaze at him through the glass.

The crystal is, perhaps predictably, a dodecahedron—the shape most favoured by the Devas—but it's a milky white, not multicoloured like their own. I gaze at the boy through

151

my crystal and he grows into a five-year-old girl. She wears a party dress, lemon yellow. She tries to re-attach the bird of paradise to its stem. When she can't, she puckers her soft lips. I decide I like her better as a boy and change her back. "Never mind," I call. "You go play at the pond. See how many fish you can count."

He drops the flower and runs off.

Devi asks, "And are there fish in the pond?"

"They're not real," I say. "Nor is any of this," meaning the flowers. "Nor is the boy." He's already headed back toward us. When I roll the crystal between my fingertips, he evaporates. The energy released by his molecules flashes. I squeeze the crystal lightly, a mere flexing of my fingertips, and the energy forms a bishop's candle tree. Its flowers are a waxy yellow.

"At the rate you're progressing," Devi says, "you won't need that much longer." She gave me the crystal to focus my thoughts when I grew bored with simple things like museum pieces; to focus my thoughts when I want to create an object—whether animate or inanimate—or to change its matter back to energy. But I can't help feeling something is missing. Something she either can't or won't give me: a secret she expects me to discover without knowing what to look for. "Soon you can simply point," she says. "Then, not even that."

"I'll keep the crystal," I tell her. "Pointing would make me feel too much like a magician." I don't bother admitting the crystal gives me comfort. It's the one thing I can touch which I haven't created: real in a way nothing I've created is real. "It's all an illusion anyway," I say. "Isn't it?"

"It's real enough for now," she says. "I assume the boy would bleed if you cut him?"

"I don't know. I haven't found any need to cut him." My tone is less dry—almost annoyed—when I add, "You know very well he and the fish aren't real. They can move, but they're incapable of growing by themselves or even reproducing."

"These are the criteria for life?" she asks. "Movement, growth, and reproduction?"

I nod, though it seems to me there must be other criteria, especially for human life. Even as I squeeze the crystal again, everything vanishes except the house I created last year. That is, I think of it as last year. I no longer need to sleep but I did take a nap after creating the house. It seemed an appropriate thing to do. Besides, I like to sleep. It stops me from thinking. I grow tired of thinking because I don't really think. I remember, and I've always remembered too much. But then, if I'd been good at forgetting, perhaps I wouldn't have been saved. Sometimes I think the Devas need my memories more than they need me. Then again, what's a man without his memory? Can a man who never remembers, or a man with amnesia, create?

I think of the Devas as being more than one though I've met only Devi. It may be she's only part of a whole, one facet of a huge dodecahedron that makes up a single, powerful being. But I doubt it. She sometimes refers to other beings—even calls them "the Others"—as if she isn't as powerful as I would like to believe. Perhaps she's modest.

Speaking of which, there is one conversation we have never had; one I have often imagined; one I suppose we will have sooner or later. It is this:

"Tell me something," I will say. "Who created the Devas?"
She will say, "A force even more powerful than us."
"God?"
"If you want to call it that."
"Then if Devas are religious enough to believe in a God," I will ask, "who does God believe in? Who created Him?"
"Good question," she will reply. "Assuming some force did create God, let us hope He—or She—is not an atheist."

Devi will laugh first. Then I will laugh, but neither with her nor at her. I will laugh in this imagined conversation because I already see there were many laws of the universe we humans never completely grasped. Here's one: that beings who create—gods if you will, though I would rather not think of myself as a god-in-training—must have a sense of humour. So many laws we never grasped, even those among us who called ourselves scientists.

I was never a scientist. I was a generalist, an administrator of the old school. I studied science but, unlike my wife, I never mastered it. She was a biomathematician, an expert on the application of what are called L-systems to life forms; on using computers to amplify cells. She was one of the best. This didn't matter when her own cells betrayed her; when they gnawed at her bones till there wasn't enough substance left to sustain life. To think we carry the seeds of life and death within us. How often we forget.

4

For once I receive more than a millisecond of warning before Devi appears. She has begun to realize I need my privacy. A light flashes briefly in mid-air to tell me she awaits an audience.

This afternoon's performance is of Glick. I've willed the space above me a rippling, afternoon blue with no sun to cast shadows. Srul Irving Glick was one of the many contemporaries I left behind. I am listening to my re-creation of the Orford Quartet perform his first string quartet. How much this piece disturbed me once; how much I need it now. The concert at which it premiered was the last concert I attended with my wife. I remember so much. Too much: the lemon yellow sari she wore; the glint of glass in the lobby; even the velour seats, which she insisted were velvet. And I remember, though not word for word, what Glick said while he introduced the work.

The first movement includes a song of resignation, a kind of funeral march, originally composed—he said—for the Martyrology of the Yom Kippur service. The second movement, in a free rondo-sonata, includes a beautiful theme of love and even attempts at humour and lightness. Throughout it, though, there are references to that first, funereal movement. The piece drives to an exhilarating conclusion.

I thought it presumptuous of him to say this last, but the piece does end as he said. More: at some point the music itself becomes a form of pure creative energy. It elevates; it transforms; it transcends. And best of all, I remember the silence which followed, the players with their fingers curled, each bow stilled while the music whirled in our minds, all of our minds, all of them suddenly as one. Then came the applause, the gratitude for a mortal who could create such beauty; the realization that two violinists, a violist and a cellist—themselves also mortals—could make mere people feel like gods. And I remember walking home, the two of us not daring to speak in case we disturbed the snow falling lightly about us. I remember the wavering of the streetlights; the memories of silk and glass and of velour. Which may have been velvet, after all.

The light flashes again to remind me Devi awaits. When I nod, my re-creation of the Orford Quartet vanishes. The energy it releases lingers, then dissipates.

Devi appears. "Another group of young ones will arrive soon," she says. "Are you ready for them?"

I nod once more and take the form of an old woman: a crone, complete with flowing, white hair and a gnarled staff. When Devi asked why I always take this form for leading tours, I said, "It feels appropriate, just as your form feels appropriate."

It does and it doesn't. Soon after we met, I grew tired of conversing with a double helix of multicoloured light. It offered to take a more human form. I imagined a four-armed goddess, none in particular. Devi, whom I named for the Indian word for goddess, copied my image perfectly. For a while her features remained faint, like a face in an underdeveloped photograph. Then I decided she should look not old but past her prime: as the French would say, "*du certain age.*" Now she rests two of her arms on the arms of a chair and holds her other two arms raised behind her. If she resents masquerading as a Hindu deity, she has never said so. She has also never objected to masquerading as a goddess or to being considered a *she*. I think she understands I can't think of her as an *it*. Any more than I can think of myself in this way.

Sometimes I change my form to look older or younger, tall or thin, but most times I take the form I had when I was truly alive. I look like Dr. S.N. Ramachandra complete with his dark skin and his paunch and his myopia. The shortsightedness, above all. S.N. stood for Satya Narayana but no one called me this. Except for my wife, everyone called me S.N. She called me Dear.

My house vanishes and I hover between the Taj Mahal and Agra Fort. This is where the young ones find me when they appear for their tour. Waving one of her arms, Devi abandons me to my duties.

"Welcome to the Wonders of the World," I say.

The young ones bob in a ragged formation of single, multicoloured helixes. A double helix, their teacher, dwarfs them.

"What's the world?" a young one asks.

"I told you," the teacher says. "It means the planet called Earth."

The young one sniffs, "Oh that."

It's true my charges have trouble appreciating what I show them but, aside from groups of them led by their teachers and aside from Devi, I have no visitors. I need no visitors. I have my solitude. It allows me to create, to re-create. Sometimes, though, I wonder whether Devi minds looking after someone as primitive as me; someone who, not long ago, amused himself with a children's park; someone who still takes naps.

After the Taj Mahal and Agra Fort, I move on to the buildings of Qut'b Minar. As usual, as soon as I turn from the tower of victory, one of the young ones causes it to lean. The rest giggle while I tilt my head patiently. "Put it back," the teacher says, and the young one does. Now the five-storey tower, all sandstone and marble, leans too far the other way. I'll have to remind Devi to straighten it. I can create a house and a garden, even a grandson, but none of them are real. Not to me. The victory tower of Qut'b Minar, like the Taj Mahal and Agra Fort, is real, though. Thanks to the Devas, these and a few other artifacts are all that are left of Earth. Though I can't move so much as a stone, they still have power to move me. And this is when—admiring the multicoloured inlay of the Taj Mahal, which looks milky white from a distance—I discover what I've been missing: the secret Devi expected me to uncover for myself.

5

This morning's performance is of Schubert. Again it's not really morning but I've willed it so, just as I've willed my re-creation of the Bishop White Gallery. Here once more are the Buddhist paintings and sculptures—among them the Goddess of Mercy, Guan Yin. The Guarneri Quartet plays in the hallway where Chopin once played. Violin, viola, cello and double bass are joined by piano for the Quintet in A, called the "Trout." Despite the presence of a double bass where one might expect a second violin, the quintet has a translucence bordering on transparence. The lumbering bass remains in the background, sonorous, and allows the cello to reach for its own upper registers. The cello was the instrument most like the human voice itself. Had I played music, I would have played the cello.

Devi appears on the bench beside me. "I am impressed," she says. "The garden, that was nice. So were the boy and the fish. But this is different. Why?"

She knows why, but I feel the need to explain. I rise and walk about the statues. There's no railing to keep me back, not as there was at the ROM. "It's not an idea of paintings and sculpture," I say. "Not in the way it was when I first re-created it. Not in the way the garden was an idea of a garden. All of this is real. You see this statue?" I point one out to her. "The fall of drapery is more smooth, more like the catenary of a chain, than the fall of drapery on that figure." She nods at the second statue. "And the pigment here is more weathered. As for these paintings—" I pivot to face the largest one, the future Buddha with disciples and attendants. "—the faces may seem alike but each one is slightly different. I re-created each face separately, each part of the painting stroke by stroke. That's why they seem so real. How long it took to discover the secret!"

"Which is?" she asks.

"The ability to hold an entire work in the mind while devoting all the energy of a moment to a single detail. And, as important, the ability to understand what each detail contributes to the whole."

Devi nods again and smiles. "You're ready," she says. "If your wife were here—"

"But how!" I demand.

"Forgive me," Devi says. "I did not mean to raise your hopes like that. It was all we could do to save you and a handful of—"

"It's all right," I say. "Really. I finished mourning for her long ago."

"Just as you've finished mourning for the others. Also why you're ready. But if your wife were here, how would she have re-created the garden?"

It's such a simple question, I wonder why Devi bothers to ask. "Using biomathematics," I say. "L-systems. Computers to amplify cells, though we no longer need computers, since we have so much time."

"And could you apply what you recall of her work? Not simply to re-create that garden with its bougainvillea but to create a new garden? A real garden?"

"Of course. I may not consciously know it, but everything I've heard or seen or sensed of the world is still in here." I tap my temple. "Every formula, every bar of music, every brushstroke." I leave the gallery, pass the performers, and leap the steps to the deck behind my house.

Devi follows.

Perhaps I'll create a garden full of plants devoted to the hour of day: the morning glory, daylily, evening primrose, nightshade. Or a garden devoted to the seasons: summer cypress, summer lilac, winter jasmine. Or to holy days: the Lenten rose, Christmas rose, Christmas fern, Easter lily. Or perhaps even a garden devoted to the beauty of time, one full of varieties of thyme itself: caraway, creeping, lemon, woolly. Thyme heals all, they say. No, that would be too clever. "I'll need to begin with something simple," I say.

"Will these do?" A dodecahedron appears in the palm of Devi's hand—one of her four hands. Floating in the centre are three blue-green spots, three cells of algae. Barely a handful. "And now," she says, "if you would be good enough to begin applying your wife's knowledge?"

Glick. I need the Glick. The quintet turns into the quartet, the Orford, and the Glick begins: the pure creative energy of his first string quartet. Soon I'll have a garden, each petal different from the last. And one day . . . No, best not to think of that. One step at a time. One cell at a time. One petal, one flower at a time.

"We need to make a record of this," I tell Devi. "A record for the future because now there will be one, won't there?"

She sits and begins to write. She writes without paper or pen, but I can see the record form between us even as I begin my life's work. My wife's work. "What shall I write first?" Devi asks. "How about, 'In the beginning . . . .'?"

We both laugh. Then it doesn't take me long, not long at all, to compose the first line of this, our record for the future:

"In the beginning, there was memory."

A Palimpsest

1

THIS IS A STORY ABOUT TWO HOUSES A thousand miles apart. And so in different time zones. It's about the people who moved into them. The people who moved out in body if not in spirit. About a sudden, inexplicable death.

This is not a nice story, though it has its moments.

The smaller house first, a character home.

- Hardwood floors.
- A brick fireplace with a tiled, ceramic hearth.
- Windows made of old glass, which bends light filtering through the branches of the neighbourhood's many elms.

Kathryn listed these and other features over the phone to her fiancé, Hugh, after her first visit. She made this visit with her mother since he was finishing his residency at a Sick Children's Hospital, far away. Kathryn told him, "I never dreamed we'd start out in such a nice place. I'm so happy, I could die."

To which he said, "Don't."

"You're such a romantic," she teased. "Did you know marriage is the second greatest adventure? After death, of course."

"Honey," he said, "sometimes I don't know about you."

"Oh good."

"So," he asked, "what about the people?"

"No major illnesses they'll admit to."

"That's not what I meant, and you know it."

She let this pass. Their enforced separation had been a trial. They had broken their engagement twice in the past year without telling anyone, especially not her parents. There were some things parents did not need to know. One more day, and he would be back in town. One more week, and they could move into the house. A month after this they would turn from a minister to face their loved ones and friends. He would say, "Please welcome Hugh and Kathryn Blunt." Everyone would applaud—even her mother, though she disapproved of their living arrangements in the meantime.

"The people," Kathryn said. "Well, they are interesting."

"Which means?"

"The husband's an artist. He's Indian."

"Oh."

"Don't worry, it not that kind of neighbourhood. I meant from India, though I think he was born here. He's, I don't know, dull, for an artist. Doesn't say much. She's the interesting one, what with researching the greenhouse effect on plants. During her sabbatical. The husband and daughter are going along."

"There's a kid in the house?"

"It's okay. The walls aren't marked up or anything. She's twelve. Quiet like her father but a different kind of quiet, like she's always watching the grown-ups to figure out where she stands. Mom didn't like her much. Says kids like that give her the willies."

"Everything gives your mom the willies."

"Now, Hugh," Kathryn said, "don't start." She waited for his, "Sorry," before going on. "They're leaving the place completely furnished, dishes and all, but I said maybe they could take some of the artwork down. All of it, in fact."

"The husband's artwork?"

"That's the strange part. Hardly any of the stuff on the walls is his except a couple of photos of mosques."

"Moths?"

"Arab temples. He said they're so old they don't bother him any more. His wife said he was being modest. He mainly paints now, and the stuff sells before it's dry. No, most of what's up is hers I think, even though it's so, well, Indian, if you know what I mean. It's just not us. I never said so but she guessed."

"Feminine intuition?"

Kathryn let this pass, too. "Once you see the house and we settle on the rent, we'll go room by room and decide how we want them left. Which bookshelves we'd like cleared out, that kind of thing. They're into Ikea. I told her we don't have nearly as much as them. She said they didn't have much, either, when they started out. Oh, but I did say we'll want to use our own bed."

"This is after I see the house, right? And what if we can't talk them down a hundred a month?"

"My dear distant fiancé," Kathryn said. "My sweet husband-to-be, whom I've known since senior high, and I do mean in the Biblical sense, if you don't like the house, the wedding is off."

Hugh liked the house. Why wouldn't he? Kathryn had impeccable taste. In response to his counter offer, the owners lowered the rent slightly as a gesture of good will. He compromised, though not at once. He didn't care for the couple—

not even the interesting wife—but Kathryn had a gift for making friends. If not making friends, then establishing a strange rapport.

They moved into what she called their honeymoon house. But life was never simple. Only people—some people—were simple. The wedding was less than a month away and, for the first time since she had chicken pox as a girl, Kathryn had fallen ill.

2

The larger house now. Not exactly a character home but not without its advantages.

- Wall-to-wall carpeting.
- Closets in every room of the four-level split.
- In one corner of the huge lot, a workshop that can double as a studio complete with skylights.

Ravi and Margaret rented the house sight unseen, but the owners had faxed more than enough information. Besides, one of Margaret's many friends—soon to be her dean for a year—had inspected the house and pronounced it fine. She'd especially liked the garden, with its wooden bridge curving over a pond.

Ravi arranged his studio first and left Margaret and their daughter, Tara, to the bedrooms and kitchen. He had his priorities, and art came before sleep or food. Still, he caught himself scowling at his easels—a small one for sketches, a large one for work he sold. He scowled because he couldn't decide whether he was battling an artist's equivalent of writer's block or whether he was facing a midlife crisis. At thirty-nine.

"If it is a midlife crisis," Margaret had said, "don't let it interfere with my work." This while he'd helped her assemble their stereo.

Opening a box of CDs, Tara made a face. When he grinned at her, she turned to begin sorting them.

He fought down his helplessness. He would have preferred a wisecrack like, "Yeah, you watch yourself." He didn't know how to cope with her silence, with her constantly turning away.

He asked Margaret, "When have I ever let anything interfere with your work? I moved too, didn't I?"

"I know, I know." She bussed his cheek while passing. "You deserve to be canonized."

"Bah, humbug." He hooked one arm around her waist, then kissed her on the back of the neck while she tried to get free. But she did laugh. He pretended not to notice when Tara rolled her eyes.

Now, setting out his books—most of them large-format art books—he tossed one into a trashcan. He'd bought this book on impulse at a store catering to self-help. It still annoyed him—the content, not the impulse. The book was called *Help Yourself Through That Midlife Crisis*. It annoyed him because most of the case studies were of successful men—doctors, lawyers, executives—who dropped out for a year to write a novel. Or weld sculptures from used auto parts. What should he do? Stop painting for a year and join IBM?

He sat back on his favourite, paint-covered stool and catalogued the equipment moved against the walls. Table saw, band saw, jointer, thickness planer, routing table, belt sander, drill press. Tools hung on pegboards above workbenches, also moved aside. Arnold Bower—not Arnie, Arnold—had said Ravi could help himself to the equipment, even the hand tools. Some of them were so old, their wooden handles were stained with honest sweat.

Arnold had made this offer the day before, just after Ravi, Margaret and Tara had moved in. Now Arnold and his wife, Dora, were flying east. Like Margaret, Dora would spend her sabbatical doing research. Not on the greenhouse effect. On the emotional stability of gifted children. She'd mentioned this while looking at Tara, and Tara had looked away. She was no genius—certainly not borderline crazy—but she was gifted. She'd also recently overcome a passing hatred for school though she still claimed most boys her age were, as she put it, intellectually challenged. Alone with Arnold in the workshop, Ravi said woodwork might just do the trick, thanks. He'd even framed in a darkroom before giving up on photography.

"This used to be a darkroom," Arnold said. "Not so long ago, either. I ripped out the inside walls. Put in this other sky-light to match." He took a dovetail saw from a pegboard and thumbed the blade. "So why'd you give it up?"

Ravi shrugged. Then he decided Arnold deserved better. "I stopped believing in the power of documentary photography to change things." He laughed over sounding like a prof, which he wasn't. "Society. Injustice. You know."

Arnold chuckled. "I was into peace marches, myself."

"And now here I am," Ravi said, "getting tired of painting for profit."

Arnold nodded with understanding.

Trying to think of what else to say—wishing he might have more time with this older, wiser man—Ravi eyed the floor between them. It was concrete. The red paint had bubbled from years of moisture. In one spot the concrete was pitted as though someone had dropped a bottle of acid. What kind of acid would leave such scars? Of course, muriatic. Arnold must have dropped a bottle of muriatic acid after cleaning an especially grimy toilet. Ravi considered buying an area rug, a gift for having survived the move. He'd seen one in the latest Ikea catalogue. It was four feet by six and would easily cover the scars. It would also be impractical in a studio.

"I took a year off once," Arnold said. "Did everything I promised myself I'd do when I retired. Sailed, played tennis. Even took up golf. That's the problem with a midlife crisis." He sighted along the dovetail saw. "It's not that you bore everyone around you. You end up boring yourself. In the end you're glad to get back to the real world, whatever your real world is." He hung the saw in its place on the board. Leaning back against a workbench, he looked about as though sorry to leave all this. "But, hey, " he added, "if you're lucky, all you've got is writer's block. Artist's block? Though if a friend of mine's right, it has less to do with not being able to paint than it does with something a hundred times worse."

"Which is?"

"Loss of faith." This time Arnold laughed, not over sounding like a prof—he taught in a junior college—but over trying to be profound.

Tired of unpacking now, Ravi left the studio. Halfway to the house he stopped to admire the garden. He caught himself imagining a boy running back and forth on the curving, wooden bridge. Four. The boy would have been four next week. Ravi could have bought him his very own paint box. Margaret could have sewed a small, blue smock. Tara could have given him her children's easel. More angry than sad, Ravi turned away. He hardly ever thought about the son he'd lost.

He wondered whether Margaret thought about him and decided yes, of course, why wouldn't she? Even if she never spoke about him.

And Tara? She had her books, her clothes, and her stuffed animals. She could trust things more than people. People left, and they couldn't be replaced.

Ravi entered the house through the back. He was heading for the basement family room—Margaret wanted it rearranged to suit Tara—but he stopped to examine the guestroom. Even with a sofa bed under the long window, the room had been Dora's study complete with a computer table. All the equipment was heading east with her. Somehow, he knew Arnold avoided this room. Arnold had even said Dora avoided the workshop, then looked annoyed with himself at having said this. Ravi hadn't wanted to pry.

He entered the guestroom and stood in front of the sliding closet doors. Margaret had suggested he put the Bowers' artwork in here because she'd brought so much of her own. "I mean," she'd added, "so much of ours." He slid the doors open. The space on the long shelf and under the hanger bar had been cleared out. Yes, the Bowers' artwork would fit in the left half and still leave the right half clear. He was about to turn away—to start on the family room for Tara—when he noticed a pile of frames.

They sat almost out of sight in a far corner of the high shelf. Only someone like him, taller than Arnold, would have noticed.

Ravi was not impressed. The frames had been piled one on top of the other and never been dusted. He simply had to set things right. He returned to his studio for cardboard and re-entered the guestroom. He took down the top frame and tried to blow dust off the glass. The dust barely stirred. It had thickened over the years into a pasty soot. He laid the frame face up on the computer table and covered the glass with cardboard. Without bothering with the dust on the second frame, he laid it face down. The third went face up and on top of this went another piece of cardboard.

He didn't care for the images. He'd liked such work once, before he'd become a serious artist. Or, as Margaret had once said, an artist who took himself seriously. The images were watercolours of a castle, a sunset, and a café, all of which he'd painted as a boy.

He took the last frame and flipped it face down. He cringed and hissed, "God damn it!"

Something sharp had sliced his index finger. The slice was like a paper cut—shallow—and it stung. The glass was broken like ice on a pond, the cracks radiating outward from the hole. He sucked on his finger while glaring at the image.

No castle, no sunset, no café. Not even a watercolour. This last frame held an informal wedding photo taken at a reception twenty years before. The man wore a wide tie. The woman wore a translucent, batik top. She was Dora Bower, no mistake: the same curly, red hair; the same broad forehead. The same eyes. In person, especially if Arnold were in the room, her eyes were a laughing green Ravi found alluring. Here the eyes were moist with a different kind of happiness, a gushing sentimentality. But the man beside her was not Arnold. This man had a sour, almost brutish face. It was hard to see more since the flash had bounced off his pale skin.

Ravi was tempted to crisscross masking tape on the broken glass but decided he couldn't be bothered. He put the photo face down, then replaced the stack of frames on the high shelf. No one else could see them now. Not Margaret. Not Tara. He guessed Arnold had never seen them. And now, though Ravi told himself not to be ridiculous, he felt as if he were conniving with Dora—as if, by hiding the photo again, he'd become an accessory after the fact.

He puzzled over this while searching for a Band-Aid.

3

Kathryn woke first on Sunday morning, the day after she and Hugh moved into their honeymoon house. The skin on her right thigh burned. Moving quietly so she wouldn't wake him, she hobbled into the bathroom. Here she sat on the toilet, lifted her nightgown past her knees, and started to cry. When she hung her head, tears ran down to collect on her chin.

Three days before, on Thursday, she'd woken with a single blister above the knee. Now blisters covered her entire thigh.

She felt like retching. Squeezing her arms against her stomach, she said, "No, not now." She searched among her toiletries in a box and found a bottle of calamine lotion. The bottle was almost empty. She couldn't bear to touch the blisters, so she used a wad of toilet paper to dab lotion on them. Without thinking, she dropped the empty bottle into the plastic wastebasket.

The noise woke Hugh. "Honey?" he called. "You okay?"

"It's nothing!" She used the toilet, washed up, and returned to the bedroom. Trying to sound casual while pulling on her bathrobe, she finally said, "It's hurting." Then she said, less casually, "Oh God, it hurts."

It had started as a tingle the previous weekend, the weekend of Hugh's return. She hadn't told her parents about the problem. Why would she? At first he had said it might be sunburn, though the skin hadn't looked burnt to her. She never lay about in the sun even at her favourite outdoor pool. She swam her laps in the morning, then showered and dressed for work. The next day he'd suggested it might be prickly heat. She'd refused to let him examine the thigh.

She never let him play doctor with her. She took their love life, on hold for months now, too seriously. The most she allowed him was the question he sometimes asked after they made love. "So, how's my bedside manner?" She would reply, playing Sophia Loren to his Peter Sellers, "Well, goodness, gracious me!" The "Doctor, Doctor" song was an old one, but all of Hugh's friends knew the words. It was a crowd pleaser at Hospital Follies. These days a female played Peter Sellers

170

and the most masculine male—Hugh, once—played Sophia Loren.

Kathryn's doctor knew the song, too. Her name was Lil. They had attended school together since grade one. In grade twelve she'd introduced Kathryn to Hugh. In those days Lil had been what people called a seasonal girl. She'd dated Hugh during the football season and dropped him after the finals. As she later put it, Kathryn had picked up the fumble and hung on for the touchdown. As Lil also put it, she wasn't seeing anyone just now. Except patients.

Kathryn had gone to see Lil on Thursday afternoon. After hearing the verdict, Kathryn had moaned, "Shingles? I don't have time for shingles." She pulled her skirt down over her knees.

"Well, they've found time for you." Lil unwrapped a lollipop. She had cartons of them because she'd stopped giving her younger patients lollipops. Now she stamped the backs of their hands. Given a choice between Bugs Bunny and Roger Rabbit, most children chose Roger. "It's a virus we've all got in our nervous system," she said. "Related to chicken pox. In fact, you can't get shingles unless you've had chicken pox. And you have. It's a real shame, Kat. I'm sorry."

"Me, too. So now what?"

Lil's tone changed, as it had a habit of changing—one moment serious, the next foolish. She could even sound offhand, though never callous. "Now? Nothing. If you'd come sooner, I could've given you an anti-viral to head off the blisters. Could be a lot worse, though. Could hurt like hell. So what is it? The wedding or the move?"

Kathryn rocked on the examining table. "It can't be the wedding. Though God knows Mom's doing her best to turn it into a circus. She's still on about that honeymoon in Puerto Vallarta. Says it'll be her present to us—from Dad, too, it's his money—but we put our foot down. Who's got time for mariachi?"

"Is that a collective foot or a royal foot?"

Kathryn managed a laugh. Without thinking, she placed her hands on her thighs. She winced. "It must be the move."

"If you say so." Lil crunched the rest of her lollipop. After pocketing the stick, she pulled Hugh's file out from under Kathryn's. "In the meantime, I wouldn't get too close to Young Doctor Blunt for the next two and a half weeks. The incubation period's three, so—"

"But we'll be living together! Finally."

"Doesn't mean you have to sleep with the guy. Or kiss him. No slurpy kisses, anyway. Don't even sneeze on him. They haven't quarantined people for this in ages but there's no point taking a chance." Lil opened Hugh's file, glanced at the contents, and closed it. "Especially with him starting work next week. All those kids. Good thing your shingles can't give him chicken pox since he's had that already. But his own nerves could act up. Mind you, knowing him, he'll refuse to catch anything."

Kathryn nodded. Even as an intern, Hugh had had his theories. He pretended to scoff at holistic medicine but his favourite theory was *it's all in the mind*. He didn't claim to be original.

"Speaking of which," Lil said. "How long are you planning to wait?"

"What brought that on?"

Lil unwrapped another lollipop. "Just an associative thinker, I guess. Young Doctor Blunt. Pediatrician. Birds and bees. Fucking."

Kathryn flushed.

"Sorry, I meant the natural instinct of *Homo sapiens* to reproduce. Carry on the line. Go forth and multiply."

"I get the point." Kathryn shrugged. "Till he gets settled. Till I'm promoted. Till we get a house. Our own house. Then we'll have time for kids. It's not like I have to look too far for the father."

"Gee, thanks. And it's not like I'm your sister or anything, but do me a favour, Kat. Kitty-Kat—"

"What!"

Lil grew serious. "Don't wait. There's a line-up at the sperm bank."

Now, while Hugh cleared away Sunday morning dishes, Kathryn sat in the kitchen and watched Lil scrawl a prescription. She'd driven over as soon as Hugh had phoned. Kathryn hadn't wanted him to phone, but she also hadn't wanted him to examine her. Even now. She'd tried not to hobble while making pancakes—like everything else in the kitchen, the griddle had come with the house—but she hadn't been able to hide the pain. He'd agreed to eat her pancakes if she would let him phone Lil.

"This is killer stuff," Lil said. She tore the prescription off her pad. "Not in all my five long years of pactising the medical arts have I seen a case this revolting. You may be unique in the annals of modern—"

"Enough already," Kathryn said.

"Liquid antibiotic," Lil announced. "To keep the blisters from getting infected and dry them up. Easier to absorb than pills, so your stomach shouldn't get too upset. Four teaspoons, four times a day. We're talking megalitres here." She slapped the prescription onto the kitchen table. "And, in case you need a good buzz, Tylenol with codeine. You don't get points for ignoring pain." Her chair scraped on the flowered linoleum. She stood and brushed a fingertip down Kathryn's cheek. "Do me a favour."

"Don't wait?"

Turning from the dishwasher, Hugh frowned, but Kathryn refused to enlighten him. She hoped Lil would control her urge to think associatively. And so Kathryn said, "Thanks for dropping by."

Three hours later she woke from a restless sleep. She'd taken the first dose of antibiotic, filled at the nearest pharmacy, and a Tylenol with codeine. She felt disoriented. She'd been dreaming about flying in deep, dark space. The tour guide had been a jolly alien with a genetically engineered microphone for a voice box. He'd been cooing about pulsars and quasars. She lay on her back with her face turned from the window. Narrow bands of light, creeping through the closed blinds, picked out the other pillow. It would soon be Hugh's. One more day, and he would be back in town. One more week, and they could move into the house. She blinked. He was back. They had moved in the day before. She was resting while he unpacked. So why couldn't she hear him moving about downstairs?

She decided he was taking a break to read—out back in the garden. During his residency he'd rediscovered the novels of A.J. Cronin. Hugh was reading *The Citadel* for the second time in as many years. When she'd asked for a plot summary, he'd said, "A country doctor becomes a city doctor and loses touch with reality." Only when she'd pressed for more had Hugh admitted, "The wife dies."

Kathryn drifted back to sleep. The next time she woke, she felt a hand shaking her left shoulder. It was a small, gentle hand: too small for Hugh's, too gentle for Lil's. Kathryn opened her eyes and squinted. Someone had opened the blinds.

A girl stood beside the bed. At least, whoever this was, she was too small to be a grown-up.

Kathryn tried to focus. She couldn't see the girl's face

because light bending out from behind her shadowed her features. She looked like Tara—Margaret and Ravi's girl—but Kathryn decided this couldn't be the Tara she'd met.

"That girl gives me the willies," her mother had said. Kathryn shivered.

This was a younger Tara, about nine. She didn't wear a loose sweatshirt, as the older Tara had, to hide her small breasts. This girl wore a T-shirt. Nor did she have short hair. Ribbons dangled from her braids. If she wasn't the Tara Kathryn had met, where had this girl come from? Of course, another house in the neighbourhood. But how had she got in?

Kathryn flinched when the small hand tugged at the comforter. And when the girl pressed Kathryn's arm, the hand felt cold.

"He won't play with me," the girl said.

"What?" Kathryn's lips felt dry. She tried to sit up and found she couldn't move. The comforter felt like a lead blanket in an X-ray lab. "Who?"

This time the girl whispered, but she sounded less plaintive. She sounded fierce. "He won't play with me!" She turned and left. Kathryn didn't hear her skip down the stairs. She'd run along the short hallway toward the front rooms.

Kathryn tried moving her legs again. The codeine had worn off. Her right thigh burned once more. She extricated herself from the comforter, eased out of bed, and hobbled into the hallway. Standing erect with difficulty, gripping the jamb, she looked at the smaller of the two front rooms. Its blinds were closed, and the room was dark.

Ravi had used it as his study but she'd guessed he hadn't spent much time here. He rented a studio in the warehouse district, he'd said. The room had looked neater than the larger one to the right—Margaret's off-campus office. Her retreat, she'd called it, from the balls of academe. Kathryn and

Margaret had laughed while Ravi, who'd likely heard the joke before, had nodded in appreciation.

Yet Kathryn sensed the girl hadn't entered this larger room. She had entered the small one, directly ahead.

A door creaked shut.

Moving slowly, reluctantly, Kathryn entered. When she switched on the light, it flashed with a fizzing click. She looked at the cupboard door. It was ajar. The cupboard looked even darker than the room.

The only time she'd peeked inside, when Ravi and Margaret had shown her around, Kathryn had found it full of boxes. They'd been marked Old Art Mags, Arches Paper. Ravi had said he wanted to leave the boxes here, and she'd said sure. He hadn't said—nor had Margaret—that before this room had become his study it had been a nursery. Kathryn had guessed this from the yellow walls and goldenrod trim. She had also guessed the room hadn't been a nursery for some time—perhaps not since Tara, whose bedroom was in the basement, had been small. Now there was still no hint of alphabet pictures taped to the walls. No hint of mobiles dangling over a crib. There were simply a desk, a chair, and Ikea shelves.

And there was the cupboard.

Hide and seek, Kathryn decided. The girl was waiting to be found. Kathryn grew impatient. She did not feel like playing games and yet she wanted to know who refused to play with the girl. A boy? Why should he? The girl hadn't looked like someone who played with other children. Especially not boys. Then again, Kathryn hadn't seen her face clearly.

Kathryn wanted to leave. She couldn't. She wanted to find the girl but couldn't do this either. Her thigh ached, and she fought the temptation to stoop. She told herself she should return to bed. What if she still were in bed? After all, she wasn't well. Of course—she was dreaming. She'd been dreaming about an alien tour guide, then dreamt Hugh hadn't returned, then dreamt someone had woken her. Still, how could she dream about a younger version of a girl she hadn't met until only weeks before? A girl who hadn't said a word then and yet, moments ago, had woken her to say, "He won't play with me."

The answer lay in the cupboard. Why else had the door creaked? Why else had Kathryn felt drawn to this room? Before she could scare herself witless, she opened the door.

This time it didn't creak. She marvelled at the design. Starting at waist height to clear the stairwell, the cupboard rose to a sloped ceiling. How clever. She was about to close the door when she saw the eyes. They glinted in the shadows above a box marked Old Art Mags. They glinted once more when whoever it was—whatever it was—growled, "No one plays with me."

4

"So what do you think?"

Ravi heard Margaret ask this even as he climbed the few steps into the living room. "Passages," by Ravi Shankar and Philip Glass, played on the tape deck.

"Nice," Tara said.

"It's definitely us," he announced.

Both of them turned before he could finish smoothing a Band-Aid onto his finger. "It's nothing," he said. "Really."

Tara rolled her eyes. "So, what do you think?"

"I said already." Stopping between them, he placed one arm around Margaret and the other around Tara. She tried to squirm away but he wouldn't let her. "Thought you were doing the bedrooms and kitchen?"

"We started," Margaret said, "but it felt as though we couldn't even relax in here."

He looked at the picture she'd taken down from above the sofa. She'd leaned it under the front windows: Constable's "The Hay Wain." Dora had brought it back from London years before. She'd said the heavy, gold frame had cost more than the glossy print. He knew the picture well though he'd never seen the original, at the British Museum. He'd spent an afternoon studying the colour sketches in the Victoria and Albert. Alone in the Constable Room, he'd made sketches of the sketches and notes of the notes. Constable had liked making notes. Wind speed and direction. Cloud formations. Light.

With "The Hay Wain" down, the room looked less conventional even with a floral sofa against the wall and a matching love seat facing the windows. Not that the Bowers had poor taste. Their tastes were simply different from Ravi and Margaret's. She'd replaced "The Hay Wain" with the largest work they owned. It was a triptych by a painter they had met, five years before, at an artists' colony south of Madras.

Ravi could never remember the man's name, and his signature was illegible. He was famous for posing Hindu gods, their images standardized over centuries, in abstract fields. In the left-hand panel the monkey god Hanuman crouched in front of a grey and green checkerboard—the tints and shades worked out as carefully as on a Mondrian. In the centre panel the bird god Garuda swooped through a viridian monsoon. And in the right-hand panel the elephant-god Ganesha danced in a swirl of blues and greens that might have been a jungle, a waterfall, or a mist.

"Amazing," Ravi said. Looking about, he realized Margaret had also installed her potted plants. "I was going to help with those," he said.

"We managed fine."

"We sure did," Tara added.

Margaret was fibbing, and not very well. He ignored Tara's

remark. The plants were small trees: fig, jade, orange. The pots were so heavy it took two adults to lift them. The shag of the carpet was flat where Margaret and Tara had dragged the pots—the orange tree to the sofa's left, the jade to the right, and the fig into a corner behind the stereo. He liked the effect. Not quite a garden, but the trees looked more vibrant than the Bowers' milk cans with their dried rushes and ostrich ferns. Margaret had moved the cans into the dining room. Tara had re-arranged the rushes and ferns. She liked arranging things, like the flowers he brought home. She especially liked the baby's breath. One sprig always found its way into her room.

Yes, it was amazing the difference a little change could make. Even with all the Bowers' furniture in place—the end tables as heavy as the sofa and love seat—the room looked transformed. Definitely us, he thought.

"Okay," he told Tara, "let's go."

Margaret had asked him to take Tara to the local video store. Tara had balked at this, but Margaret had said she was too busy. "Just one," she warned, "and remember—"

Tara chanted, "—nothing go-ry!"

A ten-minute walk downhill through a park brought them to a strip mall. While Ravi answered the elderly clerk's questions and she typed information into a computer, Tara skimmed the New Releases, then the Action, Drama and Comedy shelves. He smiled when she sat on the floor in front of low shelves marked Children's.

He still didn't understand her, though Margaret had told him not to try so hard. She'd said, "Just be there for her," and he'd asked, "Where else have I been?" To which she'd said, "Oh please." Some days Tara acted older than twelve. She'd grown up on *Classics Illustrated* comics and was reading *Jane Eyre*, the book. Next on her list came *The Secret Garden*, for the sixth time, and *War and Peace*. Other days she read comics like *Bugs Bunny*. She also liked horror comics, which Margaret refused to allow in the house. And once a month, ever since Tara's periods had begun—earlier than Ravi had imagined possible—she lay in bed with her stuffed toys and read every one of her pop-up books.

With the membership card in his wallet, he wandered about. He did this the few times she let him take her anywhere, usually to a mall, never a museum or a zoo. In a new store now, he memorized the hours of operation. He also catalogued the various sections. Most important, he made sure the titles were in alphabetic order. Tara often teased him about this—Margaret called it a guy thing, pissing around the perimeter—but for now Tara was busy.

She was reading the backs of every new children's video in reach. He smiled at this, too. Just like him, she was memorizing: star, co-star, screenplay by, music by. The videos she didn't return to the shelves remained on the floor beside her. At one point, while he wished he could get an early David Cronenberg film, Ravi heard her call to the clerk, "Don't worry. I'll put them back."

He turned to watch the woman, who looked tired. He felt sorry for her when she limped to one end of the counter.

She glanced at him, nodded in appreciation, and called to Tara, "I'm sure you will."

After scanning the New Releases, he found himself facing a pair of saloon doors. Tara couldn't see them from where she sat. Good thing, too, since the sign above them warned Adults Only.

He glanced at the counter. The clerk leaned against it with her back to him. Then he looked at the sign and frowned. He hadn't realized family video stores rented what he called, from his college days, skin flicks. Not that he was naive. He knew skin flicks were divided into soft-core and hard-core. But he'd thought they were rented only from places called XXX or True Blue, stores with silvered windows hiding customers from passers-by. Maybe these were only soft-core. There was only one way to find out. He pushed his way in quietly.

Holy shit. Holy ghosting shit.

For some reason, he'd expected to find black cases in brown-paper wrappers. Instead, he found boxes printed in full colour like those outside. The workmanship wasn't second-rate, either. No overlapping registrations or unfocused stills. These pictures were glossy and sharp.

On one box titled *What's Cum Over Her?* a man knelt over a woman. His muscled body arched over hers. His abdomen looked like a washboard. Her breasts, though she lay back, looked like rounded volcanoes. He was pumping semen onto her throat while she laughed. She was trying to catch the white stream in her cupped hands. Holy shit. Where did they find such people?

Then Ravi noticed a video called *Gulp*. The woman on this box knelt in front of a black man. She was pinching one of her pink nipples. She was also pulling on his scrotum. His testicles looked like a bull's. His cock—not a penis, a cock—looked ten inches long, thick and hard as a riot stick. Ravi thought of a horse. A God damn horse. The head of the cock—a head the size and colour of a plum—rested on the woman's sagging, outstretched tongue.

Ravi felt his penis quiver. He wanted to see more. There had to be more.

He picked up the box and looked at the back. Gulp was right. The woman's lips were almost at the man's indigo scrotum. Trick photography—it had to be—and yet, looking more closely, Ravi saw if there were some trick it had nothing to do with photography. The base of the cock glistened from the man's pubic hair into the woman's mouth. Her lips were stretched and her cheeks were taut. But how could she swallow all of that? A bull. A horse. When a wet sliver emerged from the tip of Ravi's penis, he shuddered. He could almost see the plum-sized head sliding in and out of her throat. He could almost hear her shallow breathing while she tongued hard on—

Tara called, "What's in here?"

Even as the doors swung open, he slapped the box onto a rack. Whirling, he yelled, "No!"

Her head snapped up. Her eyes fixed on his. She looked scared. She crossed her hands in front of her face with her shoulders hunched.

"Don't be ridiculous!" he said. He stood blocking her way with the doors trying to close on him.

When she lowered her hands, she no longer looked scared, but her shoulders remained hunched. She looked furious. He caught her eyeing his crotch and muttered, "Oh shit." He might as well have been naked.

"Don't worry," she said. "I won't tell."

After he stepped out of the room, the doors slapped closed behind him. He stumbled over words like, "I was just," and, "I thought," until she interrupted.

"I'll tell you one thing," she said. "There's no way some guy's going to shove that up my—"

"Tara!"

She shrugged, and her shoulders fell into place. Then she twirled on her heel and ran for the counter. Two video boxes stood ready for inspection. The clerk watched, amused, while Tara called, "So what's your vote? *Free Willy* or *Remains of the Day*?"

Ravi was shaking, and not with embarrassment or rage. He was shaking because she had no idea what she'd nearly seen. He didn't want her growing up so fast. He wished she would never grow up. He sure as hell didn't want her barging into rooms marked Adults Only, where no one could help her decide where to draw the line. Where some men might claim there were no lines. And even if he could tell her what these lines were, he didn't think she would listen. Or, if she did, she would wisecrack and roll her eyes. But he also couldn't keep blocking doorways forever.

On his way to the till, he frowned at a poster for *Jurassic Park* to buy himself time. Only moments ago, he'd wondered where they found such people. Where else but in everyday life? They weren't robots. They were real people who were sure they met a need. Or did they even think about such things? For that matter, who was he to tell anyone what the lines were when he'd wanted to see more? When he'd wanted to see the black man and the pink woman in action. Wanted to hear her gasp. Wanted to see him shoot semen—cum, whatever—into her hands, too. No, Ravi didn't want Tara growing up so fast. And this was why, though he treasured every moment Emma Thompson appeared on a screen—though he thrilled at the small gestures like that twitch of her mouth—he said, "*Free Willy.*"

After paying and signing a printout, he told the clerk, "Thanks."

She shrugged, smiling the way she might at a basically decent man. Still, he wished she hadn't said, "Never hurts to look. Sometimes." Or that Tara hadn't frowned at both of them as if she knew what he—not she herself—had done wrong.

Yes, he thought. It does hurt. He wanted to tell her this while they climbed home through the park. He wanted to say it can hurt because you always need to see more. Then, if you're not careful, even looking isn't enough. Like it or not, you become part of the madness—more than a bystander, more than a witness. You become an accessory.

5

Kathryn did not remember having screamed. Nor did she remember, until later, Hugh's taking the stairs two at a time. When he grabbed her in a bear hug, she screamed again.

"Jesus," he cried, "you nearly scared me to death!"

"You?" Kathryn pulled away, angry with him. He had strong arms, and his hug could be suffocating. Looking wide-eyed at the cupboard door, which she'd slammed shut, she said, "There's something in there."

Holding her shoulder, he pulled up the blinds. One corner dangled lower than the other and the blinds rustled. Ignoring them, he looked in the cupboard. Then he laughed. "It's a teddy bear," he said. "An old-fashioned teddy bear with glass eyes."

When he took it out to show her, she turned away. "Put it back!"

"Okay, okay." He closed the door and flicked the light switch off, on, off. Trying not to laugh, he said, "You and that bear! You nearly scared me to—"

"It wasn't there when we came that second time. It wasn't—in—there."

He tried to lead her from the room but she shrugged off his arm. Clearly annoyed, he reminded her, "You said they could use the cupboard."

She nodded slowly. Yes, she had. As long as the bookcase was cleared out, and it was.

"So? They threw in a couple of the girl's toys." He looked out the window.

Kathryn did, too. It wasn't even autumn, and leaves were turning as yellow as the walls in here. Soon the leaves would be goldenrod like the trim. "It's not hers," she said. "It's hardly been touched. Besides, it said no one plays with it any more."

"Honey," he said, turning from the window, "bears don't talk."

"Then what about the girl?"

"What about her?"

"Oh never mind." Kathryn could see he was trying to humour her, but she didn't want him to scoff if she told him about the girl. The one who might have been Tara three years before. Kathryn grew indignant. She simply had to lash out. "It sure didn't take you long," she said.

"Huh?"

"To get all the way in here. And up."

"In from where? I was in the living room setting up my stereo. Our stereo."

"So why couldn't I hear anything?"

"I was trying to be quiet."

"Oh," she said. "I guess my stereo isn't good enough?" She brushed past him and headed for the bedroom.

"Mine's got better speakers." Following her at a distance, he called, "That's one of the most important parts of a system. We're saving yours for the cottage, remember?"

She climbed into bed and straightened the comforter. Refusing to look at him, waiting in the doorway, she slapped the comforter flat well away from her legs. "We don't even have a house yet—our own house—and you're furnishing a cottage? Time to get back to the real world."

"Look who's talking." He backed to the top of the stairs. "Get some rest. You're supposed to be sick."

"And what does that mean!" She said this again, her voice shrill, while he returned downstairs. He didn't reply. She hadn't wanted a reply. She'd wanted him to admit how much she'd hurt him so she could apologize. She'd wanted him to lie next to her, to hold her close and say, "It was just your imagination." But she was sure it hadn't been her imagination. The talking bear, perhaps—she'd spooked herself silly by then—but not the girl.

Kathryn picked up a Rabbi Small mystery. Her father had dropped off an armload of books earlier in the day while her mother had waited in the car. She refused to enter the house until after the wedding. Let her be that way. Who cared? Fighting back tears, Kathryn dropped the book on the bed.

Sunday the Rabbi Stayed Home.

That evening, after another nap, she went downstairs. Refusing to clutch the handrail for support, she took one step at a time. She would show Hugh she wasn't that sick. He was in the kitchen, so her act was wasted. He'd ordered pizza and they watched *Masterpiece Theatre.* She kept shifting her feet, propped on a coffee table, because her thigh ached. At least it no longer burned. As soon as they finished, he fetched her prescriptions. She ignored the codeine, so he told her where to find it—next to the kitchen sink. When she woke in the middle of the night with her thigh on fire, she wished she hadn't tried to be brave.

She limped into the bathroom. After closing the door and switching on the light, she looked for the vial. She opened all the drawers. They were empty. Hugh hadn't unpacked the toiletries—his and hers—from their separate boxes. Then she remembered the codeine was still downstairs. She switched the light off, opened the door, and waited for her eyes to adjust.

The street lamp in front of the house bathed the small, front room in greenish light. She half expected to hear a whooshing rumble, the noise a spacecraft makes while hovering overhead, while aliens arm themselves to claim their prey. Something had happened in this house. Perhaps not something evil, but something had definitely happened. She could sense it. What if the aliens had come to play with Tara, not abduct her? No, Kathryn decided. They had abducted her and replaced her with a clone.

The real Tara was signalling for help.

A shudder brought Kathryn back to reality. Tara's bedroom was in the basement. It was a guestroom now. The walls were bare of Freida Kahlo posters; the shelves were empty of books. There wasn't a stuffed animal in sight. As for the bear, Kathryn was sure it hadn't belonged to Tara. Kathryn listened closely but couldn't hear the bear growling. He must be asleep. The house was so quiet, she could hear a clock ticking on the living room mantel. And the fridge humming in the kitchen.

Clutching the rail this time, she limped downstairs. She didn't need a light because she knew where the codeine stood, next to a glass. She ran the tap, swallowed a yellow tablet, and wiped her hands on a dishcloth. Instead of returning upstairs, she opened the back door and went outside. She sat in a lawn chair, its white plastic gleaming in the night. Looking up, she tried to identify constellations. She recognized only the Big Dipper, which she'd never liked calling the Great Bear. She couldn't see Orion but kept looking.

And she waited. If she waited long enough, the green light in the small room might start to dance.

While Hugh had been away, she'd often sat on her parents' deck and watched the stars. She'd waited for the aliens to come for her—to take her away from all of this—though she was never sure what she meant by *all of this*. Her parents, yes. Loneliness, no. Not any more. "Oh how lucky," people said. "An only child. You must have been spoiled." All her mother could spoil were Kathryn's plans, including her plans for a quiet wedding. And how she missed Hugh. If she couldn't be with him, she might as well be flying through distant nebulae. She might as well be chatting telepathically with the aliens who had chosen her, of all people, to rescue. Straightening in the chair, she winced.

"So what is it?" Lil had asked. "The wedding or the move?" And with Hugh back, what did Kathryn need rescuing from? Marriage? Certainly not. She had everything she'd ever wanted except her own house. And children.

"Do me a favour," Lil had said. "Don't wait." Though Kathryn never said so, she felt sorry for Lil. She'd treated love like a hobby for so long, she didn't know how to take it seriously any more. Now, even more than a lover, she wanted a child. She often joked about the sperm bank but Kathryn couldn't laugh about some things: love, marriage, children. She would have lots of children—three, why not four?—so none of them would ever be lonely.

She felt the cold at last. She rose stiffly, re-entered the house, and headed for the stairs. The house was still quiet except for the fridge. It hummed so loudly, she couldn't hear the clock ticking on the mantel—the loud, old clock Hugh had inherited from an uncle. Perhaps it's broken, Kathryn thought. Perhaps it can't be repaired. She smiled at the possibility, then felt guilty. She turned to climb the stairs and stopped.

Someone had switched on a light in the master bedroom. She could hear voices.

Her pulse throbbed in her throat. It drummed in her ears. Trying to quiet her pulse, she took a deep breath, exhaled, and listened. There were two voices, a man's and a woman's. Perhaps, though, the woman was a girl. What if Tara was back, visiting Hugh this time?

And what if Kathryn just left? In no time flat she could be out the front and away from this house with its faceless girls and its talking bears. And now its voices and lights. Then what? Stroll in her nightgown to a corner store? Phone her parents and ask them to drive ten miles in the middle of the night? Better to dial 911 and blubber, "There's someone in my house. My fiancé's talking to a ghost no one will play with."

She chuckled nervously. Phones, of course. Hugh was on the phone. As for the woman's voice, or the girl's, Kathryn had simply imagined it. She thought of lifting the receiver in the kitchen to make sure he really was on the phone. But what if she discovered he wasn't?

She would still have to climb these stairs.

She took another deep breath, exhaled, and made the first step. Pulling herself up by the rail—trying to ignore the thigh aching each time her knee bent—she climbed toward the light.

Something was wrong with the wall next to her. She couldn't think what, so she ignored it. She paused on the third step from the top, looked between the upright rails of the banister, and saw them. Not Hugh and the girl. Not even Hugh and Lil, though what Lil might be doing here at this time of night, Kathryn couldn't imagine. She closed her eyes and squeezed hard with her eyelids. When she opened her eyes, she knew what was wrong with the wall. Only this afternoon, Hugh had hung the first picture they had bought. It was a drawing of a sad girl, made up like a clown and holding a daisy.

The picture was gone. So was Hugh.

Ravi and Margaret were back.

Ravi was sitting on the edge of their bed. Since its headboard was too ornate for Kathryn's liking, he'd dismantled the bed and moved it into the basement. But here he was, sitting on the left side of this same bed with his back to Margaret. She was sitting up, and the lamp on her night table was on.

Kathryn pressed her brow against the rails. She wanted to rattle the banister like a cage. She wanted to scream. Hugh had said, "The wife dies," but this was worse. Far worse. In this story, she could have told him, the wife goes mad.

6

That same Sunday night, after dinner and *Free Willy*, Ravi lay sleepless in another bed a thousand miles away. Two time zones away. Just as he had in the video store, he was cataloguing, but now he catalogued the noises of the night. The leaves of all the trees on the huge lot swished in a downpour. Rain thrummed on the roof. Rain hissed while bouncing in the eaves. Rain poured its way down gutters and crackled onto stones.

Lying on her stomach with her face turned away, Margaret sighed. She hadn't done this in years but now, once again, she sighed as if trying to forgive herself.

He wondered whether she had forgiven him. She must have. They were still together, not like so many of their friends. This is why he liked the doctor and his fiancée, setting out so full of hope. Yawning at last, Ravi wondered how they were enjoying their new house.

Something clinked.

He held his breath. He didn't want to hear the sound again, but he lay awake listening for the clink. There it was. Glass on glass. Tara must be walking in her sleep.

Sometimes, in their own house, he would go downstairs and find her at the kitchen sink. She would fill a glass, drink the water, and turn without seeing him. He would follow her down into the basement bedroom with its long windows. She would climb into bed and say, "Goodnight, Daddy." She never called him *Daddy* while awake, and the next day he never reminded her of what she'd done.

Now, though, standing in her doorway, he frowned. He couldn't hear her breathing. Even if the room was too dark to see much, he knew she was nowhere near.

On his way to the kitchen, he stopped in his own doorway to make sure he hadn't woken Margaret. No, she slept soundly at last. In the orange glow of a street lamp filtering through the shutters, her light brown hair looked red. Pushed up by the covers, it looked as curly as Dora's.

After padding down the few steps from the top level, he stood in the main-floor hallway. The hallway ran from the front door, past two short flights of stairs—the first down, the second up—and into the kitchen. A coloured light flickered on the wall in front of him. Expecting to see Tara, he looked at the kitchen. Nothing there. He heard the clink again. It came from the next level down—from the family room he still hadn't re-arranged—and he glanced at the flickering light. So that was it. Tara was watching TV.

After he and Margaret went to bed, if Tara couldn't sleep she would replay whatever video they'd watched earlier. She would listen with headphones. Come morning, he would find her asleep. The video would have finished but the TV would be on, tuned to the Weather Network.

He turned and padded down into the family room. Someone was watching a video, all right. The picture was unclear because the tape was rewinding. The someone was a man.

He sat on a love seat facing the TV. The love seat was older than the one in the living room—so old it belonged in a cottage—and the man was drinking from a glass. When he placed it on the low table in front of him, the glass clinked against a bottle. He grunted and sat back.

Ravi thought of dialing 911. Then he wondered what to say. "There's a stranger in my house"? "Well, it's not exactly my house—" Ravi was neither foolish nor brave, but he decided to investigate.

He had no idea who this man was but knew he couldn't be Arnold. Arnold's hair was so blond it was almost white.

Besides, he was far away, in the east. This man had dark hair. A bald spot the size of a dollar shone in the coloured light, the only light in the room. Ravi nearly laughed. This is great, he thought. Some guy breaks into my house in the middle of the night so he can watch a video. Ravi searched along the wall beside him for the dimmer switch. A corner of his Band-Aid stuck to the knob. He froze. The man had stopped the tape with his remote control. The tape moved forward, still on play, and Ravi watched.

Holy shit. Holy ghosting shit.

A naked woman was bent over the bar of a fancy lounge. A mirror ball threw squares of light onto her skin. Her teeth were clenched on a towel, and the man behind her held its ends like reins. Her large, drooping breasts shuddered each time he slammed into her. Cut to a lower angle: her spine was arched, her buttocks high, and her labia clasped a glistening penis. Blue veins throbbed under the skin. The penis withdrew until the circumcised head bulged between her labia. Then the penis rammed into her. The sound was almost off, yet Ravi could hear her moan. She clutched her breasts to keep them from slapping onto her ribs. The penis withdrew again, slowly teasing. Cut to another angle, also low: the man's buttocks were tensed. They quivered when he rammed into her a second time. The side shot again, close up: the man half withdrawing, the woman's muffled cry of, "Harder!" Finally, in a wider shot, he slammed into her with such force, her head snapped back. Her ribs struck the edge of the bar.

Ravi winced. This was nothing like what he'd seen in the video store. There was nothing erotic about any of this. He'd wanted to see more, now he was seeing more, and he didn't like what he saw. Parts and pieces, like cuts of meat. Breast. Thigh. Rump. They might just as well be dangling from hooks.

The man on the love seat clearly liked what he saw. His right shoulder moved with a smooth rhythm. Ravi could imagine the man's large hand rising and falling. The man leaned forward, then back.

The other man—the naked one—withdrew fully. He released the towel, still clenched in the woman's teeth. Then he pumped semen onto her lower back. He plastered the semen up her spine so it glistened in the squares from the mirror ball. When she laughed at him over her shoulder, the towel fell from her mouth.

The man on the seat arched. He groaned. Then, without warning, he turned.

Ravi fell back against the carpeted steps.

The man glared as though he knew he'd been caught. His unshaven face was puffy, his lips were drawn back from his teeth, and his eyes gleamed like an animal's. A cornered animal. In a flash, Ravi knew many things he didn't want to know. Tara hadn't been sleepwalking. She was nowhere in the house. The woman he'd seen on his way to the kitchen hadn't been Margaret. She was Dora. And the man scowling at him—scowling through him—was the man in the photo, the one with the cracked glass.

Ravi had to get out of here. He had to find Margaret and Tara. He clawed his way up the steps, stumbled across the hallway, and fell. His hands skidded on the living room shag. While the room whirled—the way it did, even now, if he drank too much—he swore, "Oh shit, no."

The potted trees were gone. So was the triptych. "The Hay Wain" was back on the wall. When the print started to blur, he hung his head. All he could see was the carpet, inches from his eyes. Then not even this.

7

Kathryn stood rooted to the stairs. She bit her lip until it hurt as much as her thigh.

"But why the flowers?" Margaret asked. She said this as if she'd asked the question already, too many times.

"I told you," Ravi said. "I don't know."

"You don't know."

He sat with chin pressed onto his Adam's apple. He said something so quietly, Kathryn couldn't hear him. She climbed to the top at last. The greenish light still bathed the small, front room. At least this much hadn't changed.

Margaret looked at Kathryn and said, "He's mowing the lawn, he mows down all my perennials, and he doesn't know why."

Leave me out of this, Kathryn thought. I'm not here.

Yet they wouldn't leave her out of this, whatever *this* was. She wasn't dreaming or imagining things. Margaret really was back. So was Ravi. What if they had never left?

He looked up at her. "I felt like it," he said.

Mocking him, Margaret repeated, "He felt like it."

When Kathryn looked at him again, he shrugged. "It was sunny and bright. I was mowing the lawn and I felt this band around my head. Made of steel. It was getting tighter and I couldn't get it off. It was making me mad. Don't you see? If I could've got it off, I wouldn't have got so mad. But there I was looking at all those flowers. Foxgloves, dahlias—"

"Don't tell her," Margaret said. "Tell me. They were my flowers. I planted them."

Yes, Kathryn thought. Don't tell me. Don't even look at me. But he still did both.

"All those flowers looking bright and cheery as if nothing ever happened. What do they know? Drooping over the lawn, getting in my way. So I mowed them down. Every last one of them. They deserved it."

Margaret told Kathryn, "Flowers don't deserve anything. Not that. You should've seen Tara. She ran from the kitchen.

194

She ran screaming, 'Don't!' and he kept right on mowing. Every single flower he could get at, even under the bushes. She cried and cried. She gathered them up and took them to her room. She says she's going to press them. Save them somehow. How can she know? There are some things you just can't save. God, I could've killed him."

Both of them eyed Kathryn as though only she could help. She wished they wouldn't do this. She wished they would go away. Neither of them moved. Approaching the bedroom—their bedroom—she finally asked, "Now what?"

Ravi shrugged. "Now, nothing. Well, yes." He told Margaret, "I'll get more. I'm sorry." He flinched when she touched his face.

"We'll get more," she said. "It's my fault."

He pulled back, fierce. "Don't say that! I told you not to say that!" He rose. "It's not anybody's fault!"

Kathryn moved from the doorway to let him pass.

Margaret told him, "It's late. Come back to bed." Even as he sat down, reluctantly pulling the bedclothes out from under his feet, Margaret repeated herself. This time she sounded like Hugh.

"It's late," he said. "Come back to bed." He reached across to Kathryn's night table and switched off the lamp.

She looked over her shoulder. The clown girl was back with her daisy. The ghosts—if they had been ghosts—were gone. She entered the bedroom at last. Hugh had pulled back her side of the comforter, Margaret's side. He was asleep before Kathryn joined him.

Lying there, tracing the wrinkles of sleep on his face, she wondered whether to tell him what she'd seen. No, he wouldn't understand. She lay back and closed her eyes. She no longer felt scared. Oddly enough, she hadn't felt scared during the encounter, not once she'd climbed to the top. None of these ghosts meant her harm. They were trying to tell her something.

At least she knew who refused to play with Tara: Ravi. He was so caught up in whatever lay behind this talk of flowers and fault, he no longer had time for her. Or he hadn't, once, only a few short years ago. And Margaret? She had her work, the greenhouse effect.

Kathryn grew sleepy. Don't worry, she promised the girl. I'll play with you.

8

The following morning, when Ravi woke to see Margaret eyeing him in the broad light of day, he didn't care whether he'd fallen asleep or fainted. She said, "Forgot the bed in the guestroom, did we?" On her way to the kitchen she called, "TV off, Tara."

Ravi followed Margaret and sat, feeling silly, in the breakfast nook. He sipped coffee while she mixed batter for waffles. She had found an old waffle iron in the metal drawer under the stove. She hummed with the radio—with the "*Lacrymosa*" from a requiem—as if this were just another normal Monday and she planned to go in late.

Assuming she even wanted an explanation, what could he tell her? "There was a perfect stranger masturbating in our family room"? Or, "He didn't even know I was there"? Oh, yes, brilliant.

Entering the kitchen, Tara tsk-tsked. "Walking in your sleep again, huh? Must be genetic."

After breakfast, Margaret started on a crossword in the paper. Doing the crossword helped her focus for the day ahead. Ravi wished he liked word games. He watched through the front windows while Tara explored the neighbourhood in search of new friends. Asphalt gleamed dully from the rain.

He used the toilet, then smoothed on a new Band-Aid. Back in the kitchen, he asked Margaret, "Did you know Dora was married before?"

"Pardon?"

"Before Arnold."

"So?" Margaret raised her eyebrows when Ravi sat next to her. "We didn't have time for all that," she said. "But I got the impression she loves him more than he loves her."

"Meaning?"

Margaret frowned at a clue. "It seems in any marriage, one person loves the other one more." She penciled in the answer. "I don't mean Arnold doesn't love Dora. I just got the impression she needs him more than he needs her."

"Not like us." Ravi grinned at his own stupidity for saying such a thing. It was the closest he'd come in years to saying *I love you*. She claimed he didn't have to say so—she knew he did—but he still felt guilty over not being able to say three simple words.

She looked up at last. "What happened last night?"

"Nothing, why?"

"Oh, please. And what's happened to Mister Morning Monosyllabic? 'Juice?' 'Uh.' 'Toast?' 'Uh.' The coffee wasn't that strong!"

He inched his hand toward hers so he could drum on the back of her wrist. It was a signal they hadn't used in years, not since Tara had grown old enough to know that parents made love. Using it now had nothing to do with the video. The mirror-ball scene hadn't aroused him like the boxes in the store. The couple on screen had nauseated him. The man on the love seat had terrified him. Ravi wanted to forget.

Margaret laughed while asking, "Already?"

He thought she might add, "It hasn't been a week yet,"

197

but she didn't. Not that they rationed themselves, but their life had changed in the past three years—ever since he'd destroyed the perennials behind the house. Her perennials. Their house. Ever since the day, a year later, they had learned they could never have another child.

Margaret rose. She ruffled his hair and said, "Maybe you should sleep on the floor more often."

Rising to follow her, he said, "I will if you will."

Two days passed. Margaret settled into her new lab on campus, Tara redecorated her room, and Ravi mixed paints he didn't use. It still bothered him—the impression the incident with the man had left.

Ravi couldn't remember having been this jumpy since he'd been a boy. In those days he opened closet doors quickly to surprise the fiendish baby sitter. He turned on the light before using the toilet in case a severed head floated in the bowl. He checked for hands under the bed. They were the worst. He hadn't been able to see them, but he'd known they were there. Waiting. Now he couldn't pass a closet without opening it—carefully, so neither Margaret nor Tara would hear. As for the toilet, he switched on the light and closed the bathroom door. Then he raised the lid slowly and laughed at himself. As for beds and sofas and love seats, he didn't get down on all fours to check, but he did keep his distance. If he read in the living room, he lay with his feet raised.

His favourite spot was the sofa under the triptych, so he could look out the front windows.

Margaret's was the love seat, so she could see the painting when she glanced up.

Tara's was the family room floor. Here she read, watched TV, and did her watercolours. She was painting a picture of their home. The garden was unreal—foxgloves, dahlias, and daisies all blooming at once. She no longer seemed interested in making new friends, since the few children she'd met were boys her age. "Yuck," she'd said.

And Ravi hadn't introduced himself to the local fathers. He liked the way families went about their own lives. Here in the suburbs this involved barbecues, woodworking, and RVs. The bumper sticker on the Winnebago next door read, "Life is Nifty After Fifty." Checking the weather from the deck—it had rained every night since Sunday—he pretended not to watch the other men. They barbecued, built cabinets in garage workshops, and washed their many vehicles. The men were ten years older than him, Arnold's age, but none of them looked as friendly or as approachable as Arnold.

On Wednesday morning Ravi locked himself into the studio. He put Ravi Shankar's "Homage to Mahatma Gandhi" on a turntable from his college days. Then he turned up the volume. This was a signal. If the music was loud enough to be heard by anyone outside, it meant Do Not Disturb. But he didn't work. He paced in front of his large easel and glared at the blank centre of a canvas. He glanced at sketches tacked onto the smaller easel. They had come easily during the spring but the painting refused to come alive. Especially the central figure.

During her last phone call, his dealer had asked, "What's the problem this time?"

"Don't worry," he'd said, "you'll get your forty per cent." She'd said, "Fuck you."

He looked at the scarred floor. He still hadn't covered the scars and, yes, his dealer had deserved better. She'd got him this commission, after all, by lobbying hard.

Come next Heritage Day, a mayor would unveil a new painting in a city hall—the mayor of a city glad to celebrate its multicultural roots. Both of the daily papers had run glowing articles. Too glowing. Letters to the editor had asked why a city would spend so much on a painting when children were going without milk. Other letters had asked why the city was commissioning a "foreign" painting.

Not that anyone could guess the final image Ravi would deliver, but people knew what to expect from him. Critics who liked his work used terms like *fun*. Critics who scoffed at it used longer words like *derivative*. And people who hated art—especially art that forced them to think—used words like *pagan*.

Just now the painting didn't look foreign. It barely looked like a painting. It seemed so lifelike from a distance, it might have been a photograph except for the blank middle. Then again, the painting had begun as a photo. He'd projected a slide of twin office towers onto canvas, sketched them in with charcoal, and used oil paint so thin it was almost translucent. The towers, sheathed in blue glass, guarded one end of a pedestrian mall. The glass reflected sky and clouds and other, nearby buildings. A treed park along the bottom would hide the feet of the central figure—Hanuman, the monkey god. Mischievous Hanuman, who liked playing tricks.

Given the growing backlash against immigrants these days, Ravi was tempted to make Hanuman look evil, bent on revenge. But this would have been obviously political, and Ravi didn't consider himself political. Besides, he wanted to keep the humour. The sight of a monkey god's towering at the end of a pedestrian mall. A monkey god about to part office towers as if he were stepping from a jungle to check on civilization.

Someone tapped on the window.

Ravi whirled, his throat tight. Not with anger over being disturbed. With a sudden, irrational fear. His fear grew when he saw no one outside.

It's starting, he thought. Glass clinking in the night. Now this.

After the second tap, he laughed nervously. The branch of a tree—a young apple—snaked in the wind. His fear gave way to annoyance. Wind and rain. Rain and wind. Didn't the sun ever shine here? The only blue sky he'd seen in three days was in his own painting. An atmospheric, cerulean blue.

He turned from the window and reached for a charcoal pencil. Working quickly, he roughed in the figure of Hanuman. First the body, hunched to give the impression he was taller than the towers. Then the arms reaching forward, each paw scooping at a blue glass corner. Last, a monkey face.

Hanuman's father was the wind. Not this cool wind. A warm wind driving moonsoons across a land halfway around the world. A land Ravi hadn't visited in five years, not since he and Margaret had taken Tara to meet her cousins. A land still living in him, he hoped. Sometimes he wasn't sure. He would often put Indian records on the turntable, but lately sitars had begun reminding him how little he knew—about India, about art—and he would feel like a fraud. Then again, it took little to make him feel like a fraud these days.

"Loss of faith," Arnold had said.

"Not lost yet," Ravi muttered. "Just misplaced."

He finished drawing in Hanuman.

Ravi yawned. It was half past nine—he'd been up since six—and he was tired already. Blame it on the weather. Blame it on the move. Blame it on anyone but himself.

He tossed the charcoal onto the drill press and sat on a sofa. It was as old as the love seat in the family room, and it also belonged in a cottage. Arnold kept the sofa covered with plastic to protect its chenille from sawdust. The plastic creaked each time Ravi shifted. He stood to pull it off. Why bother? There were perfectly good beds in the house. It couldn't hurt to lie down for an hour. Who would know? His dealer? The city council? All those people who didn't know art but knew what they liked?

After leaving the studio, he ignored the back door of the house. He didn't want to pass the guestroom, with its secrets tucked on the closet shelf. And he didn't want to cross the family room though he hadn't heard glass clink for three nights now. He climbed to the deck, slid back the door leading into a formal dining room, and kicked off his sandals. He called, "Tara?"

All the lights were off. With school starting next week, she must be exploring the neighbourhood again in search of girls. Or little boys. She loved little boys. After entering the master bedroom, he stopped and eyed the bottom of the bed. From where he stood, in the doorway, he could see under the foot of the bed and under its near side. He turned on the light to make sure. Safe again, he thought. He flicked off the light, approached the bed, and sat heavily on the edge. He was about to lift his feet onto the covers when someone—some thing—grabbed his ankles.

Gurgling with surprise, he looked down. Not hands. Something worse. Much worse. Monkey paws—huge, hairy, and mean. His heart pounded. His bowels dissolved. He could barely move, but he had to escape. Somehow. But the more he tried, the more tightly the paws gripped. They would break his ankles first. They would snap his fingers one by one. He would never paint again. He knew why, too. The monkey god was furious. He was tired of waiting to be painted in.

Hanuman had come to life, and he wanted revenge.

9

Kathryn felt better. Since the weekend, she'd read mysteries, played solitaire, and resisted watching TV.

Wednesday the Rabbi Got Wet.

She'd even resisted the urge to re-arrange the kitchen cabinets. Everything seemed backward in them—pots and pans in the upper cabinets, dishes and staples under the counter. But she couldn't resist hanging her clothes in the bedroom closet. Her half of it. This was when she found the paint.

She wouldn't have noticed if she hadn't seen a white chip lying in a corner of the closet. Above the chip, on the otherwise white wall, she found a spot of blue. Its uneven edges had gathered dust. She pushed empty hangers aside, licked a Kleenex, and rubbed at the spot. The blue dissolved. Cheap paint. Her father would never have used such cheap paint. He would also have primed the wall. The spot looked purple now. No amount of rubbing would fade this earlier paint, so she stopped.

The discovery intrigued her. Seated on the bed, she tried to imagine who had owned the house before Margaret and Ravi.

An old couple, Kathryn decided. The man had come home from the war to become a travelling salesman. Calendars and pens. The woman had raised four children. Yes, here. People hadn't needed so much space back then. Sometime in the fifties or sixties, the man had painted the upstairs purple. Sixties. And just before the couple had retired, to Florida, their eldest son had come home. From a stint in Tanzania as a volunteer. He'd shaved off his beard and become a stockbroker—he hadn't been good with his hands like his father—and this son had repainted the upstairs blue. It must have taken at least two coats to cover the purple. Not only had he used cheap

paint but he'd also stinted on primer. He and his wife—
she'd been a nurse like his mother—had adopted two children from Korea. No, some place warm. Brazil. Finding the
house too small, the stockbroker had moved his family to
the suburbs.

Tara had recently been born, Margaret and Ravi had
wanted a house, and they had painted the upstairs an eggshell
white. Good for them. Between the narrow, old-fashioned
windows and the dark wooden trim, the walls begged to be
white.

Congratulating herself on her detective work, Kathryn
decided to tell Hugh. They needed something to discuss. Neither of them said so, but they were not growing as close as
they had hoped by living together. If anything, they were drifting apart. And not simply in bed, though she noticed it most
here.

Some nights he would kiss her neck and breasts and his
hand would wander down her belly, but she stopped him from
going any farther. And she never touched him where he
wanted to be touched because she knew it wouldn't stop here.
Later, when he thought she'd fallen asleep, she would hear
him in the bathroom. She wanted to tell him she was sorry—
she wanted him as much as he wanted her—but their banter
about sex stopped them from discussing it seriously.

What about Margaret and Ravi? Did they ever talk about
sex? Kathryn's face grew warm with guilt. She couldn't help
herself. Here she was in their bedroom, after all. It was still
theirs even if she hadn't seen them since Sunday night. Besides, she missed making love. Not sex. Making love. As
for them, they didn't seem passionate. Certainly not Ravi.
Kathryn had heard of men who lost interest in sex in their
mid- to late-thirties. Not her Hugh. She wouldn't let him
lose interest, not even after she had her three and four chil-

dren. She would keep swimming till the day each of them were born.

She patted her thigh through the cotton of her track suit. The earliest blisters were beginning to heal, and they itched. She wondered whether they would leave scars. Whether people at the pool would stare.

Then she looked at the mirror on a small dressing table. She could never catch her reflection before setting her face the way people do. She looked stern, and she didn't like what she saw.

She had heard some men looked at future mothers-in-law to see how their brides-to-be would age. Hugh mustn't have looked very closely. He hadn't noticed how often her mother pinched her lips, though he did joke about Kathryn's father living in fear. The day before, he'd turned from examining the loud, old clock and handed them a hundred-dollar bill. Then, having glanced through the front windows at his wife—she'd been waiting in their Cadillac—he'd told Hugh, "Whatever you buy with this, tell her it's from your folks. She'd skin me alive."

Closing her eyes, Kathryn lay back on Hugh's side of the bed.

God, no, she promised herself. She would never become like her mother. Ever. And yet she could see the signs. Mirrors don't lie. In a matter of days she'd begun turning into a bitch. There was no other word for it. Hugh was already trying to avoid her. He couldn't avoid her at night, but he gladly left for work after breakfast. He came home in time to make dinner and, after loading the dishwasher, stayed out of her way. How could she blame him? So much annoyed her. The country and western music he liked. The sports magazines he left lying about. The nightly news he just had to watch.

She knew this wouldn't last much longer. It couldn't. Two

more weeks of avoiding real contact and her nerves, fever tight, would return to normal. The virus in her system—we all have it, Lil had said—would be dormant again. Just in time for the wedding.

Kathryn looked sideways at her pillow. She told herself she should move to her side of the bed. She should also close the blinds against the afternoon sun. But she was tired from arranging her clothes. She decided to lie here for a while. Like a cat. Kitty-kat-napping in the sun. Kat on a hot tin roof. Ka-Ka-Ka-Kathmandu.

A woman screamed.

Kathryn woke with a start. Morning sun crept through closed blinds. White walls gleamed with new paint. The man lying next to her—Ravi—sat up. He looked half-asleep.

Margaret screamed again, this time a drawn out, "No!"

Ravi leapt out of bed and dashed from the room.

Kathryn followed him. When he braked in the hallway, they nearly collided. She held out her hands to stop herself—too late—and stumbled through him. She stood in the doorway of the nursery.

Margaret snatched a baby from a crib. Alphabet pictures—aardvark, beluga whale, cheeta—bordered the wainscotting. A clown mobile shuddered.

"Oh no," Kathryn said. "Oh. No."

Margaret shouted, "Call nine-one-one!"

"How can I?" Kathryn pressed her fingers through the jamb. "I'm not even here yet."

She heard Ravi dash back to the bedroom. She heard him punch numbers on the phone. Three beeps, the second and third identical. She heard him yell, "An emergency! What? No! Medical!"

"He's not breathing," Margaret cried. "I can't feel his pulse!" When she pressed her face against the small neck, her baby's head fell back. "Why's he so cold? He's never cold!" She eased his head onto her shoulder. "For God's sake, where do I find a pulse?"

Kathryn sank in the doorway and hugged her knees. She released them and covered her face. She started to cry. "We're too late," she said. "Can't you see we're too late?"

Margaret stepped through Kathryn. Still clutching the baby, Margaret ran to the bedroom. Kathryn heard Margaret shout, "Tell them he isn't breathing—"

Ravi yelled, "He isn't breathing! What?"

Kathryn covered her ears. She turned from all the useless, useless noise. Ravi stumbling over the address. Margaret crying, "How long can it take?"

Then Tara called from the main floor, "Daddy? Mom?"

Ravi yelled, "Don't come up here!"

Only the bear stayed quiet. Somehow, Kathryn knew his name. Theodore. Tara had christened him Theodore.

He'd been sitting with his back against the sunny, yellow wall—sitting up on a corner of the crib—until Margaret had snatched up her son. Now Theodore lay with one arm flopped in front of his stomach.

Kathryn wiped her eyes and looked at him.

He couldn't, or wouldn't, look at her. He was eyeing a seam in the hardwood. His glassy eyes were dull.

She lunged for him and missed. Each time she tried to pick him up, her hands passed through the plush covering and the foam beads inside. She screamed, "Don't do this!"

Theodore said nothing.

She needed to snatch him up. She needed to hug him the way Margaret, pacing in the hallway now, hugged her baby. But Kathryn sensed there was no point. She sat on the floor next to the bear, and she wept.

Margaret whispered to her baby, "It's okay. You'll be fine

soon. I'm here." She bounced him lightly, still clutched to her shoulder, and his arms also flopped—one against her left arm, one across her breast. "You'll be fine," she crooned. "We won't let anything hurt you. We would never let anything hurt you. We love you too much—"

Ravi slammed the receiver. He called, "They're on their way," and came out. He hugged Margaret from behind with one arm. With his free hand he smoothed the hair on the small, dark head. Their baby's head. Their son.

Kathryn watched them—Margaret with the baby, Ravi helpless behind her—and said, "I'm so sorry."

Margaret seemed to notice Kathryn for the first time. "I'm sorry, too," Margaret said. "There are some things a woman should never have to see."

Kathryn wasn't sure whether Margaret meant her—Kathryn—or herself. This was no time to ask. Sirens were approaching, already. They shrieked toward the house. Kathryn covered her ears and hung her head. The next time she looked up, she was sitting with her back against a desk.

The bear was gone.

Hugh stood at the top of the stairs.

"Theodore," she said.

"What?"

"The bear's name is Theodore."

"Oh."

10

During the next few days, whenever Ravi caught Tara eyeing him, he would start to laugh. So would she.

Margaret would say, "Not again!" Still, one night she told him, "It's nice to see the two of you getting along."

"When haven't we got along?" At once he said, "Don't answer that." For three years he'd kept his distance from Tara and she'd treated him like an overgrown boy. Not any more. Not since the morning she'd nearly scared him to death. But he hadn't told Margaret everything, and he sensed Tara didn't even think about it. Since life is never simple, he'd found yet another reason to keep his distance from her. This time, though, he promised himself he wouldn't back up quite so far.

On Wednesday morning he'd sat on the bed while the monkey paws had tried to pull him under.

Tara had been hoping for a scream or at least an, "Oh shit." When he didn't make a sound—didn't so much as move—she started to giggle.

He reached down and grabbed the paws. They pulled away. He sat staring at two black, hairy gloves.

She crawled out from under the bed and shrieked, "I got you!" She writhed on the floor and clutched her stomach while she laughed. "I thought you'd crap your pants!"

Furious, he threw the gloves into a corner.

"I found it in the laundry room. In a cupboard with all this Halloween stuff! A whole gorilla suit. I got you, I got you!"

"Tara!" No longer angry, he also laughed. Reaching down once more, he tried to pull her up. He fell forward onto his knees while she quivered in his arms. "You little monkey!" he said. Straddling her, he tickled her ribs until she screamed with delight.

Laughing with her head thrown back, she circled his neck with her arms.

He fell to one side.

She rolled on top of him and buried her face in his neck. They laughed together, Tara rising and falling while he gulped for air.

As a baby she had often fallen asleep like this, as light as a cushion, while he'd lain on the living room sofa and hummed with the radio. She wasn't as light as a cushion now. She was no longer a baby. Nor was she the little girl he'd taught to read.

When her small breasts shook against him, he grew cold. He bent his knees and let his head fall back. He glared at the ceiling. He'd known she wouldn't remain a child forever, but he hadn't expected her to become a young woman so soon. In a few more years she would lie on another man—a young man—and she would squirm in a different way. Ravi couldn't believe it. He was jealous of a man he didn't even know. A man Tara hadn't even met. But she would meet him and one day, in another dark room, she would cross the first of many lines.

Ravi pushed her from him and she rose. He rolled away to gain some distance, and he watched her.

Tara's loose sweatshirt had ridden up, above her navel. The skin of her belly looked like silk. Frowning, she adjusted her clothes. "Now what?" she asked. "I didn't think you were going to have a heart attack!"

Trying to grin, he said, "Why would I? Boy, you're something else." He rose to his knees, slapped his forearms onto the bed, and coughed. "How long's this been in the works?"

"Days." Moving toward the gloves, she blurted a laugh. When she bent to retrieve them with her back to him, he shut his eyes. She'd started filling out her jeans, their close fit hidden by the sweatshirt.

Three lost years. Where had they gone? Into paintings. Into shows and sales. Into classes in quaint, rural settings. All this time she had walked in her sleep and pretended she didn't care he was drifting out of reach.

"Days," she repeated. "Ever since you started acting like you saw a ghost. Dad, are you okay?"

He opened his eyes to find her staring at him with the

gloves clenched against her hips. She looked so much like Margaret now—the same self-reliance, the same bemused expression when he forgot why he'd wandered into a room.

"Just winded," he said, rising. "Coffee time."

"Oh goodie!"

"Hot chocolate for you, young lady!" He laughed at her exaggerated pout. "Okay, okay, you can have a bit of coffee in yours. Mocha. Then it's back to the salt mines."

Now he no longer acted as if he'd seen a ghost, but he did move Arnold's gorilla suit into the studio. The costume sat, hairy and deflated, on the sofa. Ravi claimed the gorilla would inspire him to bring Hanuman to life. This was not completely true. He didn't want Tara scaring him again. What if he raised the toilet lid some night and found the gorilla's head in the bowl? Not that she would do such a thing, but if he could imagine it, why wouldn't she?

And now, whatever the reason, Hanuman really was coming to life.

Ravi used undiluted paint, straight from the tube, because he wanted the monkey god to have texture. To stand out from the super real, glossy buildings. He slapped on paint, then worked it about with a stiff brush. The space between the towers grew dark in shades of brown. He painted reflections of Hanuman into the sides of the buildings. For this he once more used paint so thin it was translucent.

Starting on Thursday morning, he put in three straight, twelve-hour days. Not counting breaks for food. And rests, on the sofa with his head on the gorilla's lap.

Neither Margaret nor Tara said anything, but he sometimes caught them exchanging looks. Anxious but knowing looks. He came to bed at midnight, after Margaret had fallen asleep, and rose at six. One night, while he lay next to her and planned his following day's work—changing the curve of

Hanuman's tail—Ravi heard her sigh. She was still trying to forgive herself. Would it never end? There was nothing he could do to help her. Assuming she was the one who needed the help. He also knew she expected nothing special from him. It was enough he was painting, at last.

Twice a day he went for a walk but never down to the strip mall. He wanted to see no one but Margaret and Tara. He even stopped watching other men on the block. He didn't want to be distracted by their real world of barbecues and RVs, not while he was creating his own version of the world. "Whatever your real world is," Arnold had said. And so Ravi walked in the large garden behind the house. Often he strolled. Sometimes he strode.

One afternoon he caught himself staring at the bridge while a little boy leaned over the rail and frowned at the pond. When the boy looked up and waved, grinning, Ravi raised his own hand. Words caught in his throat. Still, he forced himself to say, "Happy birthday, son." While the boy faded, Ravi wiped at his eyes. Half hoping Tara was also outside—wondering if she ever imagined her brother growing up alongside her—he looked about. She was indoors, amusing herself somehow. He approached the bridge and looked into the pond.

No lilies, no fish. Nothing for a child.

With its backdrop of mountain ash and willows, the bridge looked like a perfect spot for wedding pictures. Watching leaves drift onto the pond, he recalled what Arnold had said about his workshop. "This used to be a darkroom. Not so long ago, either." How long ago? When had he ripped out the inside walls and added the second skylight? Before or after marrying Dora? Is this how she had known she could spend the rest of her life with him? Because he gave wood new life? Because he could do a simple thing like renovate another man's darkroom? For that matter, how did a woman know?

Ravi had asked Margaret these same questions earlier, after returning to the house for a late lunch.

"Beats me," she said. "Wonder who he was, though. The first husband. All we know is he had a darkroom."

"I don't think I want to know." Ravi still hadn't told her about the photo. Or about hearing glass clink, finding Tara gone, and realizing—too late—that the woman he'd left in bed had been Dora. He certainly couldn't tell Margaret about the man.

Before Ravi could decide why not, she asked, "Then why are you so interested in him? Assuming she was married before Arnold. And we don't even know that for sure."

Oh yes, Ravi thought. We do. "Don't you think Doctor What's-His-Name and his fiancée wonder about us? Using our furniture, eating off our plates?"

Margaret laughed as if he'd touched a nerve. She looked at the clock above the stove but he could see she wasn't checking the time. "Somehow," she said, "I don't think Dr. Blunt gives us a second thought."

Ravi knew she was hiding something, if only how quickly she'd taken a liking to the young couple. She had even told them, "If you need anything, just call." Ravi asked, "What about his fiancée, then?"

"Her name's Kathryn," Margaret said.

Now, yawning in the cool afternoon air, Ravi turned from the pond. He was tempted to enter the house—to make coffee, fill a thermos, and take it to the studio—but he couldn't afford to stall. Today was Sunday. He wanted to finish the painting so he could enjoy Labour Day. He'd also promised to drive Tara to her new school the day after.

Margaret had planned to do this but looked pleased when he'd volunteered. She had even said, "Thank you." He was glad she'd said nothing more.

Since driving meant rejoining the real world, he planned to spend the rest of today painting Hanuman's eyes. All night, if that's what it took.

He heard a titter and a whir.

A magpie landed on the crown of a pine tree. The bird perched here, rocking back and forth, like an oversized Christmas ornament. The magpie squawked and whistled as if teasing him about how close he was to the end. About how long it was taking him. Were magpies related to mockingbirds? Probably not, but everyone's a critic.

He made for the studio. Okay, so he wasn't a real Indian any more. But he could still carry on certain traditions. One of them—as he told his students every summer—was that whether an Indian painted mortals or gods, he painted the eyes last. To bring the image to life.

Entering the studio, Ravi said, "Hello, George."

The gorilla didn't reply. Tara had christened him George. Seated on one end of the sofa, he watched the door with blank, hollow eyes. He wore a sequined top hat Tara had also found in the laundry room. The hat made him look harmless, almost comical. Ravi yawned again. Maybe a nap before dinner wouldn't hurt. He had all night. But instead of lying down, he sat, keeping his distance from George.

Ravi looked at his canvas. It was his best work to date. Not really, but this was how he knew he'd come through again. If he thought a painting was his best to date, it was good enough to show. And sell. He could move on to the next work and start worrying, all over again, whether it might be his last. He wondered what the city councilors would think. Playful? Derivative? Pagan? Then again, they weren't paying for it. Taxpayers were, and they were getting a deal. One day the painting would be worth a mint. He would live on in his work, and his critics would be dead. Too bad, so sad, life is short and art is long.

He nodded off.

Half asleep, he heard a woman call, "Cli-iff!"

The voice answering her was muffled. A man's voice: "In a minute, Lee-Ann! Have a drink."

Ravi shifted on the sofa. He'd been dreaming about a garden—all the flowers mowed down yet growing back—and heard voices behind him. But when he'd turned, he'd found only George, who hadn't looked deflated. He'd looked as large and round as life. He'd been tipping his hat like a performer taking a curtain call. Like a jazz man.

"I had a drink," the woman said.

"Have two then."

A glass clinked.

Ravi jerked awake. He opened his eyes. He was still on the sofa—slouched, with his body sagging sideways—but the plastic cover was gone.

So was George.

In his place sat a woman. She looked nothing like Dora. No curly, red hair. No broad forehead or alluring, green eyes. She didn't sound like Dora, either. This woman sounded plaintive. She splashed rum into a glass and added the rest of a can of Coke. She raised her glass to him and said, "Up yours."

Wondering what to say, he straightened. Then he realized her eyes were not focused on him. Expecting another man in the room, he turned to find it smaller than it had been only moments before.

The far end of what had been his studio was now walled off. A black curtain hung in the doorway to a darkroom. His easels and books were gone. So were Arnold's tools. An etching press and worktable occupied half the floor space. Camera equipment and umbrella lights cluttered the rest. All that looked familiar was the single skylight above him. And the outside door. Even the floor looked different. Smooth. The paint hadn't yet bubbled.

As for the walls, they were covered with wedding photos shot near the bridge. Most of the frames looked cheap. The best ones held early photos of Dora. They had been made by someone she'd loved, and she looked radiant. Finally there were unframed photos of young women. Test shots of models, all glossy, all black and white.

One of these models now sat near him in living colour.

When she rose, he rose, too. She didn't notice. She was scowling at the only picture above the sofa. The frame looked new and did not look cheap. It held a photo etching of the house taken from the road. Even if the workmanship was crude—the printing irregular thanks to a poorly etched plate—the house looked like a home. In the bottom right corner were initials but no date. *CL.* C for Cliff, Dora's first husband. Ravi knew it. He also knew the type—a commercial photographer with artistic ambitions. Serious ambitions. Even used, the press must have set him back.

The woman named Lee-Ann shrugged at the etching. She raised her glass and said, "Up yours, too."

Cliff's voice came from the darkroom: "What?"

"Nothing!" She pulled at the yoke of her Western shirt. It was tight across her shoulders. She hooked a thumb through a belt loop and strutted for an invisible audience. If only she knew, Ravi thought. And that's what you call a strut. She wore jeans so tight, nothing could have fit in her back pockets, not even exploring hands. She had a body made for exploring. Her hair was dark at the roots but streaked light at the tips. He wanted to run his fingers through it. He wanted to stand behind her and mould his body against hers. To grow hard against her tight rear end.

But she also repelled him—especially her voice. No doubt about it. As long as she didn't speak, she was a stunner.

Ravi frowned. Assuming Cliff was the same, puffy-faced man who'd been watching the video, what did she see in him? Not much, probably. He was just another photographer, she was just another model. Then what was she doing here so late? And it was late. The skylight was dark. This was no time for a photo session.

Tired of examining her test shot, she yelled over her shoulder, "What are you doing in there, anyway?"

"I said already. Printing that new one of you on a copper plate. I ruined the first one. Too uneven."

"The acid?"

"Didn't leave it long enough. Look, I'll be right out."

"That's what you said when I phoned! I'll leave the door open, you said. Let yourself in, you said."

"For Christ's sake, keep your shirt on."

Ravi turned from her to look at the etching press. Next to it, on the worktable, sat a tray covered with a sheet of glass. Nitric acid. Beside this lay a half etched copper plate of Lee-Ann, her head tilted, her hair glorious, her lips parted and moist. Cliff hadn't returned the acid to its narrow necked bottle because he wasn't finished. He'd added even more acid, nearly to the brim and sucking on the glass. When he slid the new copper plate in, he would have to be careful the acid didn't overflow.

Ravi suspected Cliff would not be careful. The tray would tip and scar the concrete. Lee-Ann, watching closely, would jump back to save the polished tips of her cowboy boots. She would yell, "Watch it!" Cliff would snarl, "What's your problem?" And they would have a fight.

These people were trouble.

She'd gone back to examining the test shots on the wall. Ravi moved toward her. He was still watching her, the denim straining while she bent for a closer look, when he heard the curtain pull aside. Then he heard, "What the—?"

Lee-Ann must not have heard, since she didn't turn.

Ravi turned instead.

Cliff emerged from the darkroom. Yes, he was the same man Ravi had seen the first night it had rained. But Cliff looked meaner than ever. His cheeks and brow were puffy. His eyes were sunken—piggish, little eyes. They glowered either at Ravi or through him. Through, he decided. Lee-Ann couldn't see him, so why should Cliff?

Ravi took one step forward. Even as Cliff's hand rose in slow motion, Ravi thought he was safe. He winked. Then he sucked in his breath. The blade of an Exacto knife pressed flat under his jaw.

Oh, shit.

The blade clicked forward. One more click, and the point would puncture his skin. A hard jab, and blood would spurt. He was no longer safe. He'd never been safe.

Nor could he move.

He was still holding his breath when Cliff asked, "Who the fuck are you?"

11

Kathryn felt much better. She had finished the antibiotic and could feel herself mending. She no longer hobbled. The blisters were almost dry. She'd finally re-arranged the kitchen cabinets and was still reading mysteries.

Someday the Rabbi Will Leave.

Hugh was home. He said he liked his new job—no more working weekends and nights—and he especially liked the children. But he was still avoiding her. Each time she tried to tell him to stop, he sidestepped her hints. Let him be that way. See if she cared.

He was already up and moving about downstairs. When the phone rang, he answered at once. After his loud, "Hello?" she heard nothing more. If she could have heard him, she wouldn't have worried, and this was why she did something she'd never thought she could. Something her mother would have done without a second thought. Kathryn picked up the receiver, squeezed a hand over the mouthpiece, and listened.

Lil was finishing a question with, "—our patient holding up?"

"Fine," Hugh said. "I guess."

"You guess?"

"It's like she's always looking for something. She's got me spooked. One false move, and whammo. I'm getting tired of walking on eggshells."

Kathryn's face burned. She hadn't realized he felt so defensive. Then she grew indignant. How could he tell someone else such a thing instead of telling her?

"It'll pass," Lil said. "You know Kat."

"Yeah." His voice was dry, almost sarcastic.

"You think she's having second thoughts?"

Kathryn wanted to say no. Anything but.

He didn't answer.

"Are you having second thoughts?"

"No." He said this too quickly for Kathryn's liking. She felt her lips pinch.

"Why am I not convinced?" Then Lil said, "Want to come over?"

"Why?"

"For a chat."

"We're chatting now."

Good for you, Kathryn thought.

"For auld lang syne." Lil hummed a few bars.

The longer Hugh took to answer, the more Kathryn was tempted to interrupt. To scold Lil for playing games. To scold him for not reminding her of her place.

Kathryn started when Lil called, "Hel-lo?"

"I'm still here," he said.

"And I said—"

"I heard."

"Well?"

He tried to sound glib. "Don't tempt me."

"When have I ever tempted you?"

Kathryn slammed the receiver. She slapped the headboard. They had bought the simple, elegant headboard second-hand. Now she hated it. Her eyes burned but she refused to cry. Rehearsing what to say, she sat with her arms crossed while Hugh ran up the stairs. Two at a time. She would have to tell him to stop doing this before he ruined them. He could be so damned careless.

She expected him to be indignant, or to say something foolish like, "It's not what you think." She couldn't decide which would be worse. For him. For her. He spread his hands as if she might throw something at him. Who did he think she was? Her mother?

When Kathryn finally spoke, she couldn't help herself. "If my dad ever cheated on my mom, she would've served his balls for breakfast. On toast."

Hugh rested his brow on the open door. "I'm not your dad," he said, "and I'm not scared of you."

Fuming, Kathryn glared at the mirror on the dressing table.

He straightened and said, "I love you."

She started to cry. She slapped the comforter and wailed, "Do you know how long I've been waiting to hear that!"

"Oh, honey." He entered to sit beside her. "I've barely

been home two weeks." He took her in his arms. "I am home now. If you want me to stay."

"How could you ask such a thing!"

"You've been sick, that's all. It's okay."

"It's not okay. I love you and I need you."

"Two propositions and it's not even noon?"

Drawing back, she said, "That's not what I meant. You know it." She felt her anger growing at Lil now.

Before Kathryn could say another word, Hugh sighed. "Sorry, bad timing. You know Lil. She'd make a pass at a cadaver, then accuse him of being cold. It's just her way of covering up."

Kathryn nodded and laid her head against his shoulder.

When the phone rang once more, he answered with a brisk, "Hello?" He listened and said, "If you don't show up you'll make it worse." Then, "You know what they say. Always the bridesmaid, never the bride." And, "No, I wasn't trying to be funny. I was— Yeah. Sure. Bye."

After he hung up, Kathryn asked, unnecessarily, "Was that her?"

He nodded.

"She'll be at the wedding?"

"She cares for you a lot, you know. She's just, I don't know."

"Lonely."

"Are you lonely?"

Kathryn kissed the side of his neck. "Not any more." She made him hold her until she fell asleep. When she woke, he was gone. She couldn't hear him in the house but she imagined him downstairs. Sweeping up eggshells. On her way to the bathroom, she wondered whether he was angry with her for eavesdropping. Then again, he wasn't the kind of man who held onto things. Love, yes. Anger, no.

After returning from the bathroom, she found Margaret sitting up in bed. Her own bed, the one with the ornate headboard.

Kathryn clutched at the doorjamb to steady herself, and her fingers passed through it once more. This time she barely noticed. She was watching the baby at Margaret's breast.

Margaret looked down at him, brushed at his temple, and looked up.

"You're back," Kathryn said.

"No, you're back. I've never really left."

"You're not a ghost?"

Margaret laughed and said, "I'm not even dead yet." She grew serious. "Or maybe I was and I've started living again."

"So I'm not dreaming." Kathryn hesitated before entering the room. It wasn't really hers, after all. Not yet. She made to lean against the dresser, then remembered she might pass through it, too.

Margaret patted a spot next to her on the bed.

Kathryn sat with her left leg bent in front of her and her right leg, no longer painful but still stiff, dangling over the edge. "I don't get it. I can feel floors and beds but not walls or people?"

"Dreams are never consistent," Margaret said.

"So I have been dreaming!"

When Margaret shifted, her nipple slid out of the baby's mouth. He opened his eyes and blinked. He had Margaret's mouth and Ravi's eyes. She guided her nipple back between the baby's lips. "No," she said, "I have."

The baby's eyes squeezed shut. He tried to open his wrinkled fist but it kept closing. He was smaller than he'd been the last time—the only other time Kathryn had seen him. She liked him better this way. Needing food and warmth. Safe.

"Then what am I doing here?" she asked.

Margaret said, "You live here." She paused. "Funny, but you're the last person I ever expected to help me. I barely know you but I liked you the first time you came over."

"I haven't done anything." Kathryn wanted to touch the baby—to wiggle a finger into his closed fist—but she didn't want her hand passing through him as it had through Theodore.

"You've been a witness," Margaret said. "You're the only person who's seen what we went through. No one understood. Not our friends, not our parents. Though they lost a grandchild. There are some things even parents don't understand." She asked the baby, "Right?" Then she asked Kathryn, "But why should they? Why should anyone? No one can really understand what goes on in someone else's marriage. What drives people apart, keeps them together. Kept us together."

Kathryn nodded though she had never thought of marriage this way. She often thought people saw too much of her life. When she held her hand inches from the baby's face, he opened his eyes again but continued sucking.

Margaret smiled down at him. Looking up, she pushed her hair back from her face. "God knows it isn't easy being a mother. But there are some things we simply don't deserve. I dreamt about that morning for so long, it stopped feeling real. The same dream over and over, and I'm always too late. Then the dream stopped, but now it's started again. I know why. The move. His birthday. He would've turned four next week. He would've started play school." She paused again. "I've learned something, thanks to you."

"I thought I was the one who was supposed to learn something." Kathryn waited before asking, "So?"

"So." Margaret inhaled deeply. This pushed her breast closer to the baby's face and the soft, sucking noise stopped until she exhaled. The baby closed his eyes again. "It wasn't my fault," she said. "It never was."

They sat silently for a while, Margaret watching the baby feed, Kathryn watching their reflection in the dresser mirror. At last she said, "Does Ravi dream about that morning, too?"

"I've never asked."

"Where is he, anyway?"

"You know him. No, I guess you don't. Off in his own world somewhere."

Kathryn tried to chuckle. "There's an explanation for everything."

When Margaret said, "But that's just it," Kathryn looked at her—the real Margaret, not her reflection.

The real Margaret shook her head. "There isn't. Not for everything. That's what nearly drove us apart." Her own chuckle was a sad one. "You think you've grown up at last—you think you've seen everything, know everything just because you're a mother—and something happens out of the blue. The world ends. If you're lucky, though, something else happens and the world starts up again. Something so awful you can't imagine how it could help."

"The flowers," Kathryn said.

"The flowers. And there I thought he didn't feel a thing—he hides so much. He never said a word after the funeral. He waited till I went back to work—I couldn't wait—and he cleared out the nursery. Took the crib apart, packed everything away in the basement till we'd need it again. Then we found out we'd never need it again and we gave it all away. All except the bear. That's when he ruined my garden and I realized how much he'd cared all along. Not just over losing a child. How angry he was over what I'd gone through. How no one understood. How he thought he couldn't do anything for me except be there. I guess he didn't think that was enough."

Margaret looked down and wiped a smear of milk off the small face. "Poor baby."

Kathryn couldn't guess whether Margaret meant Ravi or their son. Watching the reflection once more, Kathryn said, "Can I ask you one more thing?"

Margaret's reflection nodded.

"You know what's going to happen. To him. To all of you—" Kathryn could not find the proper words for her last question.

Margaret found them instead. "Was it worth having a baby only to have him taken away?"

Kathryn's shoulders sagged. "Among other things."

When Margaret raised a hand to touch Kathryn's face, all she felt was a tremor. Unable to face her, Kathryn kept watching the mirror. Margaret and her baby faded. The ornate headboard dissolved into the simple one. Kathryn saw herself as if in a painting. As if she were seeing a woman she'd never known, hiding within her. This was why she didn't set her face, why she caught herself smiling sadly, and why the smile remained long after Margaret and her baby were gone.

12

Ravi heard Lee-Ann ask, "Pardon me?"

"I wasn't talking to you," Cliff said.

When she asked, "Who then?" the blade clicked back. It no longer pressed flat under Ravi's jaw.

"This guy a friend of yours?"

"What guy? Knock it off! You're giving me the creeps."

Ravi backed away from Cliff, who watched him while pocketing the Exacto knife. Frowning, Cliff told Lee-Ann, "Skip it. You wouldn't believe me if I told you."

Ravi felt safe again, almost cocky. He leaned against the etching press and crossed his arms. He could feel the floor—

he could even smell the chemicals from the darkroom—yet Lee-Ann could not see him. Cliff could, but he was shaking his head.

When Lee-Ann asked, "Want a drink?" he mumbled, "I've had plenty, thanks."

Ravi watched them—Cliff at the darkroom door, Lee-Ann near the test shots—and wondered what was happening. Again. None of this made sense. Was he a bystander, a witness, or an accessory? No, not an accessory. Whatever this was, it was going on without him even though Cliff kept glancing in his direction. A bystander. Ravi was here to listen and learn. But learn what? He was seeing nothing new. Nothing he hadn't seen in a hundred bad movies even if being part of the action made things different, more immediate. Still, it was like watching a *film noir*—sitting through all the arty angles and dissonant music, the bleak landscapes and tight close ups—and waiting for something to happen.

That's it, he thought. It's like being in someone else's dream—someone else's nightmare—but whose? Not Arnold's. All this had taken place before his time. Dora's? Ravi barely knew her. Cliff's? Please, anyone but. Or maybe none of this was supposed to make sense. What if this was the price Ravi paid—and his reward—for living in his own world? Right, sure. That's a good one.

Cliff re-entered the darkroom and emerged carrying a copper plate. He tilted it so Lee-Ann could examine his handiwork.

Ravi kept his distance. He didn't like Cliff's eyes—eyes which waited for a chance to gloat in revenge. Or gleam when something went wrong, for someone else. Ravi had seen this look on other men—losers, every last one of them—and he knew why he kept his distance. To keep from becoming like them. It didn't take much, either. Only Margaret had saved him. So had Tara.

Who would save Cliff? Dora? How could she when she didn't know what his problem was? For that matter, would she even care?

When Lee-Ann asked, "So where's the wife?" Ravi started.

"Night class," Cliff said. Making for the worktable, he carried the copper plate with one edge pressed into his gut.

Ravi stepped aside.

Cliff glanced at him, shook his head again, and muttered under his breath. After resting the plate on the table's edge, he tilted the plate and slid it carefully onto the surface.

"Sunday night?" Lee-Ann asked.

"I don't know. In her office." Cliff examined the image he'd reprinted. Ravi looked over Cliff's shoulder but stepped back when he said, "Cranking numbers. Humping a grad student."

"Somehow," Lee-Ann said, "I don't think so. Take a blowtorch to thaw out that—"

"Hey," Cliff said, "watch your mouth."

"Screw her. Look, am I here or what?"

Ravi heard a glass set down. He heard the rustle of fabric—something lighter than the curtain—but he refused to turn his back on Cliff. No one in his right mind would turn his back on Cliff.

"Keep your shirt on," he said.

"Oh, darn," she sang out. "Too late."

Looking impatient, he turned. Now he looked delighted.

Ravi couldn't help himself. He finally turned to watch her again.

She had unbuttoned her shirt and was pulling it back over her shoulders. With the sleeves caught at her bent elbows and the shirt snapped taut behind her, she strutted toward him. Her breasts swung. They were too large, too pendulous, but he wanted to touch them. To feel the nipples grow hard in his palms. When he raised his hands to cup her breasts, she walked through him. She was halfway through when he turned. She tugged the shirt down past her elbows and threw it aside. Pressing herself against Cliff, she bit his chin and said, "Gosh darn, huh?"

Ravi moved for a better view.

Side shot: full length, zoom in on the left breast. Soft, fleshy, and pillowed against Cliff. Pan, close up, to their mouths. Their kiss was so hard, so lacking in tenderness, Ravi thought their jaws would snap.

Playing the lioness, Lee-Ann snarled.

Cliff grunted like a boar.

Cut to a three-quarter side shot. His hands slid down her back and clamped onto the denim. His fingers hooked under her buttocks. Trying to pull her into him, he ground his crotch against hers. When he stopped to grin at Ravi as if saying, "You wish," Ravi shrugged. Then Cliff took her hand, guided it between them, and unzipped his fly.

She said, "Down, boy," and pulled out his penis. It was soft, soft but thick. It lay throbbing in her palm like a slug. She raised and lowered her hand, still flat, as if weighing him. When she finally made a fist, squeezing hard, he groaned.

His right hand dug through the denim into her flesh. His left hand moved, rasping across her hip, and he slammed the inside edge into her crotch.

Ravi winced.

It must have hurt, but Lee-Ann stopped tonguing Cliff's ear only long enough to say, "Harder." She scissored her thighs onto the hand. It moved like a saw, cutting into her each time she bucked.

Then the outside door opened.

Ravi turned first. He was so surprised—yet so unsurprised—he could only laugh. This was a movie, all right.

Some people's lives were nothing more than bad movies, worse than B-grade. They were schlock.

Cliff looked startled.

Lee-Ann looked outraged.

They stared at Dora, who stood on the threshold.

She looked younger than the Dora Ravi had met but older than the Dora in the wedding photo. Or framed, in here. The main difference lay in the eyes. They were tired, almost apathetic. "Didn't think I recognized that car," she said. "Working late, are we?"

Cliff fumbled his penis out of sight.

Patting his crotch, Lee-Ann said, "Oops." She turned and folded her arms coyly over her chest.

Cliff held one hand in front of his fly while zipping himself up.

Don't be a fool, Ravi thought. Don't say it. He was no longer laughing. He felt like an intruder. Any moment, the three of them would turn on him as if this were all his fault. As if none of this could have happened if he hadn't been here to watch.

But Cliff was a fool, and he did say, "It's not what you think."

"Give it up," Lee-Ann said. She headed for her shirt. Her breasts swung forward when she bent. After she straightened, she threw back her shoulders and pulled on the shirt. Slowly. Instead of tucking it into her jeans, she tied the dangling shirt front above her navel. She snapped two buttons closed but left the top three undone. She turned to pose for the camera.

Dora said, "Give me a break."

Lee-Ann tossed her hair and straightened her collar. "Maybe you should give him a break. Keeps his balls on ice when you're around, they're so blue."

Dora's eyes were no longer tired or apathetic. They were cold with fury. "So," she asked, "who pays who?"

Cliff and Lee-Ann said at the same time—

"Hey, watch your mouth!"

"You've got some nerve!"

Waving at Ravi, Cliff asked Dora, "Looking for him?"

Oh shit, Ravi thought. He relaxed when Dora, glancing toward him, asked, "Who?"

Lee-Ann cried, "I said you're giving me the creeps!"

Entering the studio at last, Dora told Lee-Ann, "Get out."

Lee-Ann moved away from Cliff but raised her chin. "Not till I get an apology."

Cliff brushed past her toward Dora. "For Christ's sake," he told Lee-Ann, "put a sock in it."

Caught in the middle, Ravi could not decide which way to turn. Later, reconstructing what followed, he couldn't imagine how everyone but him had moved as quickly as they had. Or why he'd been unable to move aside.

Lee-Ann had walked through him once more. She was headed for the car keys next to her drink. Next to a black rotary phone.

Dora had walked through him to the worktable. She looked at the copper plate.

Giving her a wide berth, Cliff had headed for the door. He stopped halfway as if unsure who to show out.

Ravi did remember he'd been careful to keep Cliff in sight. And that Cliff frowned at him one last time.

Cliff grew belligerent. He growled at Dora, "Don't touch! It's still wet."

"Looks like you're making progress," Dora said. "What's this called? Bimbo in Heat?"

"So I'm no brain," Lee-Ann said, colouring. "At least I'm no ice queen."

"Not that old cliché?"

"Easy with that!" Cliff said.

230

Ravi glanced over his shoulder. Dora was tapping on the glass covering the tray. Watching Cliff again, Ravi saw him take a step forward and quickly backed up. He didn't want Cliff anywhere near him.

Cliff didn't come any closer. He'd decided to stand his ground, to play the indignant, deprived husband. He told Dora, "If you stayed home a bit more often like a normal—" He didn't finish. His eyes grew wide, he reached out as if to take something from her, and he yelled, "No!"

Even as Ravi whirled, the glass sliced through his chest. Acid flew at him in a wave. Also yelling, "No!" he crossed his hands in front of his face. The glass shattered on the floor. The tray landed at his feet.

Cliff screamed.

Ravi staggered and fell against the darkroom wall.

Cliff had also covered his face with his hands, too late. Ravi heard acid sizzling. He smelled flesh singeing like meat. Impossible. The acid wasn't that strong. Still, Cliff screamed, "My eyes!"

Lee-Ann also screamed. She collapsed on the sofa even as Cliff shouted, "Help me! Water!" With an arm pressed against his face, he searched blindly for the curtain. "Lee-Ann? Do something!"

She kept screaming until Dora said, calmly, "Shut the fuck up." Moving behind Cliff, Dora shoved him into the darkroom.

Ravi heard Cliff blunder about. Negatives rustled on clips. A beaker fell. Then a tap opened full blast. "My eyes!" Cliff yelled. "My eyes!"

Shaking uncontrollably, Ravi stared at Dora. No, this was not the Dora he had met. That Dora—showing Margaret the good china—couldn't have hurt anyone. This Dora was bent on murder. She grabbed Lee-Ann's hair and pulled her to her feet. "Out, I said!"

Lee-Ann was crying. Mascara streaked her face. She looked as if someone had gouged out her eyes. As if she were crying blood. "The cops!"

"Don't worry," Dora said. "They'll know exactly where I am." Still clutching Lee-Ann's hair, she heaved her out.

Dora slammed the door. Then, moving along the walls, she pulled down the test shots of the models and tore the glossy paper in half. Next she pulled down the wedding photos and the pictures of her earlier self. She took special delight in smashing these. Shards of glass skittered across the floor. Slivers landed in the acid inches from Ravi's feet.

He pulled his knees to his chest and clasped them to stop shaking. When she pushed over an umbrella light, he cringed. The bulb exploded.

He heard Cliff once more. Water still gushed into a sink but now he whimpered, "Aw, Christ! Aw, Jesus!"

Dora stopped in front of the sofa. Kneeling on a cushion, she examined the photo etching of the house. "Yes," she said, "we're definitely making progress." She raised her arms toward the etching but seemed to change her mind. She sat down, reached for the phone, and dialed the Operator. "We need help," she said.

Ravi shivered. He heard the voice on the other end as clearly as he'd heard it once before: "What is the nature of your emergency?"

After clearing her throat, she said, "Oh, medical." She glanced at the darkroom. Then she looked at Ravi and he was sure she was smiling. At him.

No, she couldn't be. She wasn't really here. He hadn't crossed the line, after all—the line separating the bystander from the accessory. Not this time, and he never would. Still, he said, "Dora? It's over. You can go away now."

Perhaps she heard. Perhaps not. The question would haunt

232

him longer than the ghosts themselves, assuming they had been ghosts.

Still clutching the receiver, Dora looked up at the skylight. He watched her pat her curls as if aware of the effect she had on him. She patted her curls once more as if preparing for visitors. Police, a doctor. At last she said, smiling at him and still calm, "There's been an accident."

13

A week before their wedding, Kathryn and Hugh celebrated her recovery. They started with dinner, a three course meal from a nearby gourmet take out. The candle flickering between them threw its glow on two roses in a long-stemmed vase. The phone was switched off. The answering machine was on. A CD of country ballads spun in the living room. Hugh had offered to play classical music—something by Tchai-kovsky—but Kathryn had insisted on ballads. This is how it should be, she thought. This is what we'll look back on, years from now, when passion changes into something else. Feeling whole, feeling safe. No matter what happens a year from now, ten years from now, these will be the best years of our lives.

After dinner, he waltzed her from the kitchen into the living room. One more week, and they would rise for the first dance at their reception. She had already picked the music, the waltz from *Eugene Onegin*. The bridal party would join them for the second dance, something less challenging, yet no less romantic. She would dance with her father while Hugh danced with his mother. Kathryn's father, afraid to hold her close, would have tears in his eyes. He would forget all about her mother, who did not dance. She would remain at the head table and accept congratulations on the splendid day.

Even Kathryn would have thanked her by then.

Kathryn's father would drink all evening, dance all evening, and go home to his old life. His old wife. Some things—some people—never change.

But for now, Kathryn and Hugh danced with the lights off while a street lamp cast a shimmery green through the windows. When the music ended, she let him lift her in his arms and carry her up the stairs.

He set her down in the bedroom and they undressed one another, silently. She lay back on the bed and watched him silhouetted in the light from the hallway. Careful not to touch the scars, he parted her thighs and moved between them. He nearly broke the spell when he reached under the mattress for a condom. She closed her hand on his wrist. After coaxing his hand up toward her right breast, she steadied his palm a hairsbreadth from her nipple. Then she guided him into her. He felt silky. Hard yet silky. It was the first time she had felt him inside her like this, and she gasped.

He was trying to resist, anchoring his free hand on the bed, but she refused to let him resist. She sensed he didn't want to, not even when he whispered, "I thought you wanted to wait."

She pressed a finger to his lips. Crossing her legs around his waist and squeezing with her thighs, she pulled him as far inside her as she could. She kept him here, unmoving. Then, with her arms wrapped about his neck, she arched her back and rose.

Outside their home, outside another home a thousand miles away, street lamps cast their glow on windows reflecting the light. Green, orange—the colour doesn't always matter. What matters is that we who pass by can only imagine what goes on inside. Or what went on. Yet if we stop

long enough, we may hear the story told by the house itself, just as this story was told not by one house but by
two. If we listen closely, we may notice this much, at least:
how it is—perhaps even why it is—that the story of every
house resembles the story of our own.

Acknowledgements

These stories were written between 1985 and 1997. Excerpts, condensed versions, and earlier drafts have appeared on CBC Radio's *Ambience*; in the periodicals *Canadian Fiction Magazine, Chapman, Edinburgh Review, Grain, The New Quarterly, On Spec, Prairie Fire,* and *Rungh*; and in the anthologies *Due West, Hearts Wild, The Journey Prize Anthology, Sky High,* and *Tesseracts⁴*. As always, I received advice and encouragement from many friends and colleagues, and I'm especially grateful to Edna Alford for editing this collection.

Over the years I also received generous financial support: creative grants from the Saskatchewan Arts Board; an arts award from the Canada Council for the Arts; multicultural writing grants from the Department of Canadian Heritage; a scholarship and subsidy from the Banff Centre for the Arts to attend its Writing Studios and Leighton Studios; and a subsidy from the Writers Guild of Alberta to attend a winter retreat.

Three appointments as a writer-in-residence allowed me to finish this book. These were in the University of Calgary's Markin-Flanagan Distinguished Writers Programme, the Canada-Scotland Writers-in-Residence Exchange, and the University of Alberta's Department of English.

ABOUT THE AUTHOR

Ven Begamudré was born in South India and moved to Canada when he was six. His work has appeared in magazines and anthologies in North America, Europe, and Australia.

Oolichan Books published his first short story collection, *A Planet of Eccentrics*, which received the F.G. Bressani Literary Prize for prose, and his first novel, *Van de Graaff Days*. He edited *Out of Place: Stories and Poems* with Judith Krause (Coteau Books) and *Lodestone: Stories by Regina Writers* (Fifth House Publishers).

Laterna Magika won a 1994 Saskatchewan Writers Guild Literary Award for fiction manuscript, and the title piece shared a long short story prize from *Prairie Fire* magazine.

Begamudré has been writer-in-residence in the University of Calgary's Markin-Flanagan Distinguished Writers Programme, the Canada-Scotland Exchange, and the University of Alberta's Department of English. He has also taught creative writing through various programmes including the Sage Hill Writing Experience.